The Love for Three Oranges

The Love for Three Oranges

❧ ❦

A
John Singer Sargent/Violet Paget
Mystery

❧ ❦

Mary F. Burns

Copyright © 2019 by Mary F. Burns

Published by Word by Word Press
San Francisco, California

Burns, Mary F.
The Love for Three Oranges / Mary F. Burns

ISBN: 9781790390274

All rights reserved. Printed in the United States of America. No part of this book may be used or reproduced in any manner whatsoever without prior written consent of the publisher, except in the case of brief quotations embodied in critical articles and reviews.

Printed in the United States of America
Text Font: Garamond
Titles Font: Garamond

John Singer Sargent was born on January 12, 1856 to American parents living in Florence, Italy. Sargent became the most sought-after portrait painter in Europe and America from the early 1880's to his death in 1925. He produced some 900 oil paintings, mostly portraits, and 2,000 watercolors, which became his preferred medium.

Born October 14, 1856, Violet Paget was Welsh-English, and like the Sargent family, hers travelled throughout Europe and Great Britain, keeping company with artists, writers, intellectuals, and many socially prominent people. She was a prolific writer, using the pen name Vernon Lee, and she and John Sargent were close friends from childhood—they met when they were ten years old, in Rome. Violet died in 1935 at her villa, Il Palmerino, near Florence.

There is a glorious City in the Sea.
    The Sea is in the broad, the narrow streets,
    Ebbing and flowing; and the salt sea-weed
      Clings to the marble of her palaces.
  No track of men, no footsteps to and fro,
  Lead to her gates. The path lies o'er the Sea,
     Invisible; and from the land we went,
      As to a floating City—steering in,
    And gliding up her streets as in a dream,
    So smoothly, silently—by many a dome
    Mosque-like, and many a stately portico,
     The statues ranged along an azure sky;
By many a pile in more than Eastern splendour,
    Of old the residence of merchant-kings;
The fronts of some, tho' Time had shattered them,
    Still glowing with the richest hues of art,
As though the wealth within them had run o'er.

— "Italy" (from Ch. XI. Venice) by Samuel Rogers, 1823

PROLOGUE

THE MURKY GREEN WATERS IN THE CANALS OF VENICE hold an abundance of secrets.

In the high season, between May and early September, many an awe-struck tourist has stepped too near the edge whilst looking up at grand, decaying palazzos or despondent madonnas painted on walls, fading with age. But they are the lucky ones, as often as not pulled out forthwith, dried off, and suffering only from a night of fever-dreams in their hotel rooms.

Legendary are the tales of those unfortunates who have disappeared without a trace—one moment their footsteps are heard receding down a narrow *calle*, then a splash, then…nothing. This happens not when the city is thick with visitors of every race and nation, perspiring in the glare of the incandescent summer sun, but late in the year, in the depths of winter, and particularly, in the three days after the Winter Solstice has marked the victory of darkness over light. During those three days, in ancient times at least, not even learned astronomers could tell if the sun is making its turn and will truly come back to warm the earth.

It is a time of black despair and evil deeds.

Only on the fourth day can the naked eye discern, at dawn, that the light has seeped in a few moments earlier, and there is renewed assurance that life will persist.

Except for those who have gone to their watery graves, unmarked and unfound.

A chilling description, is it not? But it is an apt introduction to my account of the adventure that I and my lifelong friend, John Singer Sargent, embarked upon in December of the year 1879—an adventure fraught with danger, mystery and tragedy, and one which I assure you, dear reader, still sends a shiver through my bones whenever I think of it.

Come then, if you will, and enter into the madness of *The Love for Three Oranges*.

—Violet Paget, Villa Palmerino, Florence – 1926

৯ Friday, 19 December 1879 ৶
Florence, Italy

An urgent message from a friend

THE STREETS OF FLORENCE WERE BLACK WITH RAIN, and even a blazing fire hardly kept the chill off one's fingers and toes. Our house at 12 Via Solferino was a stone's throw from the muddy Arno, with a canal running alongside that lent its dampness to the villa, and heavy verdure that obscured the windows, although the upper floors were brilliant with light—when the sun shone.

I was shackled to my writing desk, finishing up the last proof sheets of my soon-to-be-published book, *Studies of the Eighteenth Century in Italy*. Only forty pages to go. I removed my eye-glasses—styled after a pair in a painting I'd seen in the *Accademia*, large and perfectly round, with silver wire rims—and rubbed my itching eyes. I settled the spectacles again, and bent my head to my task, knowing in my heart that, grumble as I might do, this first major publishing accomplishment thrilled me to the core. I had been writing and publishing the essays in this collection for a few years, and now they were to be gathered into three volumes, with a few new ones thrown in for good measure. Vernon Lee, my *nom de plume*, was becoming known.

An assertive tap at the door brought a scowl to my face, deepening to a frown as the door was thrown open and, without ceremony, my mother entered the room.

"Child, there is an enormous amount of mail for thee this day," she said. I could hear the pique of envy in her voice, embroidering the quaint Quakerish terms she affected when she was miffed. Matilda was as keen a correspondent as I, and there was—I am almost ashamed to admit it—a competition between us for both volume and content, as well as the importance of the correspondent.

I put my pen down carefully, and turned to look at her. The little devil on my left shoulder whispered in my ear.

"Is there one from Mr. Ruskin?" I asked, pretending innocence.

"I'm sure I don't know," she said, pretending indifference. "Dost think I look through thy letters?" She placed a large bundle on my desk, heedless of the papers I was examining; I had to grab them before they toppled to the floor.

Matilda gave a little cry of triumph, and held up a large, square white envelope, gilded with a coronet. "The Contessa da Chavalerio! I'm sure it's an invitation to their Christmas Day dinner!" I heard her clucking and cooing over the card as she plumped herself down on the tiny sofa in my study, near the fire, to open and savor it. I shook my head and turned to my own correspondence. Mrs. Turner, Mrs. Jenkin, Emily Sargent—I would lay most of these aside to read at my leisure—but then my eye was caught by a thin, blue missive with the instantly recognizable scrawl of my friend John Sargent. The hurried appearance of the writing communicated urgency to me, and I found that my heartbeat quickened as I seized my brass letter knife to cut the paper open. It consisted of a single page, with only three lines written on it.

Vi, you must come at once to Venice.
Take a gondola straight to Ca'Favretto, sestiere San Polo.
Please. You must come. Yours, JSS

An extraordinary note! My friend must be in serious trouble to send such a curt and mysterious missive. It was dated two days ago, postmarked San Polo, Venezia. I had thought John was still in Spain, where he'd been since October, steeping himself in Velasquez and sunshine.

I thought rapidly of what such a trip might entail—and at this time of year, with Christmas only five days away. The train north and east from Firenze to Venezia passed laboriously through Pistoia, Bologna, Ferraro, Rovigo and finally Padova before creaking its way across the recently built train bridge over the western lagoon—I had done it twice, and held my breath each time, fearing a sudden, devastating plunge into the oily waters. I glanced at the ormolu timepiece on the mantle. It was three o'clock, and if I made haste, I could board the overnight train at nine this evening, and be in Venice at this time on the morrow.

I steeled myself for battle.

"Mama," I said, rising from my chair to stand before her, using the accidental height to my advantage. "Mama, I must go to Venice tonight on a matter of great urgency."

She gazed up at me with pursed lips, narrowing her eyes.

"Nonsense," she said.

"Nonetheless," I returned, "I am going. John requires my assistance."

That gave my mother pause; John was a particular favourite. She nodded, a bit curtly, and returned her attention to her letters. I moved to leave the room, and she threw out a parting shot, albeit one that made me smile.

"Take with thee thy warmest cloak," she said. "Venezia is vile in December."

Little did she realize how prophetic her derogation would prove—*vile* was hardly the tenth part of what I was to encounter.

† September 1739 †
Venice, Italy

*The end of my three years' service.
I cast up my accounts, and reckon debts;
calculate upon the future, with a sad prevision of the truth.
My arrival in my home at Venice.*

—*Memoirs of Count Carlo Gozzi*

I AM NO VIRGIL, NOR WAS I BORN IN THE GOLDEN AGE of Augustus. Only my fanaticism for the art of poetry made me imagine that verses could be anything worth offering as a gift.

The *Cavaliere* accepted my donation, however, with affability, and then inquired whether I preferred to return to Venice or to stay in Dalmatia, occupying the post of *cadet noble* of cavalry on my promotion. I immediately begged him to take me in his entourage to Venice, and he graciously accepted.

After twenty-two days of rough crossing from Dalmatia to Venice, the wind and weather constantly beating us back, the *Cavaliere's* ship docked, in late afternoon, at his private port on the very northern tip of La Giudecca, where we—my closest friend and compatriot, Innocenzio Massimo—politely declined his offer of a bed for the night—so great was my desire to be home! We could see the dusky gleam of light on the towers of San Marco and the Palazzo Ducale, and could almost hear the great lion flag snapping in the late afternoon breeze. We found a gondoliere and headed home, entering the waters of the serpentine Grand Canal in the company of innumerable small boats and great ships.

"I am not given to boasting, *fratello mio*," I said to my friend, "but I know I can promise you a good fire, a hearty meal, and a clean bed—the best that my family can offer." I clapped my companion on the back as I gave this assurance, confident that my family's palazzo in the *sestiere* of San Polo was as grand, as welcoming, and as comfortable as when I had left it three years before at the age of seventeen.

"Anything beats the barracks in Dalmatia, eh?" Massimo, my elder by some four years, grinned and engulfed me in an embrace so hearty it made the gondola tip toward the dark waters of the Grand Canal.

"*Guardarlo, signori!*" The boatman cried out a warning, though easily righting the boat. But he was an old man, and probably had sons of his own, so he shook his head and smiled at us: two young soldiers, who sat each with an arm around the other's shoulders, looking for all the world like youthful adventurers from the olden days.

The sun was sinking behind the Dolomite mountains, and the hush of dusk peculiar to Venice settled over the watery city. I watched, almost forgetting to breathe, as the gathering autumn clouds sifted the sun's rays to create a shimmering golden light, settling like a veil of the sheerest gauze on the steeples and rounded roofs, sparks glinting from the edges of gilded crosses and flickering like candle flames in the points of the wavelets in the lagoon.

Here I sighed with relief, sharpened by desire and the ache for home—how I had longed to be back in my beloved city after three interminable years of army life in Illyria. Massimo and I fell silent as we both gazed, my eyes filling with tears, as the precious landmarks slipped by—Santa Maria della Salute on the Dorsoduro side of the Canal, the grand and stately palazzos rising from the eerily darkening waters, glimpses of *campos* and the narrow intersecting canals and *rios* depending from the Grand Canal. And the gorgeous, wondrous, haunted *Ponte Rialto*, which filled me with wild gratitude—San Cassiano was just around the bend!

"Here, here, my good man," I cried to the gondoliere, finding coins in my pocket to give him. I turned to Massimo. "Let's get out and walk the rest of the way, it's not far."

My friend assented with a grin, and in moments, with meagre belongings in hand, we set our feet on the stone pavement just under the Rialto, where market crowds and early evening strollers mingled and called out greetings to one other. Some eyed us curiously, wary of our soldiers' bearing, though we wore no uniforms—peasant or merchant, no Venetian—no Italian!—fails to spot a soldier, nor wants to cross one in any way.

I walked first at a leisurely pace, noting a few changes as we strolled—a new shop where there had been a candlemaker's, and the change of name on the costermonger's sign—had the old man died? As we neared home, I hastened my steps. We quickly crossed tiny *campos*, dodging left and right down the *calles* and through the *sotoportegos*, until Massimo, fallen behind and laughing, called out to me to wait up.

"Carlo! Don't lose me! These blasted alleys..." he stopped and coughed, a remnant of cold, damp barracks and cheap wine.

"*Despiace*, my friend, I forget you are a country boy, not used to city ways." I stopped, waiting for him to catch up, then linked my arm through his. "We are almost there," I assured him. "But I want to make one quick stop before we get home."

We came out of the *Calle Mori*, turned down *Calle di Scrimia*, and halted at the sight of a large, high, flat-fronted building with an unimpressive portico sagging from the wall, and a massive tower, built like one for a fortress, looming up into the night sky.

"This is my family's church," I told my friend, and he cocked his head, considering.

"It's very plain for a Venetian church," he said.

I smiled. "Just wait."

I led him a few steps around to the side and pulled at the iron ring of the door. It opened with a groan and a shudder. Stepping inside, the dim light of flickering votive candles made it hard to see what I knew awaited our eyes. I lifted a torch from its sconce on the wall, let it hover above some lighted candles, then held it aloft as it caught fire and flamed brightly. My friend gasped in surprise and awe.

"There will be time to see the whole church, and by daylight," I said, looking with pride on the gleaming tiles, the soaring pillars, and the glimpses of paintings and statues in the side altars and alcoves. I grinned at Massimo. "There are three Tintorettos," I said, not at all modestly.

"But for now," I continued, "let us just light a candle in gratitude for a safe home-coming."

Safe? Yes, safe enough, I was to think later. But not to the home I had hoped for.

☙ Saturday, 20 December 1879 ❧
Venice

I am introduced to the troubles.

THE SANTA LUCIA TERMINAL WAS A CACOPHONOUS RIOT of visitors departing and arriving Venice for the Christmas holidays. Thank heaven my family were never religious—and yes, I am quite aware of the irony of such an ejaculation—therefore my own luggage was minimal compared to the boxes and armloads of velvet-wrapped, beribboned gifts under which other people labored.

Although I pride myself that I speak Italian very well, I would never under any circumstances be taken for a Venetian, whose dialect is nearly incomprehensible to those who live in Mestre on the mainland, or even the neighboring islands of Burano or Murano. Pure Tuscan Florentine for me, thank you very much, the tongue of the divine Dante, Petrarch and Boccaccio, and that astute wretch Machiavelli, consequently the language adopted in Rome as "Italian." But I am a quick study, and I have picked up a good deal of *Venetan* on my visits here, and have been frequently amused by understanding the comments of servants and shopkeepers without their being aware of my knowledge.

I procured a gondola and boatman on the *fondamenta* as the winter daylight was steadily declining; it was nearing five o'clock, that dusky time of day in Venice when those who love this watery city remember exactly why they do. It was not raining, for which I thanked whatever gods are in charge of such things, although the clouds hung low and threatening; the final rays of wintery sunlight glanced metallically from rooftops and towers.

"*Ndove, siorina?*" The gondoliere asked the question in Venetan; was he testing me?

"*Ca' Favretto, vicino a San Stae,*" I responded in my best Florentine, raising my brows at him to show I would not let him get the advantage of me. I was surprised to see him react with what looked like fear—his mouth tightened and his eyes widened. Was my Italian that bad? I smiled and added, "*per piasser*" in his own dialect, at which he softened a bit, and tipped his beribboned hat in my direction. But he looked worried.

I had spent some fruitless hours on the train trying to imagine what was so urgent that John required my immediate presence. Death or illness of a family member? Not likely, as I would not be a helpful person in such a situation. Money problems? Possibly, but also not likely. Some romantic entanglement that required a woman's touch or intervention? That amused me, but my private opinion of John was that he was entirely capable in such matters, as well as a complete gentleman, and therefore could be relied upon not to get himself in such trouble in the first place. So I had given it up and concentrated on proof-reading my manuscript, which many long hours on the train allowed me sufficient time to accomplish.

The distance from the train station to Ca' Favretto, I found, was not great, as the *sestiere* of San Polo was on the northwestern bend of the Grand Canal. Amidst the calls of other gondolieres, and the shouts and clatter of the markets and shops closing at the end of day, my little barque made its way to a stately though small palazzo with a recently re-built and painted water door and wooden steps. The gondoliere grabbed onto a post to steady the boat, and at the same moment a servant in pale green livery emerged from the house door.

"Benvenuto, signorina," he said, holding out his hand to help me from the gondola. Once I was safely on the stairs, he turned away to claim my luggage and exchange a few words with the boatman. Despite the use of Venetan, I caught a few curious phrases.

The maidservant…what a tragedy! And your master…recovered?

I could not catch the servant's response, but it did not seem reassuring to the gondoliere, who muttered something and crossed himself, then shoved off and glided away a moment later.

Double doors at the top of the steps were partly open, with golden lamplight spilling out to disperse the growing gloom of the night. As I stepped over the threshold, noting with unfeigned admiration the deep, rich red color of the painted doors and the elegant stained glass windows, I heard my name called out in a familiar voice.

"Vi! Here you are at last!" John stood in the second doorway, leading to the interior of the house, smiling and holding out his hands in greeting.

"At last!" I protested, pretending to be affronted. "I could hardly have gotten here sooner had I flown through the air."

He bent down from his great height, towering above me, to kiss my cheek and take my hand to lead me into the palazzo. We passed through the small entrance porch and up two steps into a large salon, its marble floors gleaming from the torchieres set high in the walls.

John spoke briefly to the liveried servant, directing him to take my bags to my chamber, and then showed the way to another, smaller room off the main salon. I was beginning to feel the chill and fatigue from my travels, and was heartened at the sight of a good fire merrily crackling away in a stone fireplace, with comfortable chairs drawn up before it, and a hearty repast of wine, cheese, bread and winter fruits set on a low table.

"Well, this is comfort indeed," I said, sinking into the plum-colored cushions of the chair nearest to the fire. I dropped my reticule on the floor and began unhooking my travelling cloak.

"For reasons that will become clear," John began, pouring a darkly glinting red wine into two glasses, "our host isn't here to greet you." He handed me a glass of wine and sat down across from me.

"And who exactly is our host?" I inquired. The name of the palazzo, *Ca' Favretto,* of course could be a clue to the inhabitants, but not necessarily. I knew that especially in Italy, nothing was as it appeared to be. I drew off my damp gloves and reached my hands toward the fire's warmth.

Another servant appeared at the door, a young, darkly handsome man in the formal attire of a *major d'omo.*

"Is there anything you require, *Signore* Sargent?" he asked quietly, bowing slightly toward John.

"Ah, Samuel, thank you so very much," John said, "but Miss Paget and I shall serve ourselves."

"*Bene, signore.* You have but to pull the bell cord," he said, and bowed again. He had not even looked in my direction, which I thought a bit curious. The door shut noiselessly behind him as he left.

"Giacomo Favretto, the painter," John said, looking for all the world as if I should immediately recognize the name. I lowered my chin and raised my eyebrows to encourage a little more information.

"Sorry, old man, I just assumed...well, Giacomo is Venetian, he's a few years older than we are, and I met him last year in Paris—the Universal Exhibition, you know—he had quite a nice success there, and great things are expected of him."

This was a long speech for John, and I smiled at him to show I appreciated it. I took a sip of wine and a bite of cheese, and decided to have a bit of fun as well.

"I hope he is fully recovered from the late unpleasantness he suffered," I said with modest serenity. John's reaction was most gratifying.

"Why, how could you possibly know anything about it?" He set down his wine glass and looked at me earnestly. "It was indeed most unpleasant, and continues to be…how could you possibly know?" His puzzled look pleased me extremely.

"Oh, I won't toy with your good nature," I said. "I overheard the gondoliere ask the footman if his master were recovered, and there was something about a maidservant—and a tragedy? I may not have heard the word correctly, and then of course it was in Venetan, so I couldn't be absolutely sure."

John grimaced. "You couldn't be more absolutely correct, except in one detail."

I almost clapped my hands, but decorum demanded better manners. "Now, John, tell me everything—what has happened, why you're here, why *I'm* here…and what are we to do?"

John looked even more grim. "It's nothing more nor less than saving my friend's life," he said. "And we've precious little time in which to accomplish it."

I felt a shiver of dread as I took in John's words—he was not given to dramatic statements of any kind, unlike my own predilection for embellishment and the grandiose, upon occasion—therefore the situation must be as serious as his words proclaimed. I looked at him expectantly, holding my tongue for once and waiting for him to speak again.

"Two nights ago," he began, twisting a tassel on a nearby lampshade, "in the *rio* next to this house, the body of a young girl was found." He swallowed hard. "I—I was the one who saw her first—" He broke off as I gasped and leaned forward to take his hand. He squeezed mine affectionately.

"How awful for you, my dear John," I murmured, and watched his face carefully, reading there his evident distress.

"It took some doing to pull her from the water," he continued. "Her clothes—so heavy and wet—and she wasn't wearing any shoes." He seemed most distressed about this small fact, as if it added dreadfully to the poor girl's fate. I waited a moment for him to speak again.

"There was something else," he said in a low voice, looking away from me. I froze, fearing I would hear of some unnatural violence done to the girl.

"Her mouth," John said, forcing the words out, "her mouth was filled with orange peels."

"Orange peels!"

John merely nodded, and we were both silent for several moments. Then I asked the first of the many questions crowding into my brain.

"She belonged to this house?" I asked.

John nodded. "She was one of the maids here, a very nice girl, I met her last spring when I was visiting here. Her name was Anna."

"I presume the police were called," I said, and when he nodded, I spoke again, frowning at the simple but cynical arithmetic I then instantly accomplished. *Death plus police equals...*

"And the police think that *Signore* Favretto...?"

"That's why he's not here to greet you himself," John said glumly. "He has been taken into custody by the police, on suspicion of murder."

† September 1739 †

My arrival in my home at Venice.
Disagreeable discoveries relating to our family affairs,
which dissipate all illusions I may have formed.

—*Memoirs of Count Carlo Gozzi*

DAYLIGHT WAS FADING FAST AS I LED MY FRIEND Massimo to the modest courtyard door of my family home. The palazzo fronted the Grand Canal, where suitably there was a grand entrance with marble steps leading up to the main salon, but for everyday activities, the family and servants used the doors that let out on the *Calle del Rosa*.

The lamps in the courtyard were not lighted and, despite the gathering shadows, I could see it hadn't been swept for days; spiders were busy in the window frames, cobwebs draping the corners. I pulled the house bell sharply, grimacing apologetically to my friend. Deep inside the house I heard the clang of the bell, lonesome and dolorous. I pulled the rope again, harder, and stepped to a side window to peer into the house. At last, a small and wavering light, a candle, flickered as someone drew near to the door.

"Who is it? What do you want?" An unfamiliar female voice growled the suspicious demand. I stepped back from the door and bellowed my answer.

"It is I, Carlo Gozzi, second son of this house and your master! Open and let me enter!"

There was silence from the other side of the door.

THE LOVE FOR THREE ORANGES

"How do I know you are who you say you are?" She thumped the door from her side. "You could be that ruffian Perugino, come to cause me grief again."

Massimo and I exchanged looks; he shrugged. "This one's a real hard case," he said, starting to laugh. I grinned broadly then—the two of us had got up to many tricks and games in our time in Dalmatia, and we were used to laughing outright at peril and destruction—this little obstacle was a mere trifle, after all.

"Tell me, good woman," I said, in my most commanding and persuasive voice, "does the family cook still keep the blue clay pot for the Friday fish stew in the cupboard with the missing handle, with the yellow flowers painted on the front?"

For answer, we heard the massive iron bolt scrape against its fastening, then the iron peg in the floor was lifted and turned aside, and the door was pulled open into the house. A large woman of middle age, whom I did not recognize, stood filling the doorway with her body, clothed in a variety of shawls and headscarves over a house dress and an extra skirt. She peered short-sightedly at me and Massimo.

"Why are you here?" she said, looking us up and down in the coolest manner possible. "The family are all in Friulia—you should be there."

"By God and all the saints, woman," I said, laughing. "And so I should be, but as Fate would have it, I am here, and would like to enter my own house, if it so pleases you, you dragon of the gate."

She scowled at me for a moment, then with a short bark of laughter, she stepped back to let us enter.

"Come, come, young masters, I imagine you are who you say you are," she said, closing the door behind us quickly and with great firmness, locking it up tight again. "I'm only doing the best I can to keep the place together. No one else would come here, with the family away—though not all, not all." She muttered this last phrase almost to herself, but I caught at it.

"Not all? Is there some one of my family here, then? Gasparo, perhaps?" I named my elder and much esteemed brother eagerly, hoping that he alone of all my numerous and fractious family members would be in residence.

"Yes, yes, it is himself," the woman answered, beginning to show us further into the house. "Not here at the moment, he's not, but he'll be home soon, you'll see." She looked us up and down again. "I suppose you'll want rooms freshened up for you—and some food and drink."

"That's exactly what we want," I said. A sudden thought struck me, and I turned again to the woman. "Is his wife here, too?" I asked in great trepidation, and was vastly relieved when she shook her head. "He is here alone, *Signore*," she said.

I took Massimo by the arm. "I'm delighted that Gasparo is here—or will be here—he's the very one I want to see first, and to introduce to you—he'll be able to help dispatch that debt of mine I owe you, right away."

Massimo cuffed my arm in mock anger. "I told you there's no hurry—I'm well provided for, and we'll be friends for a long time, so I won't let you forget!"

"Debts between friends hang about the neck like a rope, tightening with every little strain—I won't let that happen to our friendship," I said, completely serious. I caught up a torch from a sconce in the hallway, and used the woman's candle to light it. When it was blazing well enough, I bowed to Massimo in a courtly manner.

"But come, let me show you some Gozzi hospitality," I said, waving him away from the entrance hall toward the marble staircase that rose from this floor to the next, two curved sets of steps, left and right. In the center of the curve my mother had planted a small garden of trees and urns with flowers in them, to catch the light at the top of the house, three stories up, where there was a round window to let in sunlight. It was nearly my favourite spot in the house, and I walked toward it eagerly. As we approached the staircase, I stopped short to gaze in wonder at the parched and leafless trees and empty urns that filled the center space.

I turned to ask the house servant about this, but she had disappeared, to the kitchen I hoped.

I continued to lead Massimo to the first floor—where were the public rooms for visitors, and my father's library, but all was dark and gloomy, and we could see little in the poor light of my torch—and then to the second floor, where there were several bedrooms. Above that was the small penthouse, which was used for servants' rooms. The staircase seemed in good condition, but I noticed with increasing unease that there were bare spaces on the wall, discolored rectangles and squares, which formerly had held large and beautiful portraits of my family's ancestors—where were they? Taken away to the country house in Friulia? Or, God forbid, sold for whatever pittance the frames would bring?

We gained the second floor landing—I stood appalled and amazed at what had once been a wide and gracious hallway, leading to handsome, comfortable bed chambers along both sides. Even with the dim light of my torch, I could see holes, actual holes in the floor, the parquet broken and gnawed away by vermin, the plaster on the ceiling chipped and marring the once fresh murals, the wallpaper peeling and mildewed. I stepped into the room that had been my very own throughout my childhood and early adolescence, and couldn't hide my shock and dismay.

"Where is the furniture?" I turned around and strode to the corners of the room, gesturing fiercely. "There, there was my wardrobe, and my desk, my chair, there by the window—nothing!"

"There's a bed," Massimo said, trying, I think, to sound hopeful. "That's a good thing."

I stopped and looked at him, then at the bed—the hangings were drooping at the corners, but there were still pillows and coverlets on it. I looked back at Massimo, and felt that all I could do was take it in stride.

"Well, my friend," I said, walking over to him and clasping him on the shoulder. "We've slept in much worse places, haven't we?" I waved the torch at the ceiling. "At least there's a roof over our heads, and I expect there will be something hot to eat—and something cold to drink—in a very short time."

"And what more do we need?" cried Massimo, smiling with all good cheer.

I nodded, and we embraced, but I had to swallow hard to keep down the sob in my heart that threatened to burst forth in unmanly tears.

ॐ Saturday, 20 December 1879 ॐ

I hear what has occurred

"Murder!" I exclaimed. I put down the piece of bread I was about to consume, and tried to organize the onslaught of questions in my mind.

John nodded tersely, and drank from his wine glass. I noticed he hadn't touched any of the food, and on closer examination, I could see he looked terrible—pale and shaken. I gave the plate a nudge in his direction.

"The *rio*," I said. "Is it accessible from the house?"

John shook his head. "There's no door or entrance of any kind on that side, only windows," he said, gulping down his wine and leaning forward to pour another glass. He looked at me, distress clear in his eyes. "There was a window on the top floor, the penthouse floor, that was open—the window in Anna's chamber."

I thought about this. "Is there any possibility that she ended her own life?"

John stood abruptly and began to walk about the room; I could see he was making a tremendous effort to master his emotions.

"It is possible," he said at last, coming to a halt near my chair, looking not at me but at the dark beams of the low ceiling. "But not very likely. You see," he continued, sitting down again and this time looking straight at me. "This is not the first time—this is not the first young woman—to be found in the *rio* alongside this palazzo—though by great good fortune, the first one was found in time—she lived." He sagged back in his chair, weary and spent.

"Good Lord!" I exclaimed. I decided that I clearly had to take hold of this situation if I was going to make any sense of it.

"John," I said, a trifle severely, "let us start from the beginning, shall we? When did you arrive here, and was it at your friend's request? Tell me everything."

I poured more wine into our glasses, and sat back to listen.

"Giacomo wrote to me about three weeks ago," he began, calmly enough. "We had become instant friends last year, in Paris, and I stayed with him earlier this year." He sipped his wine.

"His is a most gentle, kindly spirit," he continued. "There is a kind of innocence, of wondering dreaminess, about him, that is most engaging." He paused, a slight smile on his face. "He comes from a poor family, but was fortunate in having his talent recognized as a young boy, working in a stationer's shop, cutting out silhouettes, if you can imagine! His patron enrolled him at the *Accademia*, under Molmenti, and he has become the center of a new movement, here in Venice, a new way of painting, that has brought him fame as well as fortune."

John stopped to take a breath, that being a longer speech all at once than was customary for him. I smiled encouragingly, but felt my usual impatience about getting to the point.

"So he wrote you…?" I prompted.

"Yes, I was in Madrid, just about to head south to Morocco," he continued. "His letter came to me as I was on the point of departing. Beastly weather in Spain, by the way, wet and cold as the devil, couldn't wait to get across the Straits." He caught the glint in my eye and took up the tale quickly.

"He said he'd been receiving odd letters, notes really, that were vaguely threatening and seemed written in an older style of Italian, talking about water and resurrection, and oranges, of all things."

"Oranges?" I spoke aloud in my surprise. "Why oranges?"

John shook his head. "No idea, I mean, Giacomo had no idea about anything the notes said. But you'll see—no, wait, I'll try to relate things in order." I was concerned to see how disorganized my dear friend's thoughts seemed to be—he appeared to still be suffering from the shock of this sad event. I nodded as he continued.

"At any rate, he didn't pay much attention to them, he figured it was some rival from the *Accademia*, envious of his success perhaps, or maybe even mistaken identity."

"But then..." I said, eyebrows lifted.

"Yes, well, at the end of his letter to me, he said that a young woman, just recently hired by his cook to work in the kitchen, had been rescued late one evening from the *rio* next to his home, incoherent and babbling about ghosts and such nonsense. Giaco wasn't there—here—at the time, he was in Rome, but he heard through neighbors—you know how small a city Venice is—that she was quite off her head, talking about oranges and spirits and things that went bump in the night, apparently."

"Was it possible that she merely fell in and, frightened as anyone naturally would be," I pursued the thought, "just said bizarre things as part of an hysterical reaction?"

John shrugged. "She insisted she was pushed, by 'an unseen hand' from behind her, as she was shaking out a rug on the landing, which is where the *rio* meets the Canal. Evidently she was so shaken that, though physically not harmed, she insisted on being taken back to her parents' home in Mestre, never to return."

"How very strange!" I pondered the story as I reached for a glass of water, sipped it carefully, then spoke. "Ghosts and oranges! And your friend connected that detail to the notes he had received?" I paused, thinking. "And now, of course, with the oranges in poor Anna's mouth…."

"Yes, yes," John said, "although he admitted he couldn't for the life of him make any connection with anything. So," he continued, "he wrote asking me to come to Venice, to help him discern what was going on."

I thought about this a minute and then said, with all my usual bluntness, "But why would he ask *you* to come?" I belatedly heard the inherent insult in my question, and hastily added, "Not that of course you wouldn't be of great service and support, but—surely he has other friends here in Venice who could help?"

John smiled slightly. "I think he felt he could not trust anyone in this city," he said. "And besides," he added, somewhat sheepishly, "I had told him about our…adventure…in the north of England last year, and I guess he thought I might have some…detecting abilities…or something like that." He reached for his wine glass, and I saw a mischievous glimmer in his eyes as he glanced sideways at me. His allusion brought vividly to my mind the sad death that had led us to a nearly incredible experience centered on events some four hundred years before our own time. I brought my attention back to the present.

"However," he continued, "as soon as I arrived, and after finding Anna—I could tell that I needed the help of my brilliant and insightful partner, so I wrote to you."

He leaned forward to pat the back of my hand. "And you, my illustrious Twin, came as called, as we promised each other so long ago."

I nodded, and touched his hand in return. "*To fight for truth, to conquer with mercy,*" I said.

"To die with honour." We recited the last line of our childhood pledge together.

"Let's hope it doesn't come to that," I said dryly, but I felt a great misgiving in my very bones—with a young woman drowned just outside this house, and perhaps a failed attempt on another, Death lurked very near—and it seemed likely that his work wasn't finished yet.

† 30 October 1739 †

A heartfelt discussion with my brother.
More disagreeable discoveries relating
to our family affairs. I learn how things stand in
Friuli, our country home.

—Memoirs of Count Carlo Gozzi

MY BROTHER GASPARO ENTERED THE HOUSE not long after my friend Massimo and I had settled into what remained of the family's dining room, eating the surprisingly well-cooked meal the old door-dragon had conjured up, and beginning to relax under the influence of a long-hidden bottle of wine I unearthed in the cellar—I remembered the hiding places.

Gasparo strode past the servant who had opened the door, and greeted me with surprise, wonder, and reproach.

"Carlo, my dear brother, how came you here?" He embraced me warmly as I sprang up from the table to meet him, although his greeting spoke to me of an elder brother's inherent criticism of a younger. "You sent no notice—I at least heard nothing—but you see, taken all unawares, the state of our house." And with that, he burst into tears.

"Here, here, none of that, my good brother," I said, trying to soothe him. I turned and led him to a seat at the table, put a goblet of wine in his hand, and exchanged rueful glances with Massimo, who remained tactfully silent. "I am home now, for good—or ill!" I laughed, and patted his shoulder as he drank the wine. He seemed to me so much older than when I had last seen him, and weary to the bone. "We will sort this out together, but first, drink, eat, calm yourself."

I seated myself and pulled a platter of grilled onions and potatoes closer, spooning some onto a plate for him, and gesturing to Massimo to pass the branzino my way as well, giving my brother time to compose his feelings.

"You must forgive me," he said, looking up from his kerchief, and then he started, having noticed my friend at the table for the first time. "And you, my brother's friend and comrade-in-arms, are you not? I beg your forgiveness as well, put it down to a lengthy illness I am barely rid of—the dampness, the chill—and the lack of hospitality that we can offer…" Gasparo's voice cracked and ground to a halt.

"Brother," I said, "we will talk of all our family matters in due time. But for now, please allow me to introduce my dearest, closest friend and fellow-soldier, Innocensio Massimo, late of Dalmatia and the Count's glorious army there…" Massimo rose, formally bowed to my brother, then sat down again. My brother seemed completely overcome, and was drinking his wine with great single-mindedness.

"Let us regale you with stories of our travels," I said, raising my glass. "But first, a toast! We are blessed to be home again!" Gasparo and Massimo raised their glasses too, and drank. "Second, we are overjoyed to *not* be in Dalmatia, all due respect to the Count!" We drank again. "And third, I offer my personal assurance to you, my dear brother, that whatever has befallen our family fortunes, I will do my best to restore and raise them again, all in good time, and with the help of our Blessed Virgin Mother, Mary Queen of Heaven!"

"Here, here!" They both called out their approval, and after a second glass of wine, my brother began to look and speak more like himself. The servant came and went, filling our glasses, taking away plates, until finally the cheese and fruit were on the table, with a little bottle of fine lemon liqueur that I recognized immediately.

"Maria's limoncello!" I cried, looking at Gasparo for confirmation. "There is still some left from the summer crop?"

"It's the last bottle, at least, here in this house," Gasparo said, smiling sadly. "I was saving it for a special occasion." He nodded in a friendly way to Massimo. "The homecoming of you two soldiers is certainly special enough!"

I pulled the cork from the bottle and delighted in the pungent fragrance of lemon that sprang into the air. I doled out the pure golden liquid into tiny crystal glasses, and handed them to my two dinner companions.

"To better times!"

Later, after I had seen Massimo as comfortable as could be in a hastily made-up bed in a guest room, I wished him a hearty good night, and walked down the creaking, dimly lit hallway to my brother's room. There was a guttering, smoky fire in the hearth in his room, and he was sitting in a big chair, already again despondent, wrapped in an old cloak, and facing the fire. I pulled another chair away from the window and sat next to him, where we could both look at the fire together.

The silence grew as the flames threw flickering shadows on the walls around us.

"So, little brother," Gasparo said at last. "There is shame in what I must tell you...shame in what has happened to our family."

I held my breath, and waited for him to go on.

He buried his face in his hands, as if he couldn't bear to speak.

"Gasparo, my brother," I said, as gently as I could manage. "What has happened, please, just tell me."

"Our father," he said, after a long silence. "Our father is...unable to speak, paralyzed, immobile on his bed of pain."

The shock I felt upon hearing this news almost slayed me on the spot. It took several minutes before I found my voice. "What...how...when? How is it I have not heard this dreadful news? It must be recent, then...did you send news to me in Dalmatia?" I stammered to a stop, and turned to look at him. "Tell me!"

Gasparo sighed deeply. "It started after you left...but was worsened by the marriage of your two elder sisters."

I nodded, again surprised that I had heard nothing of this, but a growing sense of understanding of the state of my family's fortunes arose in my brain.

"The illustrious Conte Giovan-Daniele di Montreale has married your eldest sister, and the younger is now the Contessa Michele di Prata."

I was puzzled. "How did these fortunate events cause my father to fall ill?"

Gasparo sighed again. "The dowries...ten thousand ducats...each."

I frowned at this. I knew my family had land and estates, here in Venice, and also in Padua, Pordenone, and the farm estate in Friuli—but not much ready money. My mind raced.

"My father sold off portions of the estates to raise the money," I said. It was a statement, not a question. Gasparo nodded, his eyes closed.

"But it still wasn't enough," he said, taking a deep breath and speaking in a rush, to get it out and over with. "We are in debt for another two thousand ducats, at nine percent interest, and creditors are hounding our family daily. The Conte di Montreale—pernicious bastard of a brother-in-law!—is suing us for dowry money promised but not yet paid. And then there are our three younger sisters! Laura, Girolama, Chiara—they are of an age to marry, and we have nothing for their dowries!" He passed his hands over his eyes. "Our father succumbed to melancholy, then silence, then stillness."

"And our mother?" I thought of that indomitable woman, whose form and mien still, at this remove of time and distance, struck me with awe and fear.

"She rules, as she always has, with a penurious and rigorous hand," Gasparo said. He lifted his own hand, gesturing to the ruins of the once beautiful palazzo, ancient and stately. "She has given up on this home, and is happy to see it fall into the canal. The family resides in Friuli now."

As hard as it was to take in all the dreadful events that had befallen my family, I was young, and strong, and a soldier—I still felt hope and strength in my own spirit and bones.

"Then let us go to Friuli—tomorrow, or the next day, when you are well enough to travel," I said firmly, leaning over and laying my hand on his knee. "I must see my father—and Mother as well." I gave Gasparo an encouraging smile, then a wink. "You've always been able to get around her, you know that! Together, we'll turn this around—we'll get back on our feet, you'll see!"

Gasparo laid his hand on mind and grasped it tightly. "I rejoice that you have returned to us, little Carlo," he said, and let the tears flow once more.

I didn't know how I was going to fix things, but I knew that I would—that it was my duty and perhaps, my destiny.

☙ Saturday, 20 December 1879 ❧

The scene of the crime – a famous palazzo

THE HOUR WAS NOT SO LATE—AND I WAS NOT yet too fatigued from my journey, the excitement of the situation having revived my spirits greatly—but that John was willing to show me through the palazzo and discuss the case more thoroughly. We finished our light repast, John assuring me that there would be a more appropriate, and abundant, dinner served later in the evening, and he called the servant to have me shown to my chamber. We agreed to meet in twenty minutes; John said he would remain in the comfortable sitting room until I returned.

A pleasant-looking woman, perhaps nearing fifty, curtsied briefly as I met her at the door, and gestured that I was to follow her. She said her name was Jocasta, and she was the housekeeper. My things had already been placed in my room, she told me, in passable Italian with only hints of Venetan, so she was easy to understand. I thought for a moment to ask her some questions about the unfortunate maid Anna, but I held back out of respect for the woman's feelings, and also because I felt I didn't know enough yet to ask intelligent questions. Nonetheless, it struck me that Jocasta did not look as if she were grieving; but some people are more reserved than others, even Italians.

Jocasta led the way toward the staircase, which immediately struck me when I saw it. It was composed of two wings of shallow marble steps, to the left and the right of a circular garden that, as I looked up, I could see was lighted during the day by an enormous skylight some three stories above. There were green plants and some unusual flowers blooming in the garden, cascading over the edges of marble and stone vases and pillars. Sconces set in the walls were filled with beeswax tapers to light the scene.

My gasp of astonishment caused Jocasta to pause and look at me questioningly.

"*Perdonne*," I said, still gazing in awe. "I am struck by this staircase—it resembles in every detail the one described by Carlo Gozzi as ornamenting his family home in Venice." I had just three days ago finished the proof-reading of that particular chapter in my *Studies in the Eighteenth Century in Italy*, in which I had referenced the memoirs of that illustrious playwright—the very page on which he describes the staircase was before my eyes, although in his description it had fallen into disrepair and all the plants were dead.

Jocasta looked a little blank, but I could tell she understood my words; then a light broke through, and her eyes seemed to narrow in distaste. "Ah, *si, si, Signorina*, Carlo Gozzi, *si*, this was his family home—San Cassiano—though long, long ago, very long before *Signor* Favretto bought the palazzo."

"Yes, that's it!" I cried. "San Cassiano, like the church nearby, yes?" I was gratified beyond measure to realize that I was actually in the family home—one of the Venetian homes, I corrected myself inwardly, with the Gozzi's main seat being in Friulia, out in the country—of one of the greatest lights of the comedic theatre of the 18th century. I marvelled now that I had not thought to visit the place before, but my researches had concentrated chiefly on his writing and his plays, not his personal life. I realized I was standing open-mouthed at the foot of the staircase, lost in reverie, while my patient guide indulgently waited for me to move on, though watching me closely. I shook myself and smiled brightly at her, and we began to walk up the stairs.

We paused only briefly on the landing of the first floor as I peered left and right, remembering Gozzi's descriptions of the lovely space and furniture as it had been before the family fortunes began to fail. As we proceeded to the second floor, I could see there was only a sort of truncated half-floor, possibly the servants' quarters, on the third floor above us.

"*Signora* Jocasta," I said, as she opened a door a little way down from the staircase, "do you happen to know which of these rooms might have been Carlo Gozzi's, when he lived here as a boy?" I'm sure the foolish hopefulness in my face was apparent to the good woman, but she did not disdain my interest, only shook her head apologetically.

"*Sono così dispiaciuto*," she said. "That was a very long time ago, *Signorina*." Now there was a hint of impatience.

"Yes," I sighed, then laughed deprecatingly. "Only about a hundred and fifty years!" I looked sideways at her, wondering if she had a sense of humour. "Not so long in the minds of native Venetians, I dare say."

Jocasta smiled, but her eyes glinted with a flash of steely light. "Not for some things, *sì, Signorina*. Some things we never fail to remember."

I was shown into a lovely room, the wall sconces already lighted, and a well-made fire warming the space. The bed looked comfortable, my clothes were already aired and hanging in the wardrobe, and the Persian carpet beneath my feet gave warmth and elegance and color to the room, which I appreciated greatly.

"This is charming," I said, and Jocasta showed me the water closet and other necessaries, and I was able to dismiss her, feeling I would be as comfortable—nay, more comfortable!—here than in my mother's rented house in Florence.

I took as little time as possible to refresh myself and change from my travelling clothes to more appropriate indoor apparel. I aspired more to functionality than to fashion, and had my dresses made so that I could easily don my own attire without a chambermaid fussing about. Neatness and propriety were all I aimed for, especially in my early years—it was only later in my life that I became playful and daring, adopting a mannish style of clothing that was highly practical and utterly scandalous—but I'm getting ahead of myself.

John was pacing the floor of the decorative sitting room when I returned, full of my discovery about the palazzo's former owner, but he immediately took me by the arm and led me to the doorway leading to the water door on the Grand Canal. We stepped outside, and, despite the cold air, I was assaulted by the rank smell of the murky waters at this time of the evening. There was little traffic—the black surface was smooth as a mirror, reflecting the lights from palazzos that seemed to rise out of the inky depths. The cold beauty of a winter night played against the dissonance of a strong odor of fish, and perhaps worse things.

Keeping my thoughts to myself, however, I let John lead me to the end of the deck-like platform that ran the width of the house, with high, wooden railings to keep one from falling into the Canal. At the farthest end, we stopped, and John stepped behind me, telling me to lean out and look to my right.

"That is the *Rio di San Cassiano*," he said softly. He reached past my left side and pointed to the water, some six feet below us. "That is where I saw Anna," he said. "I had come out to smoke—it was rather late, past two—and as I tossed my cigarette into the water, I saw something white." I could feel the shudder that raced through him at the memory, he was leaning against me so closely. He swallowed hard. "It was her hand, at first, then her arm—then I saw her white gown floating all around her." He shook his head. "It was horrible, horrible."

"My poor Twin," I said, and turning, I put my hand gently on his arm. He laid his hand over mine, and struggled to regain his composure.

I began to shiver, probably from a combination of the night's chill and the wretched end of that poor girl. John noticed immediately.

"How vile of me to bring you out here, without a coat or shawl," he exclaimed. He put his arm around me and led me back into the house. Once inside, he closed the canal doors and walked with me slowly toward the grand staircase.

"I roused up the house, as you can imagine," he continued. "The servants were all crying and carrying on, but two of them came round in a boat, and I went with them, and we fished—we brought her out of the water."

He sighed deeply as we came to a stop at the foot of the stairs. My gaze was drawn to a bright orange flower, some exotic thing, like nothing I had ever seen, which bloomed at the end of a long, leafless stalk. But my attention was all for John's narrative.

"Someone had sent for a doctor, although it was clear she was beyond help—quite, quite dead." He paused.

"Did the doctor say she had died from drowning?" I asked.

John frowned. "Well, at first he did—it was natural to assume that, we all assumed it," he said. "But then, when we had laid out the body"—he gestured to a door across the hall—"down there, in a large stillroom of sorts, we could see there were marks, on her cheeks, as if she had scratched at her face—and then—" He paused once more, controlling his voice. "That's when we saw—the orange peels stuffed in her mouth, so terrible!" He shook his head and fell silent.

I reflected on this gruesome fact; it seriously piqued my curiosity. John roused himself and spoke again.

"The doctor was very concerned, and said as it wasn't clearly a natural death, or a simple accident, the police had better be called."

"Didn't anyone call the police when this happened before, to the other young woman?"

He shook his head. "I think everyone just assumed she was, as you said, merely hysterical after her ordeal. And the fact that Giacomo was in Rome at the time, naturally the police didn't take any particular interest in him." He looked darkly at me. "But this time they did—I suppose the police always assume the worst."

I nodded. "Especially for the blustering *ignoranti* who are the Italian police," I said, absently. My mind was clicking fast, taking in facts and possibilities. But I kept them to myself for the time being. "And so they arrested him—they actually charged him with murder?"

At this, John took a step onto the staircase, and I eagerly moved with him.

"There was—apparently—no actual charge, but they have him in custody," he said. "Giacomo's *avvocato* was with him there this morning, and we had hopes he would have been released to come home tonight—he still may be," John said. "You never know, with the police."

"True, true," I said. "They are as likely to let him go as to keep him for a week—it all depends on the right word in the right ear, the right payment…" I broke off at the look on John's face.

"How do you know about those sorts of things?" he said, smiling faintly. "You never fail to amaze me."

I smiled back, and patted his arm, but didn't expatiate on the subject. "Where are we headed?" I said instead. I looked at the staircase that rose up and up to the penthouse.

"Anna's room," John said, with an unreadable look on his face. "It remains untouched since she died."

☦ October 1739 ☦

Fresh discoveries regarding the condition of our family.
Travel to Friuli and back to Venice with new hopes.
I abandon myself to my old literary studies.

—Memoirs of Count Carlo Gozzi

WE TOOK LEAVE OF MASSIMO SOON AFTER we left Venice, as he was headed due West, toward Padua, and we turned our horses north and east to the lush farming plains below the mountains.

"The crossroads of the barbarians," Gasparo muttered as we reached the top of a hill, and stopped to look at the rivers and plains laid out before us. I knew whereof he spoke, and in my mind's eye I saw the Roman Legions massing to the East to face the Huns pouring down over the mountains from the West—centuries ago.

"It was always thus," I said with a sigh, and a sad smile. "But we are still here—we Friulians, are we not?"

Gasparo smiled at this, and nodded, and we clicked to our horses to trot down the road towards home.

A jubilant, warm and ecstatic welcome awaited us, and especially, me—the returning hero of the Dalmatian wars. Sisters and brothers, servants, tenants, neighbors—all gathered to embrace me as dogs and pigs and cows scattered and lowed and squealed and barked all around us. It was pure family chaos, and I drank it up, laughing and hugging—until I caught sight of my aged father, struggling to stand at an upper window, held up by two manservants, feebly waving a hand to me. I flew across the farmyard and up the stairs to my father's room. There I fell at his feet, grasping his hand to kiss, while both of us dissolved in tears of joy and grief.

He was only fifty-five years old, and yet he looked so ancient and wasted! Speechless, he was led back to his bed by the servants as I followed, still clutching his hand. Though he could not talk to me, he could listen, and I could see in the gleam of his eye that he wanted to hear my stories of military life, of exploits large and small, of all the glory and folly that a young man experiences when away from home for the first time. I did my best to entertain him, but his attention span was limited, and soon he was snoring in his bed. I kissed him gently on the forehead, and went back downstairs to rejoin my family.

I soon found myself, over the next few weeks, at the center of a domestic whirlwind of recriminations, accusations, gossip, ill will, tattered dreams and vitriolic resentment. My sisters—especially Girolama, the youngest at fourteen, who like me was an intense reader and writer, and also like me, had a mischievous, obsessive streak that did not bode well for her, especially in regard to a future marriage partner—my sisters, I say, each came to me in her turn, pouting and wheedling and gossiping about our mother and her relationship with Gasparo's wife.

"She's so tight with the purse strings!" This was a common complaint from all my sisters, reiterated with tears and wails about not having proper clothes or a carriage to take them visiting.

"Gasparo lies down like a whipped dog, he won't do anything against them!" After witnessing a few confrontations between my elder brother and his aristocratic wife, I could see the truth of this—and how poor Gasparo only wanted to be left in peace to read and write his philosophical treatises.

I tried my best to smoothe over all the ruffled feelings, counseling Christian patience and Roman fortitude, charity and kindness and familial love—but I might as well have whistled my breath away. The only relief in sight was that the family was determined to move back again to Venice, with the winter approaching in the country and the City preparing to celebrate its unique blend of the Christmas holidays and the ancient pagan rites of the Solstice and its aftermath. My mother hinted that due to better than expected harvests that Fall, there would be some additional money to re-furbish the house and make some repairs. My sisters looked forward to parties and dances where they would be on parade in full glory—to catch a suitable husband.

Despite our differences and complaints, we were yet a family, and a merry one. The journey to Venice took place over a few days with much laughter, games and puzzles to keep our wits sharp and our spirits high. Servants had been sent ahead to prepare the dreary palazzo for our coming, and I hoped that this time, there would be more of comfort and good cheer in the ancient home of our ancestors than I had experienced at my recent homecoming there.

I took immediate possession of a small room at the very top of the palazzo, a little penthouse with a window embedded on each of three sides—south, east and west, the north side being taken up with the door to the hall, the staircase and the skylight above. I set my desk, during this wintery time, at the south window that looked across the narrow *calle* to the palazzo next door; when the sun shone, it wasn't unbearably cold. There I could retreat from the bilious arguments of my extended family below and concentrate on writing—at first just poems and ditties that came to my youthful mind, then later, more serious essays about art, literature and culture. No politics or religion for me! I was young, fancied myself intellectual and above all, rational—alas, as I see it now, it was the failure of Cupid's arrow to have pierced my untried heart that gave me such airs and confidence. That, and the mere lack of years living in the world.

That youthful arrogance and sense of immortal invulnerability were soon to be sorely tested.

Unbeknownst to me, but as I was soon to be informed, my mother and sister-in-law had all but signed a contract with a local well-to-do merchant for him to take over our palazzo in Venice, the entire property and every floor and room, in return for a handsome quarterly rent! So much for the maintenance and new furniture being for the use of the family! These crafty, unfeeling women had intended for us all to either return to Friuli or disperse to the homes of other relatives while this lucrative bargain gained time and money for the family to recoup its fortunes. But there was a problem—they needed the signatures of *all* the male heirs—Gasparo and me, and my two brothers. Apparently these vixens had already obtained my brothers' signatures or approval (one of them living far distant at the time, and utterly careless of the family's woes), and I was the only one left.

Well, I told them I wouldn't sign. In the short time I had been at home, here and in Friuli, I had discovered that the monies gained from the sale of much land, and also from personal items such as furniture, paintings and even linens, had been squandered and ill-managed by the scheming untrustworthiness of my sister-in-law (I hesitated to overblame my mother), and therefore I was determined that she should have no more access to riches that would be frittered away again.

Everyone in my family united against me, except Gasparo, who merely wept and turned away, too distressed to either importune me or castigate me—and not at all inclined to bring his wife to task for her schemes and machinations. Even my beloved sisters turned on me, calling me selfish and cruel, depriving them of what could be critical dowries. I was roundly despised by all, and everyone took every chance to calumniate my name even to my own father, despite his growing weakness and senility. Nonetheless, I thought perhaps I had been successful in stopping this atrocity, but one morning a few days later my sister-in-law swept into my little upstairs room, sneering and waving a paper in my face.

"All your selfishness is for nothing," she said triumphantly. "*Signore* Mercato has agreed to the terms without your signature!" She looked as if she would spit on the floor. "It turns out it's not really required for *all* the sons to agree!"

"*Signora*," I said, rising from my seat and trying my utmost to speak with civility, for the sake of my dear brother her husband. "I would appreciate it if you would depart from my presence at once, and never speak to me about this subject—or any other subject—again."

"You should be ashamed of yourself, young man!" she cried, and waved a hand toward my desk, covered with paper and pens. "You live off the kindness of your family, yet you bring in no income! You practically take the food from the mouths of your sisters, and your unhappy brother, and yet you do not lift a hand to help this family!"

The anger I felt at her words was tempered by my better self, my rational self, saying to me that this was in fact not far from the truth. Although I tried to hide my feelings, I believe my sister-in-law could see the flush of shame in my face as, with another smile of derision, she turned on her heel and marched back down the stairs.

But before any action on this heinous contract could begin, everything came to a sudden halt by the inestimably sorrowful death of my dear father, a few days later. He died in my arms, the dear man, while I was visiting him in his room and attempting to cheer him by reading a poem I had just written. I was glad, at least, that he had not lived to see us all turned out of the palazzo by the greedy calculations of his own wife and daughter-in-law.

However, a curious and ancient provision of the Venetian law of inheritance, at that time, came into play, and much to my satisfaction, overthrew the females' plans. This law required that all property leased or rented by non-family for the life of the owner (i.e., my father) was to be immediately restored to the heirs, without any penalty due, upon the death of said owner.

Signor Mercato was at first furious, then threatening, then morose…and then resigned. I myself acted with admirable restraint in not mentioning the change in situation to my mother or sister-in-law, merely giving them a gracious smile and nod of the head whenever we passed near each other.

Privately, though, I was determined that I must make some money to help my family, and set myself seriously to the task of finding out a way to do so—using my literary talent, of course.

❧ Saturday, 20 December 1879 ❦

Looking for evidence in Anna's room

WE MOUNTED THE MARBLE STAIRCASE WITH SLOW STEPS, engrossed in our separate thoughts. I wondered at John's strange aspect when he spoke of the maid Anna, but decided it would be indelicate to pursue the subject just now.

"Is there a *Signora* Favretto?" I asked as we gained the landing of the first floor, and turned to continue up the stairs. John nodded and spoke after a moment.

"Giaco married, I understand, earlier this year, although I've only just met his wife, a few days ago." He shrugged. "She's Venetian, from an old family." He glanced at me, an amused gleam briefly lighting his eyes. "With new ideas, apparently, as she's gone and married a poor artist."

"The oldest idea in the world," I scoffed, waving at the gallery of gilt-framed paintings lining the walls of the stairwell, and encompassing the whole palazzo in the sweep of my arm. "The *poor artist* is probably doing better than her family, I imagine, despite their lineage."

John nodded his agreement. "He's fitted up this house especially for her," he said. "It was quite a wreck when he purchased it, like much of this old *sestiere*." He glanced at me, a spark of humour in his brown eyes. "Wait until morning, when you can go out into the neighborhood and see what I'm talking about—it's barely changed in two hundred years—maybe five hundred!"

"Exactly what you love to paint, of course," I said, smiling at my friend. "So where is she, *Signora* Favretto?" I pursued my subject. "Is she with him at the *Questore*?" I looked around as if to spy her out. We stopped for a moment at the second floor, where there were the family chambers and guest rooms. "She doesn't seem to be much in evidence here." I paused, waiting for John's response, which was not forthcoming "She *does* know of her husband's arrest—detainment, that is, does she not?"

Still he hesitated. I couldn't help but wonder at his reticence, but I waited in silence. We began the ascent to the third floor penthouse, and stopped at the landing halfway to catch our breath.

"John?" He looked as if he were trying to figure out how to say something tactfully.

"Caterina—*Signora* Favretto—left the house immediately upon the discovery of Anna's body, although it was the middle of the night," he said. "Her widowed mother lives in Dorsoduro—Caterina stays there often, apparently, and she went there even before the doctor arrived, she was so keen to leave the place."

"Really? She just up and left her husband at such a moment? She must be a fine lady indeed."

I'm afraid my reply showed a certain disapproval of the lady's lack of courage and loyalty.

"Well, Anna apparently was a particular favourite of Caterina's," John said, almost apologetically. "And, from some things Giaco has said, in unguarded moments," he continued slowly, "I get the sense that his wife is, well, *troubled* might be the best word for it." He paused. "She is a study in contrasts, I would say."

John rested his hand on the curled newel post at the beginning of the final wing of steps, leading to the truncated penthouse floor. He glanced up at the skylight, larger now that it was so near, glinting like a black mirror against the night sky.

"She is uneasy in this palazzo, which I could see for myself," he said. "Something about it unsettles her, I can see it in her face, her bearing, when she is not aware she is being looked at. And yet, this is the home her husband prepared especially for her—and she had a great deal of say in the furnishings, which you would think would please her." He paused, motioning with a tilt of his head upwards, to see if I were ready to continue the climb. When I nodded, he spoke again. "One can hardly blame her for not wanting to stay in this *house of death,* as she called it, the last few days." He shook his head. "I must admit I have no idea whether Giaco has informed her of his current state." He shrugged. "My guess is that he has not. He wouldn't want to add to her distress."

We stepped into the small space that comprised the top floor of the palazzo. The wooden planks were uncarpeted, the walls bare and whitewashed, but it had the benefit at least of the rising heat from the fires on the lower levels, and was not unsuitably chilly. As I had surmised, the area consisted of two servants' chambers and some closets for storage. The light from the stairwell sconces threw flickering shadows onto the plain walls. It must be insufferably hot in the summer.

John turned to the left, and stopped before a plain wooden door, his hand hovering over the knob. With a sigh, he turned it, opened the door, and stepped back to let me inside.

"Oh, wait," he said abruptly, turning away. "I forgot, we have no light." He stepped quickly down the stairs to the second floor, and returned in a moment with an oil lantern that adorned one of the ornate marble tables in the hallway. Its light was more than sufficient to illuminate the very small room that served as Anna's bedchamber—John held it aloft as I stepped inside the room and looked around.

A narrow bed, the covers thrown back, as if in haste; the pillow on the floor. There was a small window in the center of the far wall; it was closed and latched. I stepped further into the room, carefully, so as not to disturb anything that might yield some evidence of foul play or crime. A rag rug, oval in shape, was shoved part way under the bed. Bending down a little, I could see a pair of pale slippers under the bed as well. I remembered John's distress at poor Anna's bare feet, and shook the dismal thought aside.

A very slim cupboard stood in a corner of the room. I moved toward it, and opening the long door, saw inside two dresses, both black, a pair of heavy black shoes nestled at the bottom, and a single shelf with neatly folded undergarments. The sole ornament poor Anna seemed to possess hung on a nail above the shelf—a pink ribbon upon which was strung a silver medal, some religious personage, I imagined, the Blessed Virgin or a favourite saint. I am not well versed in those sorts of things. I felt around the sides and floor of the cabinet, searching for a hidden panel—and was rewarded when I felt a small indentation at the edge of the floor board. I pressed it with two fingers and pulled back—the panel was on a kind of spring, and popped up.

"What have you found?" John was hovering over my shoulder, peering in.

"Hidden panel," I said, trying to suppress my excitement. "These old wardrobes often have them." The space under the panel was shallow, and about eighteen inches across, somewhat less than the width and depth of the wardrobe floor.

"There's nothing here," I said, disappointed. "Completely empty."

I re-situated the panel, and closed the wardrobe door softly. I looked around at the rest of the room, and spoke to John.

"That window," I said, pointing to it. "Was it open or closed when you—after the girl was found in the water?"

John rubbed his forehead with his free hand. "It was open. Someone must have closed it since." He motioned for me to take a look. "Undo the latch and you'll see that it looks out on the *rio*."

I moved toward the window, which was set above middle height in the wall, and noted that the single, small wooden chair in the room was pulled up close under the window, set sideways, as if someone had placed it there to step onto, to gain access to the window.

"Is this window really large enough for someone to go through it?" I wondered aloud. "Here, John, bring the lantern closer." With one hand on the back of the chair and the other on the windowsill, I stepped up onto the chair, unlatched the window and peered out. Standing on the chair, the bottom of the frame was slightly below my waist, and it was, I judged, about eighteen inches across.

"Anna was about your size and height, Vi," John said, his voice mournful in the quiet room.

"Then she could easily have climbed out this window," I said. I leaned out farther and listened to the sounds of the winter evening—I could see lights reflecting on the water below, which seemed very far away. How would it feel to fall into it from such a great height! The thought made me tremble, and I pulled my head back in and latched the window again. I dismounted, and looked up at John, standing forlornly holding the lantern.

"Or she could have been pushed," I said, "although that would take a certain amount of strength, especially if she were fighting back and struggling."

"But she couldn't have been," John said. "Struggling, I mean. There were those damned orange peels in her mouth—surely they had been put there after she was dead?"

"Or unconscious," I said. I thought a moment. "Could she have been poisoned? Or strangled? Were there marks on her neck?"

John shook his head. "I don't really know—there were scratches and bruises on her face, I remember that—but we would have to consult the coroner, if they have even bothered to have an examination of the body."

"Surely, for a murder, the police would—" I broke off. "Pardon me, this is Italy, not England. Who knows what they'll consider it appropriate to do? Or when?"

We stood in the middle of the small room, looking at each other. A thought occurred to me.

"Wouldn't it have made a huge splash, a body falling from this height?" I said. "Didn't you say you were out on the terrace, smoking? Wouldn't you have heard a splash?"

John thought this over. "I was out there for no more than fifteen minutes," he said finally. "And I did not hear a sound. It could certainly have happened some time before that—the *rio* is sluggish, especially at that time of night, so the body could take some time to drift forward into the Canal." He shrugged. "People are always throwing things into the *rios*," he said. "It's a common sound, that sort of splash."

I nodded. "We need to look over every inch of this room," I said. "Something happened here, and we need to find out what it was. Did the police search here?"

John laughed dismissively. "Not what you could call a search." He looked around the room, saw a lantern hook near the door, and carefully positioned the light on it.

"What are we looking for?" he asked.

"I really don't know," I admitted. "Just look." I surveyed the tiny space. "It won't take long."

Stepping away from the bed, I bent down and carefully tugged at the rag carpet, pulling it out from under the bed and smoothing it out. One of Anna's slippers came with it, and in an attempt to get the other one, I gathered my skirts and knelt on the floor, reaching far under the bed. My fingers grasped the slipper and I pulled it out. Something inside it touched my hand, and I yelped.

"What?" John cried.

"Nothing," I said, relieved that it wasn't a mouse or any other living thing. I shook the shoe over the rug, and the offending item fell out.

It was a long, curled orange peel, dried out around the edges but still supple. The faint, citrusy smell was released into the air as I touched it.

"Oranges are readily available, at Christmas, aren't they," I mused. I was still kneeling on the floor by the bed, and John came over and bent down beside me.

"I remember them as stocking gifts, don't you?" he said, taking the peel from my fingers and looking at it. "Exotic and marvelous, in the depths of winter…"

"So anyone can get an orange in the market, this time of year." I paused. "There was an orange on the platter of fruit we had served to us just now." I looked at my friend, who then straightened up and put out his hand to help me rise from the floor. I dusted off my skirts, and took back the orange peel from John's hand.

"This means, I believe, that whatever happened to poor Anna, happened in this room," I said. The thought chilled the blood in my veins. That poor girl!

"But what, exactly?" John said, frustrated. "And who could have come up here, unseen, unheard, and gained access to her room? Wouldn't she have screamed? Wouldn't the other servants have heard something?"

"Perhaps," I said slowly, "unless it was someone she knew." I glanced quickly at John, then away. "Even someone she was expecting? Or, maybe it was one of the servants themselves?" I glanced out the door into the dark landing. "Whose room is across the hall?"

John thought a moment. "I believe it is another maid, Maria, I think it is." He looked at me, warily. "The male servants, and the housekeeper, all sleep below stairs. The cook, I believe, has a home nearby."

I smiled at him. "You have been doing your groundwork, Inspector John."

John nodded, but again that unreadable, closed look came over his handsome features. "The police did not talk to the servants," he said at length, "other than the briefest of questions. Once they had decided their murderer was Giaco, they didn't bother with anyone else."

"Well," I said, "we're going to have to do all that ourselves, then." I thought of something I had forgotten momentarily.

"Those notes," I said, "you said that your friend had received some letters, strange letters?" John nodded, and I continued. "Do you know where they are? Can we see them? We must see them!"

Just then there was a gentle tap on the door, which startled both of us in the extreme. It was Samuel, the Favretto's *major d'omo. Curse the man,* I thought, *how long has he been standing there, and what has he heard?*

"*Perdonne, Signore* Sargent, but *Signore* Favretto has come back—and the *Signora* is with him." The servant delivered his news, I perceived, with suppressed excitement, while trying to appear indifferent. Although he was a young man—maybe around twenty?—his hair was beginning to grey at the edges; he had smooth-shaven cheeks, and a suave manner. But I didn't like the glitter in his eyes, and I very much didn't like the way he continued to ignore my existence. He hadn't once looked at me; he directed his message entirely to John. "They are in the small sitting room, and sent me to fetch you."

"Excellent!" John cried, less disconcerted than I, apparently. "Please tell him we will be down in a moment."

Samuel bowed and retreated as silently as he had come.

"I don't like that man," I said to John, once I was sure the *major d'omo* was out of hearing.

"What, Samuel?" John said, retrieving the lantern from its nail, and preparing to leave the room. "He's a little stiff, like most butlers, I imagine. Giaco says he couldn't manage without him, says the man took charge the minute he walked in, some months back, and everything's running like a Swiss clock."

"He's awfully young to be 'in charge'," I sniffed. "More to the point, he doesn't like me."

John stared at me a moment. "He doesn't know anything about you," he protested.

"Oh," I said, "I think he's about to find out, but I don't think that's going to make him like me any better!"

✝ Early December 1739 ✝

Dismal Winter in Venice.
I am Distracted by a Fair Neighbor.

—*Memoirs of Count Carlo Gozzi*

BY THE END OF NOVEMBER, DESPITE THE EXPECTED gaieties of the coming Christmas season, most of my family had departed Venice again for Friuli. In the main, I think my sister-in-law, in concert with my mother, intended to retreat and re-group out in the country—where they could live more frugally—and from there, eventually, to renew the attack on me in the city, perhaps in the Spring. There were few cordial farewells directed to me, although everyone had been able to maintain at least outward civility during the funeral and interment of my dear father in the family crypt at the church of San Cassiano. Indeed, my elder brother and I held each other tightly, our tears of grief dampening our faces and collars. I had little hope from him of his being able to become the master of the family, with such a wife and mother leagued against him, but I loved him with all my heart.

The funeral was truly a magnificent ceremony, attended by the better members of society whose memories of my father's generosity, dignity and love of Venice had lasted beyond and despite the wreck of our family's fortunes and reputation in recent years. My mother was suitably attired in black lace and silk, as were my lovely sisters. No fewer than ten cardinals were sent from Rome, carrying a special blessing from the Pope, and concelebrated the lengthy Mass, watched over by the splendid Tintorettos and statues of saints ranged all round the altar. My three brothers and I bore the coffin up the steps of the dilapidated portico and through the high, main door, then down the aisle, lighted by candles on either side. Afterwards, a funeral collation was laid out at our palazzo, unusually clean though draped in black, and was enjoyed by all comers, whether they were known to the family or not. It is the Venetian way.

When my family left, only I and Almarò, my youngest brother, were left to inhabit the crumbling palazzo, and even he was intending to leave soon, to stay with relatives in Milano. I retired to my little hermitage at the top of the house, surrounded by my books and letters, intent upon finding a way to make money to support my family, and after a few days, I was completely alone. Only the housekeeper-cook and one manservant remained to support me.

At times I began to think I was going mad. I ate little, drank too much—raiding the cellars for long-hidden bottles of wine that even my sister-in-law had not been able to find—and kept myself sequestered, cloistered even, in my little penthouse high above the green waters of the Grand Canal. I penned poem after poem, wondering even as I wrote them, what was driving me on? To whom were these fervid poems written? What was this great longing in my heart and soul that seemed to burn within me—it was not religious fervor, no, far from it! I began to ask myself, was it Love I was yearning toward? And if Love, was it the pure enlightened spirit of *Agape* or the dark, lustful urgings of *Eros*?

I was soon to find out.

The sun had actually made an appearance that day, a watery, thin sort of light peeping through the grey clouds above the city in the first days of December. It was early afternoon, and the congealing remains of my poor luncheon lay mouldering on the plate by my desk.

I had opened the shutters above my desk, which faced south, allowing me to gaze with pleased melancholy across the rooflines of the city. Slightly below the level of my own window, however, I could see a shuttered window, like my own, belonging to the palazzo across the *Calle del Rosa* from our own. Unlike our home, I noted that the palazzo was in excellent condition, with fresh stucco and paint, and flowers in pots on rails in front of all the windows. It was much grander than our humble home, with two *piani nobile* rising above the second floor, which was the one almost level with my own little penthouse.

My misery and loneliness had blinded me to anything around me for some time, and I felt a stirring of curiosity about the people who lived next to us. I was to be richly rewarded on the spot—as if my thoughts flew with wings to the window across from mine.

A shutter was flung back, and I gazed in fascination as a slender white hand and arm, revealed by a sleeve of shimmering blue silk and lace falling back, reached out to open and fasten the other shutter. To my delighted eyes, the most beautiful face appeared at the window, upturned to the glimpse of sunlight—a pale and perfectly proportioned face, with dark, wing-like brows, a red pouting mouth, opened slightly to show perfect, even white teeth. This lovely vision was completed by the sight of a swanlike neck, plunging down to a décolletage like two plump doves snuggled into silk and lace. Her luxurious reddish-blonde locks were tied back loosely with a blue ribbon.

I must admit I probably looked like a schoolboy drooling after pastries in a baker's window, and I caught myself quickly before the young lady—for lady she clearly was—could catch sight of my face. Composed, therefore, and looking (I hoped) like the scholarly gentleman I intended to be, I nonchalantly reached out a hand, as if to close my shutter, thereby contriving to catch her attention.

"Oh!" Her startled exclamation was pure music. She gazed up at me as if I were an apparition. *"Oh, Signore, perdonne me,"* she murmured, and cast her eyes down shyly, drawing one hand, clutching a white lace handkerchief, across her bosom.

I looked at her with what I thought was princely courtesy, and academic indifference, and gave a slight nod of my head. "Not at all, *Signorina*," I said, and made as if to continue closing the shutter.

"Wait!" she called, blushing prettily. "It's actually…*Signora*," she said, and drew her left hand from beneath the handkerchief to briefly display an enormous diamond and sapphire ring—I could make out the individual jewels from where I sat, it was so large—but then, we were at most six feet apart, the upper stories of the palazzo being somewhat nearer to each other than at the level of the street, where the walls were perhaps eight feet apart.

She was so young, and shy, and freshly innocent, that my heart was inclined to soften my imperious manner—young men can be so ridiculous in their sense of personal dignity!—so I spoke more graciously.

"Your countenance is so very young, my dear *Signora*," I said (and I, all of twenty-one at the time!). "I could never have imagined you a matron. You must forgive a dry old scholar who does not mix with the world."

She blushed again, even more becomingly. "Indeed, sir," she said, looking down at first, "Indeed, I am but six months a bride." Her eyes, a clear, startling green, lifted and showed me a luminous and somehow wise depth to her I had not seen at first.

I was entranced.

"You have my congratulations, *Signora*," I said. "And my good wishes to you and your husband for a long and happy marriage."

Despite my suddenly intense infatuation with this charming creature, I was determined not to give myself away, and reached again to close the shutter, when I was caught by the sound of a sorrowful sigh, and glancing down, I saw one crystalline tear drop upon her rounded cheek.

"What is it, my dear *Signora*, that can cause such a sorrow that makes you weep?" I leaned forward and partly out of the window, to be nearer to her, as she seemed disposed to speak in low tones.

She shook her head, and sighed again. Then she, too, leaned forward into the window frame, causing (I saw with delight) her creamy white bosom to swell with the pressure against the wood. It made me quite faint with a sudden burst of desire.

"Oh, sir," she said. "A scholar and philosopher such as you has no time for the sad domestic plight of an ordinary woman like myself."

I started to respond, but saw her glance into the interior of her room, then hastily move away from the window. I heard her address someone, a maid perhaps, and I quietly leaned back from the windowsill so I would not be seen, and perhaps, betray her to a servant—or maybe her husband! I heard the shutters of her window close with a bang shortly thereafter, and decided it was for the best. I tried to settle back into my studies, but the memory of her lovely voice, and all her various charms and mysteries, preyed heavily on my mind. Try as I might, I couldn't help but form fancies in my head about a continued liaison with her.

☙ Saturday, 20 December 1879 ❧

I meet Giacomo and Caterina Favretto.

A DEEP SILENCE REIGNED IN THE SITTING ROOM when John and I entered to meet our hosts, although there was, to my sensibilities, a pressure in the very air, a weight as of overcharged emotions, held tightly in check. I admit I had by this time all too lively an interest in both members of this Venetian duet, and I eagerly, but politely, surveyed them closely in turn.

John immediately addressed his friend, without even properly introducing me. Under the circumstances, however, I felt it was an understandable breach of propriety.

"Giacomo, I can't tell you," he said, "but of course you feel it more than I—how relieved I am to see you released and at home again." John strode forward and embraced the Italian painter, a man not much taller than myself and who, therefore, appeared but a youth next to John, although I knew he was several years our senior. His tousled, tumbled brown locks gave him the look of a Venetian Byron, but the true Italian appeared in his well-trimmed mustache, its ends twisted and waxed into tiny points. He was impeccably dressed, almost dandyish, and wore a brown velvet smoking coat with deep pockets over a spotless white blouse. He must have been arrived some time in the palazzo before we were informed of his presence, I surmised; time enough to change into more comfortable clothing that what he'd been wearing, no doubt, when he was carted off by the police.

"*Signorina* Paget," he said to me when he stepped back from John's embrace. He gave a quick little bow, his hands at his sides. "My wife and I are delighted that you have come to visit." Then, turning to his wife, "Caterina, my dear, *Signorina* Paget is a childhood friend of our dear John, and is a well-known author of many excellent and insightful essays about Italy, primarily the 18th century."

Caterina remained seated as I advanced further into the room. I nodded my acknowledgement of Giacomo's lovely compliment, and then bent my knees in a slight curtsey to his wife. She said nothing, but I didn't take that as haughtiness or pride; rather, her vague look and effort to focus on what was being said soon made me feel a kind of pity for her—she clearly was very distressed. A brief glance told me she was younger than her husband, but not younger than I—she looked to be about twenty-three, and was quietly though expensively dressed in some pale, muslin-y thing which draped attractively around her curvy figure. Her hair was a gorgeous, sunlit golden-red, as is the case with some Northern Italians, and fell in curls and wisps about her exceedingly white, fragile cheeks and liquid green eyes. In all, a lovely creature! I immediately took back my hard-hearted judgement of her reaction to the death of her favourite maid.

I seated myself on the sofa next to her, and was favoured with a watery smile. I perceived what I interpreted as a "prompt" from her husband, and she immediately turned to me and spoke. "Miss Paget," she said, her voice light and pleasing—she spoke a pure Florentine tongue—"I have not read any of your works, but I am now eager to do so. Please tell me what would be the best one with which to begin."

Flattered by this bewitching appeal, I nonetheless modestly protested.

"*Signora*, I fear that my Italian studies are probably a pale imitation of works you have doubtless read by the great masters, in your native tongue," I said. "My audience is, rather, the readers outside of Italy who wish to be enlightened about the greatness of her art and music and literature."

I glanced away to see if John had heard my response, but he and Giacomo had retreated to the far end of the sitting room, and seemed deep in intense conversation.

"However," I continued, turning back to the lovely Caterina, "one chapter of my forthcoming book is all about Carlo Gozzi, the re-inventor of the *Commedia dell'Arte*?"

I was amazed to see Caterina's pale cheeks flush with a slow-rising blush; she became visibly nervous although she tried to hide it by dropping her handkerchief and then moving to pick it up. Curious! I decided to pursue the subject.

"Of course you must know this, but I was so pleased to learn that this very palazzo, which you and *Signor* Favretto inhabit, was once the family home of the Gozzis." I watched the lady keenly as she straightened up—she tried to avoid my eye, but one glimpse told me she was exceedingly disconcerted. She opened her mouth to speak but nothing came out, and then she—I believe—pretended to cough, delaying her response to me and in the course of it, gaining her husband's swift attention.

"What is it, my dear?" Giacomo sounded not merely attentive, but worried—he positively rushed to her side, kneeling down before her on the sofa. "Caterina, my darling, you are not well!" He snatched up a cup with warm tea in it and held it to her lips; she sipped at it, her cough subsiding, and sank back upon the sofa pillows with a wan look and a barely audible *grazie mille, amore mio*.

I stifled an unladylike snort. Why on earth would she be distressed upon hearing Carlo Gozzi's name? That she knew the palazzo's history was clear to me, but what could be problematic about that? I was determined to find out.

My nemesis, Samuel the *major d'omo*, appeared in the doorway to announce dinner was served. Giacomo tenderly raised his wife from her sofa, and all but carried her into the dining room.

John hastened over to me and offered his arm. As we passed out of the room, he bent his head to catch my low tones. "*Signora* Caterina is hiding something," I said. He looked at me in wonder, then his eyebrows drew together most threateningly.

"Don't worry," I assured him. "I'll be very nice to her."

✝ Early December 1739 ✝

*The history of a brief love affair which,
though true, may be considered as fiction.*

—Memoirs of Count Carlo Gozzi

THE NEXT MORNING I WAITED IN AGONY AT MY DESK, my spirit hungry for another glimpse of the lovely *Signora* next door. Soon I heard the click of the interior latch on the shutters, and saw them begin to open. Hastily, I looked down at my papers and books, not wanting to appear too eager, as if I had been waiting for her. When I heard the shutters fall open, I raised my head, as if startled by the noise, and looked directly into the upturned eyes of—a blowsy, fat-cheeked female servant, who appeared to look at me with a calculating and even leering eye. With a bare nod of her head, she continued with the shutters, then turning back into the room, I heard her say loudly, "You must sit at the window, my lady, with your needlework, the light is so much better here." Moments later, the vision I had encountered the day before took a seat at the window. She did not look up for many minutes, but after a while my own steady gaze at her drew her attention to me, and she looked up.

"Good day, *Signore*," she said simply, but accompanied with the sad smile I had noted yesterday.

"And to you, *Signora*," I said, with dignity (I hoped). "We are blessed with fine weather, somehow, despite it being December," I continued, "when Veneta is usually dripping with cold rain and fog." I hesitated. Was I talking too much? But the lady's smile grew a little, and she looked up at me encouragingly. I decided a little gallantry couldn't hurt. "No doubt the sun shines in the hope of shedding its warmth on such a lovely lady as yourself, and to draw you to the window where you may gather its rays to yourself."

I held my breath; I had gone too far, I feared. My fair neighbor's gaze was withdrawn, but I noticed a fine blush suffuse her long neck and slowly color her face. As I watched, emboldened by this enticing response, I could see one corner of her mouth twitch upward in even more of a smile.

"Sir," she said at last, "you do me great honour to take notice of a mere housewife at her duties."

I answered with what I thought was an even better compliment, and so, gradually and by increasingly intimate degrees, the *Signora* and I began to converse with one another—first about the weather and the town, the preparations for the coming Christmas festivities, and then on to higher matters of politics, religion and philosophy. I was amazed to hear her discourse—erudite and thoughtful—she had evidently been well-educated, and had a curious, stimulating mind.

We talked eagerly until finally, as she turned her head to respond to a summons by her maid, telling her that her husband was asking for her, she quickly took her leave.

I sat, gazing at the now-closed shutters as the darkening sky shrouded the city in dusk and fog—the winter was closing in, and the longest night of the year would be upon us in about three weeks.

And I realized I was hopelessly in love.

For the next three weeks, my *Signora* and I had nearly daily conversations at our open windows. I was delighted with her manner of speaking, as well as the substance, and her sense of humour. She had excellent taste in music, theatre and the arts—and soon I was bold enough to read her a poem or two (secretly dedicated to her, though I think she began to perceive the secret), and she was intelligent enough to appreciate them and discuss them with spirit and knowledge.

Then, one day, her shutter did not open. I sat yearning at my desk all the morning and into the afternoon, but not a sound did I hear nor a light did I see in her upstairs room.

A second day passed, and still no *Signora*. Could she have left the city for a visit? But she had not mentioned any such thing. Surely, she could not be ill! I paced my room, wondering if I could be bold enough to go downstairs, cross the *calle*, and knock on her husband's door. Undetermined and worried, I sat back down, and tried to read a treatise on the medieval practice of *Commedia dell'Arte* that I had come across in a bookshop recently.

I must have fallen asleep at my desk, the window still open to the elements (foolishly, what with the damp evening air and all the dire spirits of the Solstice soon to be abroad), when I was abruptly awakened by something light hitting me on my head—I roused up, and saw a small rock with a note tied to it with a delicate blue ribbon, like the one in my lady's hair, lying on my desk.

What could it mean? It was so dark outside I couldn't see if the *Signora's* window was open or closed.

My heart beat fast as I untied the ribbon and smoothed out the paper. There, in feminine handwriting most exquisite, were the following words:

Dear Signore, I beg of you—have I displeased you in any way? Why have you not answered my note? Did you not receive the miniature that you requested? The last two days have been agony, and now I feel I have no choice but to throw myself upon the mercy of one whose honour, dignity and wisdom I have heard much about, and witnessed a little myself—you, my neighbor and hopefully my friend! If you would not thrust me into utter despair, please meet me at the sotto portico by the ponte storto at S. Apollinare; look for the gondola with a white handkerchief hung out one of its windows.

It was unsigned.

What was I to do? I was unaware of any note of hers having reached me! I could not imagine that either of the two house servants would have failed in that duty to me—there was little enough for them to do, and yet they were paid as if they worked day and night. My poor *Signora!* What kind of trouble must she be in? As a young man of a romantic and gallant nature, I could do no less than to fly to my fair neighbor's side in her time of need, though I did not even know her name.

❧ Saturday, 20 December 1879 ☙

Dining at Ca' Favretto

THE DINING ROOM WAS GORGEOUS IN ITS APPOINTMENTS: yellow satin on the walls, fluted half-columns in the corners with elaborate Corinthian capitals, an ornate marble fireplace, gilded and polished, and a three-paneled bow window that overlooked the Grand Canal. There stretched before us a dining table that could easily seat twenty people. Happily, the four of us were arranged at one end, two on each side, John next to me and the wedded couple across from us.

"You must excuse the unorthodox arrangement, *Signorina* Paget," Giacomo said, holding out a chair for his wife, while John did the same for me. "You see, we treat you as a friend, and do not stand upon ceremony."

"I find the arrangement delightful," I said. "Much more conducive to conversation, which is above all what I prefer to dine upon, rather than mere fish and vegetables."

Shortly after we had been seated at the dining table, and the first course was beginning, the door was opened and an extraordinary looking woman sailed into the room. Giacomo, who sat facing the door, instantly rose to his feet, as did John after a moment.

"Mama! We did not expect you…but of course you are welcome!" He turned to me and John, saying, "Allow me to introduce my mother-in-law, *Signora* Maria Angelina di Contadini. Mama, this is the distinguished artist, *Signore* John

Singer Sargent, and the esteemed writer, *Signorina* Violet Paget, that is," he caught himself, and nodded to me, "Vernon Lee."

John bowed and I nodded my head, noticing at the same time that the *Signora's* daughter looked caught between relief and terror at the sight of her mother.

And what a sight! The woman was tall but thickset, very unlike her daughter, with a piercing eye and far from gentle manner. Imperious was the word that came to mind. She had peacock feathers in her headdress, which perched atop a pile of dark brown ringlets; her gown was simply cut, but of a violent magenta color with contrasting deep blue piping and buttons scattered here and there. Her complexion was rather darker than her daughter's, and to my untrained eye, she appeared to be wearing rouge! I gazed at her in mute astonishment—was she an actress? An opera singer? At any rate, I imagined she was going to provide at the least some diversion for our fairly somber party. It was enough to make one forget there had been a murder.

The ever-vigilant Samuel was already leading in servants to lay a place at the end of the table for this formidable person, and in scarcely the time it took for *Signora* to present her cheek for her daughter to kiss, the place was set, and Samuel was pulling back the chair for her to be seated. It could have been a trick of the light, but I thought I saw a look of some meaning pass between *Signora* and the *major d'omo*—and did his hand linger for a moment on hers when he laid the napkin in her lap? *Tut tut, Violet Paget,* I told myself—*surely you are imagining things!*

The topic that had been so studiously avoided amongst the four of us was, without ceremony, brought forward by *Signora* di Contadini.

"Let us settle this outrageous accusation against you, my dear Giacomo," she said, taking up a fork and waving it in the air. "The police—those buffoons—how can they possibly think you had anything to do with that wretched, unfortunate maid!"

"Mama!" Caterina protested. "This is not a thing anyone wishes to discuss, and certainly not over dinner." I was surprised at her assertiveness, although on a closer observation, it seemed more the result of nerves stretched to the breaking point than any kind of inner strength of character.

"No, no, my dear," her husband said, soothingly. "Your mama is only interested in my welfare, understandably." He looked apologetically at me and John. "This is indeed most distressing, but I'm hoping that with your assistance, we may be able to make some sense of this evil chaos."

Signora di Contadini looked coolly at me over the rim of her wine glass. "Is *Signorina* Paget a policeman?" Her tone was dry but civil. She turned her gaze to John. "Or this handsome gentleman? Perhaps he is a special investigator of crimes for the *Questore*?"

I choked back a laugh at this portrayal of both of us, which made me cough, then hiccough.

But I could see immediately that John did not find her questions amusing.

"Murder is not a matter for comedy, *Signora*," he said, rather stiffly. "A young woman is dead, another claims an attempt on her life, and your daughter's household appears to be at the center of this mystery."

"My apologies, *Signore* Sargent," the lady returned, looking actually repentant. "I did not mean any disrespect for the dead, and of course you are correct." She leaned back slightly to allow the servant to offer her a platter of roasted vegetables; she transferred a few spoonfuls to her plate, and took up the subject again.

"And how did it come about, my dear Giacomo, that the police were so good-natured as to allow to you return home?" I thought with philosophic amazement at the prerogatives of this formidable mother-in-law, who ignored her daughter's wishes and continued to discomfit her son-in-law in his own home. I nudged John discreetly with my elbow, as he looked about to intervene—I wanted to hear his friend's answer to this question.

Giacomo sipped at his wine, patted his mouth with a snowy napkin, and sighed. "I don't know, Mama," he said. He looked very tired. "They asked me the same questions over and over, all day long, and I think eventually they became tired of my answers."

"What kind of questions?" I asked, hoping to steer the conversation to something useful, although I feared that I would be as irritating as the *Signora*.

Surprisingly, Giacomo answered without seeming annoyed. "Oh," he said, "such things as *had I or anyone heard anything? Had the girl been lately distressed or frightened? Had anyone noticed anything suspicious that day, or any day? Who were her friends? How long had she been in my employ? Did she have a lover?*" He waved his hand to dismiss it all, and I discerned a faint blush as he stated this last question.

We paused momentarily as the fish course was brought round and served. When the servants retreated, the mother-in-law started up again.

"And *did* she?" *Signora* di Contadini asked sharply. When Giacomo looked a little puzzled, she said, even more sharply, "*Did* she have a lover?"

At this he blushed more thoroughly and shook his head. "That is, I do not know, but I'm sure she did not—Anna was not—she was a very good girl."

Caterina spoke up. "Mama, you are intolerable. What is it to you, whether our servants behave themselves or not?" She, too, was flushing with rising color. "Anna was a good girl, just as Giacomo says. This must be the work of some insane person who got in somehow and killed her." She was fighting back tears.

Her mother looked at her coolly. "And the other maid, the little kitchen girl, six weeks ago, was that another insane person who tried to murder her? Or perhaps the same one?" She emitted a low sound of derision—what would be called a snort in a person less distinguished looking. "You are overlooking the obvious, my dears," she said, calmly taking a bite of the cream-soaked plaice. "Someone who lives in this house—or who has regular access here—committed this murder."

Caterina's eyes rolled back in their sockets, and she fainted dead away. Luckily, she leaned toward her husband so he was able to catch her in his arms and keep her from falling to the floor. Two footmen standing at the sideboard sprang into action and swiftly but gently carried the poor lady away, with her husband following immediately, after glancing his apologies in our direction.

The *Signora* had put down her fork and ceased eating to watch the sad spectacle, but she seemed unconcerned. *Was this a common occurrence?* Had the fragile-looking Caterina actually fainted? I'm sorry to be so cynical, but there you have it—I have never been very sympathetic with women who make a habit of fainting, particularly at convenient moments or to garner attention, and although there was something in Caterina's looks that betrayed a true nervous sensibility, perhaps even stretched beyond endurance, I remained suspicious of her behaviour.

John had leapt from his chair to be of service, but the footmen had precluded any need for his assistance. He seated himself again, but signed to the servant to pour more wine in his glass, and he left the rest of his meal untouched.

The *Signora* continued to eat with a hearty appetite. I decided on my course of action.

"*Signora* di Contadini," I said accordingly, "I would greatly appreciate hearing your views about this murder, and the attempted murder, if that's what it was. It appears you have given it some considerable thought."

Her dark eyes flashed with a spark of amusement. "Yes, I have," she said. "And I see no reason not to tell you my thoughts on this matter." She looked around the room, found the face of Samuel and motioned to him a gesture that he, at least, understood immediately, and John and I did moments later, when all the servants left the room. When the door clicked shut, the *Signora* turned her gaze upon us, pursed her lips, her chin resting on pointed hands, and nodded, as if making up her mind about something.

"There is a curse on this palazzo," she said abruptly, and I could see there was no gleam of amusement in her eyes now. "A curse of death and revenge—and it has fallen now on my daughter and her husband."

✝ Late December 1739 ✝

The Night of the Solstice

—Memoirs of Count Carlo Gozzi

I LEFT THE HOUSE MASKED, AS WAS THE CUSTOM for that time—Venice had maintained certain traditions, now seeming so quaint and medieval—and most persons, especially women, who went abroad in the night in the weeks leading up to Carnival (and throughout that particularly bizarre time) were granted permission to wear masks. Full costumes and outlandish regalia would be worn when Carnival itself began after the first of the year, only to culminate on the eve of Ash Wednesday. Women would dress as men, men would dress as women, masters and servants would change places—all the better to deceive and trick each other into licentious behaviour while remaining anonymous. As a youth, I was not immune to the excitement of such risky, unorthodox behaviour, but I have come to see it differently now.

But this is not the time for a lecture on cultural mores.

I wore a simple black mask, which obscured most of my face, leaving only my eyes visible. By donning a cloak with a hood, and wearing black clothing, I easily concealed my identity—not that anyone would probably know me after my four years' absence, and having grown and changed during that time, as youth will do. I was not intent on trickery or bad behaviour, but this modicum of disguise would suit my main purpose—meeting a married woman in secret.

THE LOVE FOR THREE ORANGES

I hastened to the little bridge of S. Apollinare, an obscure *ponte* reached only after several twists and turns, far into the interior of San Croce *sestiere*. I met several parties of men and women on the way, some gaily costumed and already quite inebriated, though it was barely seven o'clock.

I approached the edge of the *riva* cautiously, looking about me for any possible witnesses—there were none. Then I spied, by the steps leading to the *rio*, the very gondola my *Signora* described, with a white handkerchief tied to the window frame. The gondoliere tipped his hat to me, his face unreadable (I believe they are accustomed to at least *appear* to take no notice of their passengers or what they might be meeting for), and I drew aside the heavy velvet curtain that hung across the entrance to the *vendado*, wherein my lady was situated. A lantern on the table held a fat candle, by whose light I could see that the *Signora* was splendidly dressed, with jewels at her throat and hanging from her ears, and her magnificent wedding ring flashing as she extended her hand to me. I bowed over it with awe and a feeling akin to a fevered, frightened ecstasy.

She invited me to sit beside her, then raised her voice slightly and told the gondoliere to row toward the Giudecca, naming a centuries-old monastery she intended to visit. Then she turned back to me, speaking in a low voice that throbbed with emotion.

"I hope you will forgive me," she began immediately, casting down her eyes. "I realize that I have foolishly compromised myself, in ways which I will confess to you soon, and of course, that by asking you to meet me in such circumstances, I am putting my reputation in danger again. Not that I have ever heard any ill opinion of you, Count Carlo Gozzi, that would make me feel myself at risk being with you."

I assured her of my most complete discretion and good will, which raised a deep sigh from her breast. We were silent a moment, and then I decided I could dare to ask the main question on my mind.

"May I know your name, *Signora*?" I said. "It appears you have knowledge of me, and I long to have us treat each other as equal partners."

She nodded her head slightly. "I am *Signora* Caterina Maria del Rosso, née Chavarria; I am a native of Venice, and married *Signore* Tomaso del Rosso six months ago."

Then it all came pouring out, as I sat back and listened with great interest to her little history—how she was the only daughter of a miserly, wicked man who had already estranged his only son and heir, her older brother who had fled the city; how she had been forced at a very young age into an arranged marriage by her father, but the man had died within a month; and how she had been saved from her father's machinations, by the good offices of *Signore* del Rosso, an old colleague of her father's and a very wealthy merchant, though exceedingly old himself—forty years her senior!—who had come forward to offer his hand for her, and actually paid her father for the privilege; and how, sadly, her husband was now ailing and probably near death, and who, she insisted with a shy and blushing glance down at her beringed hands, had ever treated her as a good father would have done, and had not approached her as a wife would expect of a husband, but instead showered gifts upon her and treated her kindly. She then subsided into a fraught silence.

I gave her a few moments to compose herself, then asked her gently, "And what is it you can tell me about this strange note and miniature you indicated that you had sent to me, and that I swear I never received?"

She looked up and set her gaze pleadingly upon my face—even in the candlelight, her green eyes were pure and full of life. "Ah, *Signore*, I hope you will understand and continue to forgive the weakness of a young woman unacquainted with the wicked ways of the world! I received this letter," she said, and opening her velvet reticule, she took out a much-folded piece of paper, and handed it to me. She bowed her head. "A man, who is a servant in our household, and whose wife is our housekeeper, brought it to me a few days ago, swearing that it was from you."

With her permission, I read over the letter, soon finding it hard to keep from laughing out loud—as if such a puerile, deficient, and grammatically poor missive could have ever come from my hand! But to spare her feelings, I kept my amusement to myself. The letter was replete with meandering protestations of the kind spouted by a most consummate lady-killer, full of panegyrics on the fair one's charms, oceans of nauseous adulation, stuffed out with verses filched from Metastasio. The concluding moral of the letter was that I (who was not I), being desperately in love with her, and forecasting the impossibility of keeping company with her, saw my only hope in the possession of her portrait; if I could obtain but this, and keep it close to a heart wounded by Cupid's dart, this would be an immense relief to my intense passion.

"Is it conceivable, madam," said I, after reading this pretentious effusion, "that although you have conceived a gracious inclination toward me, grounded on my discretion, on my prudence, on my good principles, on my ways of thinking, and that after all this you have accepted such ridiculous and stupid stuff as a composition addressed by me to you?"

"So it is," she answered, looking ashamed but trying to maintain a semblance of dignity. "We women cannot wholly divest ourselves of a certain vanity, which makes us foolish and blind. Added to the letter, the man who brought it uttered words, as though they came from you, which betrayed me into an imprudence that will cost me many tears, I fear. I answered the letter with some civil sentiments, cordially expressed; and as I happened to have by me a miniature, set in jewels, and ordered by my husband, I consigned this to the man in question, together with my note, feeling sure that if I were obliged to show the picture to my husband, you would have returned it to me."

She looked me in the face, one last hope visible in her eyes. "It seems then that you have received neither the portrait nor my letter in reply?" she said. "Could your servants…?"

I shook my head vehemently. "I trust them as I trust myself," I said. "But is it possible," I continued, "that you are still in doubt about my having written this literary atrocity? Do you still believe me capable of such an abomination?"

"No, no!" she said, shaking her head sadly, all hope gone. "I see only too well that you have nothing to do with the affair. Poor wretched me! to what am I exposed then? A letter written by my hand…that portrait…in the keeping of that man…and if my husband should find out!…. For heaven's sake, give me some good counsel!"

She clutched at my hand, holding it close within both of hers, and abandoned herself to tears. My heart was wrung with her innocent foolishness, and I murmured many endearing things to her bowed head, stroking the beautiful red-gold locks to soothe her, all the while thinking furiously about what could be done to save her reputation, and perhaps, punish the scoundrels responsible for this betrayal of their mistress.

☙ Saturday, 20 December 1879 ❧

The Signora and The Curse

SATISFIED WITH THE SURPRISE AND HORROR she perceived in our demeanours, the *Signora* sat back in her chair and sipped at her wine.

"A curse!" I repeated. "Pray, *Signora*," I said, trying to keep a caustic tone of utter disbelief from my words. "What manner of curse is this? And how do you come to know about it?"

John spoke immediately after me. "I cannot believe that Giacomo would countenance such an idea!" He said it scornfully, though politely. "Is he aware of this notion of yours?"

The *Signora* shook her head sorrowfully. "Oh, you English," she said. "You take such pride in being rational and scientific."

"John is actually an American," I said, feeling mischievous, and not at all insulted by the slur of rationalism upon my home country.

"Even worse," said the intrepid *Signora*, shrugging in that incomparable Italian way, not only with the slightest lift of her shoulders but seemingly with her whole being.

I was silent and thought for a moment—Italians, not only from the effects of nearly two thousand years of Roman Catholicism and all its various superstitions, but also from the inheritance of the pagan religions, time out of mind— were inclined to posit great powers in the utterance of a curse, the same as with a blessing. And often, I knew, the power of suggestion was enough to make a "cursed" person behave in ways that could lead to the fulfillment of the prophecy. These thoughts ran swiftly through my mind, and ended with my deciding to encourage the *Signora* to explain her idea. "On what evidence do you base this theory of a curse?" I said, laying my hand lightly on John's arm, to keep him from interfering.

"Evidence! Pah!" said the *Signora*. "Murder should be evidence enough!" She watched me with steely eyes.

"The murder is evidence of a crime," I returned evenly, setting down my wine glass, which I had just taken up. I needed a clear head for this pursuit, and reached for the water goblet instead. "What is the curse, and how do you know of it?"

The *Signora* glared at me a moment, then gave in with a good grace. "My family," she began, "has lived in Venice since it was a marshland full of fishing shacks." She looked up at the painted ceiling of the dining room and smiled. "Through the centuries, the di Contadinis—they took their name from the peasants they used to be, back in the 7th century, on the mainland—have helped build this beautiful city." She had leaned forward to speak, and now leaned back again, more relaxed. She looked at her empty wine glass, then glanced at John, who was seated to her right. He took the hint, and refilled her glass.

"We built her—we fought for her—we died for her," she continued. "The di Contadinis lived in cottages, in small houses, in palazzinos, in palazzos. We fished in the waters of the lagoon, we became glass makers, voyagers and merchants—we married into other old families and produced heirs who made fortunes—and lost them." She gazed into her wine glass with a melancholy air, as if seeing there the reflection of her illustrious ancestors.

I bit my tongue in my impatience for her to get to the curse. I must have made some little movement that exposed me, as the *Signora* focused her glittering eyes on me.

"You, *Signorina,* more than anyone, should know the value of a story, a good tale, and one that is only enriched and deepened through years of retelling," she said. "Listen with your heart, and your soul, not just your intellect, and you may learn something worth knowing."

Her admonition startled me—was she a fortuneteller too? It is but too true that I had spent many a year delving into old folk and faerie tales—German, Italian, English and French—in my quest for knowledge and the mastery of languages. And these tales of old informed my dreams, my goals, my writing—so I shivered when the secret impact of her words came over me—despite my outward protests, deep inside I longed to believe in these tales, these ghosts and spirits, their curses and protections. The late adventure in the north of England had affected my previously unshakeable denial of the possibilities of spirits and ghosts and other-worldly phenomena, and I was not as certain as I used to be.

The *Signora* was watching me closely. I shuttered my face and smiled pleasantly. "As a writer," I said, "I am indeed aware of the importance of atmosphere, mystery and depth in any good story." I took a sip of water, and willed my hand not to tremble. "Do go on, *Signora.*"

I noticed John looking back and forth between the two of us, as if he didn't quite know what was going on, and certainly wasn't of a mind to get in the middle of whatever it was. So, being an intelligent gentleman, he held his tongue.

"Because my family has lived in Venezia forever, there is very little about this city and her inhabitants—through the centuries—that we do not know. This house," and again she cast a glance at the ceilings and the yellow silk on the walls, "is not so very old, by some standards, having been raised to its present glory only in the last few years—by my illustrious son-in-law." She tapped a solid finger on the table, once, twice, thrice. "But before that, going back to the 18th century, this house has decayed and rotted from the inside out, all because of the hardness of the heart—if it can be called a heart—of that dog Carlo Gozzi!"

I was taken aback at the *Signora's* disparagement of Carlo Gozzi—my studies of this illustrious gentleman and playwright, renowned for reviving the *Commedia dell'Arte* in the mid-1700's, had, to me, revealed him to be a studious, polite, though canny and competitive, down-at-the-heels aristocrat. I searched my memory for clues in his famous *Memoirs* for any tale that could relate to the *Signora's* ire. I took another sip of water.

I noticed John looking at me questioningly—of course, he knew I was writing about Gozzi in my book—but I shook my head slightly at him, to indicate he shouldn't interrupt now and that I would talk to him about it later. He nodded briefly to show he understood. What a delight and convenience it is when one can converse with one's closest friends without saying a word! I returned to the *Signora*.

"You speak, *Signora*, as if he had done some unpardonable wrong to you, or your family, as lately as a few weeks ago," I said. "Surely there are no grudges that last a hundred and fifty years?" But even as I said this, I knew that what I said was foolish—such grudges, especially among Italians, were treated as present insults, and although often the exact nature of the quarrel was lost in time, the emotions it had raised continued in force.

The *Signora* sniffed contemptuously. "Surely you know better than that," she said. What an acute sense that woman had! She narrowed her eyes at me. "I know that you have written about Italy—and Carlo Gozzi as well—so don't act as if you don't understand the vengeful soul of the Italian race!" She signed to John to refill her wine glass again, and I marvelled at how the woman could drink so much and still appear relatively sober—one glass of wine was enough to overturn me!

"*Perdonne,*" I said humbly, but I caught her eye with a gleam in my own. "Please tell me what wrong Carlo Gozzi has done to make you hate him so."

She smiled. "That's better," she said. Then, looking around as if to make sure no one else was near, even though she herself had sent the servants from the room, she spoke in a loud whisper. "He broke the heart—and ruined the reputation—of an ancestress of mine—a young, beautiful and virtuous lady—and among other valuable things, he stole a bejeweled portrait of her!" John and I exchanged amused looks at this. The lady continued.

"And until the portrait, with its jeweled frame, is restored to her family, this will be a house of death," the *Signora* continued. Her face grew troubled. "As you can see, the curse has come alive again, the ghost of my ancestress has returned, after all these decades—and I fear that my own daughter is in grave danger, unless we find that miniature, and perhaps the other jewels."

John spoke up, hesitating only slightly. "And do you think, are you saying, that these items are still here—in this palazzo?"

The *Signora* nodded curtly. "I know they are, I can feel them calling to me."

"But what has all this to do with the murder of this unfortunate girl?" I said, and John nodded in agreement. "Anna was not killed by a ghost," I scoffed. "There is very definitely a human hand behind this crime." I thought a moment. "And why would Caterina be at risk—isn't the ghost her ancestress, too? Why would she want to hurt Caterina?"

In our rapt attention to the *Signora's* story, we had not noticed that the door to the dining room had opened quietly.

"Who wants to hurt Caterina?"

† December 1739 †

The Night of the Solstice (continued)
—*Memoirs of Count Carlo Gozzi*

AFTER A WHILE SIGNORA DEL ROSSO RAISED HER head from my lap and began to dry her tears—although I was more than delighted to be the pillow for such a beautiful head—and compose herself. The gentle rocking of the gondola was soothing, and peace reigned in the canal, broken only by a raucous cry or muffled laughter from the *rivas* we passed, the only indication other than the darkest of nights itself that we were at the Solstice. I had pondered well my lady's dilemma, and when she seemed able to attend, I spoke aloud my thoughts.

"If I am to give you advice," I said, noting at once the gleam of hope in her bright green eyes, "it is necessary I should be informed about the man and wife who occupy your house, and about the intimacy you maintain with them."

She shrugged slightly and replied that the husband seemed to be a good sort of fellow, who gained something by a transport-boat he kept.

"The wife is a most excellent, poor creature," she continued, playing with the rings on her hands, "and a devoted daughter of the Church. She is attached to me, and I to her. I often keep her in my company, have often helped her in her need, and she has shown herself amply grateful."

She paused to take a sip of something from a flask that I noticed for the first time, secreted under her voluminous skirts. "You know that, between women, we exchange confidences which we do not communicate to men. She is aware of certain troubles which beset me, and which I need not speak to you about; and she feels sorry for me."

I saw a blush rise from her creamy bosom to her throat and cheeks, and she turned her head away a little. "She has heard me talking at the window with you, and has joked me on the subject. I made no secret to her of my inclination, adding however that I knew my duties as a wife"—here she looked at me earnestly—"and that I had overcome the weakness. She laughed at me, and encouraged me to be a little less regardful on this point. That is really all I have to tell you, and I think I shall have said perhaps too much."

So she spoke, and dropped her eyes.

"You have not said enough," I said. "That excellent Christian woman, your confidante—tell me, did she ever see your portrait set in jewels?"

"Oh, yes! I often showed it to her." She looked at me with the most innocent, questioning face. "Does that matter?"

"Well," I said, quite sternly, "I will lay out the story for you—your 'excellent and so forth' woman has told everything to her equally 'excellent' husband. They have laid their heads together, and devised the roguery of the forged letter to abstract your jewelled miniature."

"Is it possible?" exclaimed she, staring like one bewitched.

"You may be more than sure that it is so; and shortly you will obtain proof of this infallible certainty."

"But what can I do?" The *Signora* wrung her hands in dismay.

"Give me some hints about your husband's character, and how he treats you."

"Oh, my husband adores me! I live upon the most loyal terms with him. He is austere, however, and does not wish to be visited at home, nor receive guests, nor give dinners. But whenever I ask leave to go and pay my compliments to relatives or female friends, he grants me permission without asking further questions."

I mused over this information for a few moments, then addressed her in a voice of authority. "I do not deny that your want of caution has placed you in a position of delicacy and danger. Nevertheless, I will give you the advice, which I think the only one under these uncomfortable circumstances. That excellent Christian woman, your confidante, does she know perhaps that I was going to meet you in this gondola to-day?"

"Oh, no, sir! Certainly not, because she was not at home."

"I am glad to hear it," I said, thinking rapidly. "This, then, is my advice. Forget everything about the miniature, just as though you had never possessed it; bear the loss with patience, because there is no help for it. If you attempted to reclaim it, the villain of a thief and his devout wife, finding their roguery exposed, might bring you into the most serious trouble. If your husband has a whim to see the miniature, you can always pretend to look for it and not to find it, affect despair, and insinuate a theft."

I now watched her carefully, and spoke most seriously, though in a gentle voice. "Do not let yourself be seen henceforward at the window talking with me. In fact, go even to the length of informing your confidante that you intend to subjugate an unbecoming inclination towards me. Treat the pair of scoundrels with your customary friendliness, and be very cautious not to betray the least suspicion or the slightest sign of coolness. Should the impostor bring you another forged letter under the same cloak of secrecy, as I think he is pretty sure to do, take and read it, but tell him quietly that you do not mean to return an answer; nay, send a message through the knave to me, to this effect—that you beg me to cease troubling you with letters; that you have made wholesome reflections, remembering the duty which an honest woman owes her husband."

Did I see a flicker of shame cross her lovely face? How I wished I could take her in my arms and assure her of my ardent affection and esteem. But I soldiered on, saying with a little laugh, "You may add that you have discovered me to be a wild young fellow of the worst character, and that you are very sorry to have intrusted me with your miniature. Paint me as black as you can to the rascal; if he takes up the cudgels in my defence, as he is sure to do in order to seduce you, abide by your determination, without displaying any anger, but only asking him to break the thread of these communications which annoy you. You may, if matters take a turn in that direction, waste a ducat or two upon the ruffian, provided he swears that he will accept no further messages or notes from me."

Signora del Rosso was now gazing at me in a kind of rapture, awed, no doubt, by my cleverness and care for her. I spoke once more, and to myself I sounded like an uncle or an older brother—but how I longed to be related to her in a different way entirely!

"This is the best advice which I can give you in a matter of considerable peril to your reputation," I finished up my long speech. "Pray carry my directions out with caution and ability. Remember that your good name is in the hands of people who are diabolically capable of blackening it before your husband to defend themselves. I flatter myself that before many days are past you will find that my counsel was a sound one."

I took a deep breath, having delivered this admonitory and advisory speech at such great length that I was a bit winded.

My young lady, though looking somewhat overwhelmed, declared herself convinced by my reasoning. She promised to execute the plan which I had traced, and vowed that her esteem for me had been increased.

At this point we reached the Giudecca, where she had to disembark. With a modest pressure of one of her soft hands on mine, she thanked me for the trouble I had taken on her behalf, begging me to maintain my cordial feelings toward her, and assuring me that she prized our friendship among the great good fortunes of her life.

I left her gondola, and returned to Venice by another boat, considerably further gone in love, but with my brain confused and labouring. Love and the curious story I had heard kept me on the stretch.

I barely noticed the crowds of people I encountered in St. Mark's Square, but in the *calles* and *rivas* as I made my way home, my ears and my heart heard the small cries and moans of various couples sequestered in shadows, kissing and fondling each other, licensed by the Solstice night. My blood thrilled to the touch of the arrow of *Eros*, but my dry intellectual mind and academic spirit persuaded me that it was *Agape*, a pure and unsensual love, that was piercing my heart.

Such fools we mortals be!

☙ Saturday, 20 December 1879 ❧

*We hear more about the family's Past,
and I am visited by an Apparition.*

WE ALL TURNED TO SEE OUR HOST standing at the door, a puzzled look on his face. He repeated his question.

"Who wants to hurt Caterina?"

"My dear Giacomo," John said, his tone derisory, "it appears that your palazzo is haunted, and in order to solve these murders, we must find a ghost who is bent on vengeance." He took a long drink from his wine glass.

Giacomo came further into the room, frowning at his mother-in-law. "Mama," he said, "you are not telling my friends that old story of yours, surely?" He shook his head in resignation as he spoke to her.

"Old story!" The *Signora* flamed at the words. "You of all people should know how true this story is—and why Caterina is in danger."

That struck me. "Why you, Giacomo?" I asked, using his first name, although my sense of propriety suggested we were not familiar enough for that—but he didn't seem to notice, or mind if he did. "Why should you *of all people* know this?"

Giacomo sighed, and pulling out a chair, sat down where his wife had lately been seated. He ran his hands through his curly, brown hair, then leaned back. He looked exhausted. Poor man, I thought, he's been through hell, and here we are, still tormenting him. He should be in bed.

"It's because," he said, his low voice strained with weariness, "somehow or other I am a descendant—many, many times removed—of Count Carlo Gozzi, who has so injured my mother-in-law's family."

"You, Giaco?" John said, surprised. "I thought...that is..." he floundered to a stop, turning a bit red at his *faux-pas*.

Giacomo waved a hand, kindly, at his friend. "No, no, it's all right," he said. He turned to me. "You see, *Signorina* Paget, I come from poverty, a sickly waif let out to work in a printer's shop by distant relatives who no longer could afford my maintenance—and yet, through the grace of God and the Blessed Virgin, I succeeded where so many of my family had failed through the centuries." He paused a moment, poured himself some wine, and sipped at it.

"I realize that my own personal history makes it hard to believe that somewhere back in the very distant past I have a connection to an aristocratic house—one that has also known decline and poverty and...death." He looked up at the ceiling. "I have been blessed to restore this palazzo to some of its former beauty in the early decades of the 18th century, when Carlo and Gasparo and all the Gozzi family lived here, wrote their plays and books here, and entertained the cream of Venetian literary, musical and artistic society."

"And now you, too, feel the curse of Caterina del Rosso, my ancestress," muttered the *Signora*, but clearly enough to be heard.

"*Basta!*" Giacomo cried out, sitting upright and looking menacingly at his mother-in-law, who started back in surprise. "Enough superstition and fear! We live in enlightened times—I banish your talk of curses with the light of Reason and Science!" With that, he stood, swaying slightly, and bowed to me and John.

"You will excuse me, *Signorina*, my dear John," he said with the utmost courtesy. "I must attend to my wife, and it is long past time that I myself find some rest and silence."

John stood and accompanied his friend to the door of the room, his arm around his shoulder. He saw Giacomo out the door, then turned back to us in the room.

"Vi," he said, "I'm going to have a smoke, then I'm going to retire as well. You will forgive me if I don't stay any longer here?" He didn't even glance at the *Signora*, nor take leave of her, possibly the only deliberate breach of civility I have ever witnessed in my dear friend.

"Of course," I said, pushing back my chair and rising. "I was just going myself." John held the door open for me, and I paused at the *Signora's* chair before I left the room. "*Buona notte, Signora,*" I said, and bowed my head slightly.

The *Signora* acknowledged my words, but said nothing. Her dark eyes gleamed with a pointed light that made me think, with a shiver, that I certainly wouldn't want to be on the receiving end of her wrath.

John and I exchanged silent glances once we gained the hall, but we parted without speaking—he looked too burdened with unsaid emotions, and I desired only peace and solitude, the better to review the evening's events and information and start making some sense of this sad and mysterious affair.

After I dismissed the sleepy maid who was waiting in the upper hall for me, I dressed in my nightclothes, and seated myself on a pillow before the fire, cross-legged, as I had recently learned to do from a strange but interesting acquaintance of my mother's. Matilda was always meeting up with the most preposterous and unusual people—a feature of her character that I rather liked, not that I would tell her so—and this one, a foreign man, a Hindu, had spoken at length one evening in Florence about the virtues of meditating in silence accompanied by certain postures of the body to help quiet the mind. He readily demonstrated these positions for the company, and although I declined to perform in the drawing room, I had subsequently tried the experiment in my own chamber.

And found it useful for thinking.

The wood in the hearth burned with hardly a crackle, making only a soft fluttering sound from time to time as the flames consumed the well-seasoned logs. Gradually, I felt my body relaxing and releasing some of the tension, both from my long journey and from the fractious family encounters at dinner. I let my mind drift, let it range and wander, as it were, over all the conversation and statements I had heard since I arrived at Ca' Favretto.

My wandering brain lighted upon an enigma—not unusual for me, as I was always alert to errors and anomalies—I should have made a good lawyer, seeking out the soft places and the inconsistencies. *Signora* di Contadini, the formidable mother-in-law, had accused Count Carlo Gozzi of somehow possessing her ancestress's bejeweled miniature portrait illegally, by trickery or theft she didn't say. Now, in all the research I had done for my soon-to-be-published book on the 18th Century in Italy, I had never read anything that suggested Gozzi was anything but a most upright person of integrity, and certainly well-off enough (at least in his middle years) to not be needing to stoop to taking a woman's jewels. He had a sterling reputation, a long if colorful family history in Venice and Friulia, was a renowned playwright and author and an esteemed son of Venice.

With my eyes closed, I skimmed over the pages of his two-volume *Memoirs*, which I had read in the original, trying to pinpoint any sections that may have alluded to this bejewelled miniature. At last the page swam before my eyes…I have something of an eidetic memory…and I saw a passage wherein Gozzi described conversing with his "fair neighbor" at the window of his little penthouse room—it was a description of his "third love affair" while still quite a young man.

That was all I saw. I opened my eyes, remembering now that I had skipped that section altogether after the first paragraph, not finding it relevant to my critique of Gozzi's theatrical works and contribution to reviving the *Commedia dell'Arte* in the later 18th century.

If only I had the books with me here, I could consult them immediately and find out Gozzi's side of the story, so to speak. But then, there are plenty of libraries in Venice, and surely one of them held copies—if not the original itself—of Gozzi's *Memoirs*.

But why on earth should I follow up on such a preposterous claim? An old family legend, a ghost story! Surely this could have nothing to do with the murder of the maid Anna. Then that little nagging voice inside my head countered the thought by pointing out that one never knows when it comes to murder, and every idea—intuitive or factual—should be given room to develop. I made up my mind to visit the principal library of Venice tomorrow to get a copy of the *Memoirs*.

A second thought struck me, out of the blue—and I inwardly cursed myself for having missed it from the start—the orange peels! Could that be some as-yet-unexplained reference to Gozzi's most famous play, *The Love of Three Oranges?* I recalled that his *commedia* was based on a centuries-old faery tale, told no doubt at the bedsides of countless children by their countless nurses or mothers or grandmothers. As always, it was a cautionary tale about love and pride and over-reaching—in this case, a prince looking for a bride finds three successive faery-women encased inside oranges. With strict instructions (from the typical old crone) to make sure he peeled the oranges near water, of course he ignored the instructions the first two times! The orange-faeries required water to drink immediately upon being unpeeled, so when that did not happen, they shriveled and died. Oops. Third time being the charm, faery lives, love at first sight, then on and on, betrayals and reversals, la-di-da, happy ending—although I vaguely recalled something about a maid who was executed for her treachery.

The fire was cooling down, only a slight flickering of warmth and light. I stretched my legs and arms and prepared to rise. A lamp was lighted on the table next to the bed, so I was well able to see my way across the room. Halfway there, just steps from the bed, I was stopped by the hairs on the back of my neck and on my arms rising and prickling as at the presence of danger—an other-worldly presence—behind me. A coolness, as of night air coming through a window, enveloped me, brushing against my legs like a purring cat.

Should I whirl about and confront it? Should I pretend I felt nothing? A little thrill of fear and delight shot through me, and my rational self tut-tutted at my emotions—*affected by the ghost stories at dinner, are we?*

Readiness is all! I turned quickly about, and saw nothing—except that the door to my room was open, quite fully open, without having made a sound. I started at that but, more curious than frightened, I took up the lamp by the bedside and went to look into the corridor.

The long hallway was dimly lit by one sconce near the staircase, and the even dimmer light of stars looking down through the skylight at the very top of the house. My lamp created too much illumination near me, throwing the farther reaches into shadow, so I turned the key and put it out. Darkness loomed and after a moment, there! At the staircase landing, a pale and ghostly shape, a woman in a light-colored dress, a good century or two old in fashion, with white hair piled high; her face was averted from me as she began to mount the stairs to the next floor, the servants' floor, where Anna's room was.

I tried to speak, to call out to the spectre, but found myself unable to utter a sound, so mesmerized was I by the ghostly creature. I watched as she ascended the stairs and then, suddenly spurred to action, I ran down the hall to see her more closely, heedless of my nightgown and my lack of a lamp.

When I reached the foot of the stairs and looked up, I saw no one and nothing—she couldn't have climbed the remaining stairs so quickly! I blinked and rubbed my eyes. Had I really seen anything? Was is mere imagination, heated by the family stories of vengeance and sorrow?

Suddenly there came upon the very air all around me the scent of oranges—spicy, crisp with citrus and redolent of hot southern climes. I sniffed, and turned my head, and the scent disintegrated as if dispersed by a breeze.

I admit it, I couldn't talk myself into going up that staircase on my own, and perhaps encountering the spirit—or, what might be worse, a murderer in the guise of a vengeful revenant.

I crept back to my room, closed and locked the door, put the key on the table with the lamp beside it, and crawled under the covers, feeling doomed to stay awake all night.

✝ December 1739 ✝

The Night of the Solstice (continued)

—*Memoirs of Count Carlo Gozzi*

I WAS TOO RESTLESS TO RETURN HOME IMMEDIATELY, after the long talk I'd had with my lady. I had met her early, around seven o'clock, and it was barely two hours later when I found myself in the precincts of the Rialto, not far from my home. I had donned my mask and black cloak again after leaving *Signora* del Rosso at the monastery, where she was visiting an elderly cousin, a nun, and so I was dressed for the revelry that had begun earlier in the evening, to usher in the Solstice.

What can I say? I was young, had been living a soldier's hard life in grimy barracks far from home, and was presently without the comfort and stability of a genial family home to which to return. As I stood musing at the nearly pointed top of a bridge above a narrow canal, a group of people intent upon pleasure swarmed toward me.

"*Signore!*" Two of the (apparently) female persons addressed me in merry tones. "*Signore*, why are you alone on this night of all nights? You must join us, please! Come along with us!"

A chorus of voices from the six or seven people gathered on the bridge echoed the same invitation. They seemed a jolly, harmless group—and it had been a long while since I had indulged in mere silly carousing and drinking.

I thanked them with a low, sweeping, gallant bow, but I said nothing. I decided on the spot to be mysterious and silent.

"Oh, ho! A man of mystery, then," said a fellow wearing a white mask with ruby lips. His deep voice and curling beard below the edge of the mask gave him away as definitely a man. "Well, come then, *Signore* Darkness! Join our little clique!"

I bowed again, and one of the women linked her arm in mine—clearly a woman by her curvy figure and gentle chin, which showed below a three-quarter mask with silver gilt sparkling on its surface, and a bright array of pink feathers for a head-dress. Her hands were gloved, as it was a chill night, and she wore a furred cloak wrapped tightly around her. She was nearly as tall as I, and quick in her movements, graceful too.

"You are mine," she whispered in my ear. I shivered slightly at the touch of her lips against my cheek. Inwardly, I laughed at myself—she could be a lady, a married woman, a girl who worked in a café or a shop—but the deceptive aspect of this annual playing in the streets seemed to fit my mood tonight. I didn't have to be Carlo Gozzi, aspiring writer, former soldier, son of a time-honoured Venetian family, not tonight! I placed my hand over hers and we swept along with the rest of the group, heading toward the Rialto, where I knew there would be singing, dancing, music, food and wine on the wide *rivas* to either side of the famous, haunted bridge. I had little enough in the way of money, but I could contribute my mite to the festivities to ease my pride and not appear miserly.

A huge throng awaited us at the Rialto, and my companion clutched at my arm tightly as we fought our way across the bridge to the other side. One of the men, though he was dressed as a serving woman, with a distorted mask-face and wig, seemed to be in charge, and was directing us over to a well-known restaurant on the far side of the bridge.

Dancers and singers, jugglers and fortune-tellers surrounded us, clamoring for attention and tips, as we tried to walk carefully down the broad, steep steps of the Rialto. With so many bodies jostling, it was impossible to tell exactly who had grabbed lasciviously at my backside and given it a healthy squeeze, or whose body pressed against mine from behind and made lusty thrusting movements against my cloaked back. My companion squealed once or twice as she was similarly accosted, but everyone seemed to take it as expected, and no harm was intended.

We reached the restaurant, lively with lights and noise, and waiters scurrying to and fro holding huge platters of savory food and large bottles of wine over their heads as they expertly wove their way among the patrons. Apparently, our colleague-in-charge was known at the place, and we were shown to an alcove on the side, with a banquette against a wall and a large table. It was possibly meant to hold up to eight people, but by the time we reached it, our group had swelled to ten or more, and we crammed in as close together as we could, with my companion and I squeezed together in the corner of the banquette.

Several bottles of wine appeared very soon thereafter, with a tray of glasses which the waiter merely left on the table for us to divide up and share as we would. I managed to grasp two for myself and the woman with me, and after a few moments, a passing bottle came our way and we were able to fill our glasses in time to toast with the rest of the company.

Our little corner allowed for some semblance of quiet, and I found my companion once again whispering in my ear. She had a clear but soft voice, with a genteel accent, so, not a servant or a shop girl, I guessed. My eyes couldn't help drifting to her pushed up bosom below her rather low-cut dress, visible now that she had thrown back her furry cloak. I felt her hand drift back and forth upon my thigh and make light, tickling movements with her fingers. So, not likely a virgin either—that was a practiced, knowing hand on my leg.

Platters of octopus and pasta with scallops were on the table, and my costumed lady ate hungrily, removing her hand from my leg in order to eat, but daintily and with humourous gusto. She talked and laughed with the others in the group while I maintained my silence, which she teased me about from time to time.

Finally, in a bit of a lull at the table—some of our number had gotten up for various reasons—to dance, to get more drink, to step outside for a necessary visit—she returned to her fond tickling of my thigh, and leaning into me, her bosom pressing against my arm, she said in a low voice—a little more than inebriated at this point, "I know who you are, my dear."

I allowed myself a low chuckle and shook my head.

"Ha!" she cried. "You have a voice! Let me hear you, I beg of you, I'll bet your voice is manly and musical."

I think I was a little past merely drunk myself, so I answered her, whispering in her ear. "My voice is only for your ear, my dear one."

Then I hiccoughed, and we both burst out laughing.

"Still," she said, after a moment, her hand warmly caressing my thigh and moving inward, "do you want me to tell you your name?"

I shook my head. "This is not a night for names," I said, and reached for another glass of wine.

"How about a warning, then?" she said, her voice suddenly very clear and quiet, as if she were sober on the instant. I drew back from her, puzzled, and looked into fierce dark eyes through the eyeholes of her mask.

"Beware your fair neighbor, Carlo Gozzi," she said. "She is not who she seems to be."

I stared at her, incredulous and puzzled. "What....what do you know of her...or me?"

She shook her head and leaning up, she kissed me full on the mouth, a deep and insistent kiss that made me feel I was drowning in her, enveloped in flesh and sweetness, pulling me down...down.... The room whirled around me as I opened my eyes and tried to get my bearings, but my *signorina* quickly shrugged her furred cloak back on, and begging some of the group to pull the table back so she could get up, she slipped away before I was scarcely aware she was moving.

Above the din in the restaurant, I heard church bells tolling the hour—probably midnight by the sound of them, though I was too drunk to count. Our odd little company were putting money on the table, and I, in an excess of pride and *brio*, pulled out my purse and contributed several ducats beyond what I probably had consumed myself, for which I was heartily thanked and pounded on the back by my fellow revelers.

The cold night air hit my face like ice water when I stepped outside the steamy restaurant. People were beginning to straggle homewards, and I thought it was high time I did the same.

Had my companion actually said what I thought she did? It happened so fast...and how could she know who I was? And who my neighbor was? And why would she say I should be wary of her? I shook the cobwebs from my brain as I stumbled home, though instinctively mindful that cutpurses and muggers would be waiting to pounce on people who looked like they were too drunk to be cautious. I pulled myself upright, straightened my mask and cloak, and walked purposefully, with dignity—and my right arm was crossed over my waist as if I clutched my dagger under my cloak, ready to use it should anyone approach.

I made it home safely, God and the saints be praised for looking after a poor young soldier, and was inordinately touched to see that my housekeeper had waited up for me, and was ready to open the door and bring me a hot posset to warm me. As I dozed toward sleep, the seriousness of the masked woman's warning dimmed in my mind, and I dismissed it as some Solstice play-acting nonsense. My lady was a lady, an innocent maiden, I felt sure, and I would not hold with any slander of her character or her person. I fell asleep with a longing to see her the next day as soon as possible.

☙ Sunday Morning, 21 December 1879 ❧

The Solstice Begins

I ENTERED THE ORNATE, GILDED BREAKFAST ROOM—a smaller version of the elaborate dining room of the night before—and was not surprised to see *Signora* di Contadini already seated and busy with newspapers and coffee. Other than the servants, it was just the two of us.

I decided a direct attack might work best, to begin with. I had no intention of revealing the uncanny vision I had glimpsed in the night.

"*Signora*," I said, as I sat in the chair held out for me by the servant, "tell me more about this curse of yours."

The *Signora's* eyes held fast to her newspaper, as if she intended to finish a paragraph before she responded. She sipped at her coffee, then said, "It is not *my* curse, *Signorina* Paget."

Drat! I thought. One for the *Signora*.

"It is, however," I said, helping myself to a platter of cooked eggs which the servant held for me, "one in which you have a certain sense of ownership, is it not?" I darted a quick glance at her as I sprinkled salt on my eggs.

The *Signora* put down her paper, leaned back in her chair, and regarded me with interest, her black eyes keen and piercing. "What has happened to you since last evening?" she said calmly.

Drat again! The woman must be part gypsy!

"Why, whatever do you mean?" I said, feigning nonchalance. "I am the same person now as I was last night."

Signora's mouth twitched as she tried, apparently, not to smile. She shook her head slightly.

"Come," she said, "let us not parry like boys playing soldier with wooden swords." She leaned over to lay a beringed hand on mine. "I know this palazzo—I know its inhabitants…." She paused for a long moment. "Isn't there something you'd like to tell me?"

This conversation was not going the way I had intended. I didn't trust the *Signora*—I couldn't quite put my finger on it—maybe it was just the overwhelming Venetianness of her, the centuries of intrigue and spying, deceit and plots and yes, death! The watery city positively dripped with hidden crimes and cruel revenges.

I smiled at her, and patted her hand with my other hand—so condescendingly.

"And what is it you think I have to tell you?" I said, lifting an eyebrow with, I thought, subtle elegance.

She withdrew her hand, frowning.

"You do not trust me," she said flatly.

A servant stepped forward to deliver another coffee and she dismissed him abruptly, waving her hand. I saw her throw a glance at Samuel, the *major d'omo*, and in a moment the room was cleared of servants, and we faced each other alone.

"You do not trust me," she said again.

I met her gaze with equanimity. Fortune teller or not, the woman was a good reader of her fellow humans.

I decided to be bold.

"Yes. I do not trust you."

The *Signora* nodded once, as if satisfied she was right, and content that I had admitted it.

She reached for a buttered roll and put it on her plate, her eyes fixed there as she spoke.

"What do you think you have to lose by at least appearing to trust me with a confidence?" she said.

I rejoined immediately. "What do you think you have to gain by having me tell you—whatever it is you think I want to tell you?" I almost smirked. "Or rather, whatever it is you think I *don't* want to tell you?"

"Oh," said she, "I am an old woman, with nothing to gain or lose, only a bit of gossip, perhaps, with which to entertain myself, or my friends when we play piquet."

We both looked at each other then, warily but with a sense of amusement.

"Very well," I said, abruptly abandoning my hesitation—what, after all, *had* I to lose?

"Last night," I said, slowly and with great deliberation, "in the hallway by the staircase, I saw—I believe—the celebrated ghost of your poor, ruined ancestress."

Signora nodded, smiled, and leaned forward with eagerness, her eyes bright. "White gown of an ancient cut? Hair piled high?"

"Of course," I said, dismissively. "How else?"

Signora had moved beyond fencing and dodging. "Did she speak?" She grasped my hand tightly. "*Did* she?"

How I wanted to recount some haunted, whispered words of doom—or enlightenment—from the long-dead Caterina! But alas, I would not stretch the truth. I shook my head.

"No, *Signora*, I heard nothing, only saw what I took to be the figure of a woman standing at the foot of the stairs, then slowly mount, then disappear."

The *Signora* nodded again. "She seeks the upstairs room, always the top of the house," she said.

In my mind's eye I reviewed the pages of Gozzi's *Memoirs*. "That is where Count Gozzi had his penthouse room, where he wrote his plays and letters." I made it a statement, not a question.

THE LOVE FOR THREE ORANGES

We looked at each other, again wary but amused. She answered my unspoken question.

"We have searched that room many times," she said. She broke the spell of stillness, and reached for the cream pitcher. I waited for her to say more, and when she didn't, I spoke again.

"Which room up there is his, the one he wrote in?" I tried to sound merely curious, but I really wanted to stand in the room where the famous playwright had penned his creations—a kindred spirit!

The *Signora* looked as if she were debating whether to tell me, then she shrugged.

"It's the room that is used as a storage closet currently," she said. A fierce light flashed in her dark eyes. "Would that he had died there, before he met my ancestress and ruined her reputation!"

"Have you read Gozzi's *Memoirs* yourself?" I asked cautiously. "I think I remember that your ancestress lived in the palazzo just next door?"

She tossed her head in contempt. "I would not give his ghost the satisfaction of reading them." She narrowed her eyes. "And yes, the Palazzo Cornero is where my ancestress used to live, until she was driven out because of the monster Gozzi."

That remains to be seen, I thought to myself. I couldn't wait to get hold of a copy of the *Memoirs,* then we would see about that.

The *Signora* shook herself a little, as if to disperse her anger, and then, surprisingly, she crossed herself in the Catholic fashion. "The Pope took it into the Church's possession some eighty years ago," she said, "that palazzo, and now the holy Cavanis use it as the order's domicile in Venice." She paused. "They are quiet enough, and orderly," she added, grudgingly.

A sudden thought darted into my head, and I quickly looked at my plate and pretended interest in the toast and egg—I didn't want to give the *Signora* a chance to read my mind. Could the presumably purloined miniature lay hidden somewhere, lost perhaps long ago, in the palazzo next door? Perhaps the ghostly ancestress, rejected by Gozzi as a lover, had only accused him of stealing a precious object that she had carelessly lost? Fanciful thoughts, yes, but anything was possible, and I felt convinced that Gozzi was not a common thief, so there must be another explanation.

We were rescued from any further *tête-a-tête* by the arrival of the master of the house and also John, along with an influx of servants bringing fresh, hot food and more coffee.

I was grateful for the respite, and glad to see that the mistress of the house had chosen to be absent, as I wanted to ask her husband some questions that would be more difficult in her presence.

"Good morning, *Signorina* Violet," Giacomo said, and bowed slightly in my direction. He looked better for a night's sleep, and was dressed immaculately in dark trousers and a lily-white shirt, with a maroon velvet morning jacket for comfort. He sat down across from me and at his mother-in-law's right hand. John pressed my shoulder sympathetically with one hand as he passed behind my chair, and muttered under his breath so only I could hear, "Been braving it out with the *Signora* alone, eh?"

I smiled, but addressed our host. "How is your lovely wife, *Signore*, I hope she is feeling better this morning?"

He looked grateful for my interest. "*Si, Signorina*, my dear Caterina is much better this morning." He looked slightly embarrassed for a moment as he added, "She usually takes her breakfast in her room, and I urged her to do the same today, presuming the liberty to tell her that you and John would not feel slighted by her absence."

"Not at all, not at all," I assured him.

The gentlemen helped themselves to the food the servants were holding out to them, while I glanced at the *Signora*, who had not spoken a word other than of the slightest greeting to her son-in-law. She looked to be in what I believe is called a "brown study," lost in her own thoughts.

I took the plunge. "Giaco, I beg your forbearance in raising the subject, but I hope you will not take it amiss if I ask you some questions about the…recent events here."

"Of course, *Signorina* Violet, I am at your disposal." His eyes looked weary and sad, and I redoubled my determination to help this poor man solve his tragic dilemma.

"First," I said, after thanking him for his consideration, "may I see the strange notes that you received in the last few weeks?" On seeing his knitted brow, I added, "John mentioned them to me when he was telling me about all that had gone on."

"Strange notes?" We had the *Signora's* full attention on the sudden. "What is this, Giaco? I never heard of any notes."

Giaco took a deep breath—I think he was trying to stifle his impatience—and spoke. "I did not want Caterina to be distressed, I never told her about them."

The *Signora* drew breath to speak again, but I interrupted.

"You still have them?" I said. "I think it would be important to read them."

"Yes," he said. "They are in my strongbox in my study." He started to rise, as if to retrieve them at that moment.

"Oh," I said, "please, do sit and have your breakfast, there is no need for you to hurry yourself for them right now."

"On the contrary, *Signorina* Violet," Giaco said, getting up and pushing in his chair. "The sooner we find out as much as we can about this sad affair, the better we all will feel." He bowed his head, and quickly left the room.

The three of us at the table ate in silence for some minutes. We heard rapid footsteps coming back down the stairs, and the breakfast room door opened suddenly. Giaco stood in the doorway, an open strongbox in his hands.

"The letters are gone! Someone has taken them from the strongbox!"

† December 1739 †

Three Days before Christmas

—Memoirs of Count Carlo Gozzi

I WAS MORE THAN USUALLY EAGER TO SPEAK with my lady again, especially in light of the strange message whispered to me by the masked woman at the restaurant. With a sore head from the Solstice revels, I sat at my desk, the window open to the dim and overcast day; the clouds looked heavier than the weight of sin.

At last *Signora* del Rosso showed herself, late in the afternoon, in her workroom; I was passing along by my open window and glimpsed her as she quickly threw a paper tied to a pebble into my room, then disappeared. I picked the missive up and read the scroll, of which the purport was to this effect: "I must pay a visit to a friend after dinner; my husband has given his permission; could you, dear friend, meet me within the hour, and at the former *ponte storto*? The gondola will be waiting with the former ensign of the handkerchief. Please come, I am sorely pressed to tell you something."

My heart leaped in my breast, but my rational self warned me that I needed to exercise some caution and restraint. Such was the effect of that mischievous whisper in my ear! That calumny I tried hard to dismiss! I hastened to my chamber, threw on my warmest cloak and, hesitating a moment, picked up the black mask from the night before.

People went about with masks in daytime as well as night during these lost days between the Solstice and Christmas Day—when we could all rejoice at the return of the Light, both physically and spiritually.

I didn't want to arrive at the *ponte storto* before my lady did, as it would look bad to be simply hanging about. As I left my own poor palazzo, it occurred to me that I had not taken time to visit the family church, San Cassiano, since my father's funeral. Perhaps I could find some respite from my anxious thoughts, or a strengthening of resolve, with a few prayers and lighting of some votive candles.

Slipping quietly out of the house, although the housekeeper and manservant never questioned my actions, I strode down the very dark *calle* outside our gate, made a left turn, the dripping, dark brick walls seeming to close in above me; darted right, then left around a chimney, then left again into the *Calle dei Morti* which led to the bridge over the *Rio Cassiano* and directly into the small space in front of the church. The crumbling portico, in the gathering gloom, looked ancient and unfriendly, and I saw figures, like shadows, seeming to be embracing furtively behind the large columns. They scattered as I approached the main door.

Humble and plain as it was on the outside, the interior of the church was always a revelation, despite time and soot and smoke—both from candles and from the occasional fire in the *sestiere*—having made their mark on the once gleaming surfaces.

I made my way quietly to the jewel-box of a side chapel that was especially beloved of my family—below its altar several of my more illustrious ancestors reposed. I knelt on the worn velvet cushion, crossed myself, and tried to pray. But the devil had me in his sights, and with the lingering befuddlement in my mind from too much drink the night before, all I could conjure were my lady's dovelike breasts, her innocent eyes—and then the lascivious kiss of the masked *Signorina* last night. My blood ran hot, and I felt as if a kind of madness was overtaking me. I shook my head in vain to free it of such thoughts, and begging God's forgiveness, escaped from the church and the thrust of guilt that pierced my soul.

I found my lady at the rendezvous point. She seemed more beautiful than I had ever seen her, because her face wore a certain look of cheerfulness which was not usual to it. She ordered the gondolier, who was not the same as on the previous occasion, to take a circuit by the Grand Canal, and afterwards to land her in a certain *rio* at Santa Margherita.

Then she turned to me and spoke most animatedly. "*Signore*, I must now address you as an illustrious prophet of events to come!" From her bosom she drew forth a folded note and handed it to me. "This was brought to me first thing this morning by my husband's servant, whose wife is my maid."

It was written in the same hand as the first fraudulent note supposedly from me. The caricature of passion was the same. I, who was not I, thanked her for the portrait; vowed that I kept it continually before my eyes or next my heart. I read with increasing indignation that the letter-writing scoundrel was begging the dear *Signora* for the loan of twenty sequins, promising to repay them religiously within the month! She might give the money to the bearer, a person known to me, a man of the most perfect confidence.

"This is the rankest insult and skullduggery!" I cried, giving way volubly to imprecations on this villain's character, status and ancestry, as my lady laughed a silvery, delightful laugh.

"How did you deal with the impostor?" I asked her.

"Exactly as you counselled me," she said. "And you will have to excuse me if I painted you as black as possible to the fellow," she said with a shy but merry smile. "He stood confused and wanted to explain; but on seeing that my mind was made up, he held his tongue, completely mortified."

She reached out her hand to take the note from me and I re-folded it and gave it to her.

"And what did you say then?" I asked.

"Oh, I ordered him to talk no more to me about you, and to accept no further messages or letters," she said, highly pleased with herself and the acting she had done. "Then I gave him a sequin, on the clear understanding that he should *never* utter a word again to me concerning you. I told him that I was resolved to no longer be acquainted with you."

My face must have revealed what a traumatic thought that was to me, for she shyly touched my hand with her (properly) gloved one, and said, "To what extent our relations have been broken off, you can see for yourself now in this gondola; and they will only come to an end when you reject my friendship, which event I should reckon as my great disaster. I swear this on my honour."

I bent and kissed her hand with fervor, feeling all the delight of the soft glove against my lips, and dreaming of the skin beneath it. After a moment, she gently pulled her hand free.

"I must report another favourable circumstance," she continued. "This afternoon, my husband surprised that same rogue in the act of stealing some ducats from a secret drawer in his bureau. He told the man to pack out with his wife, threatening to send him to prison if they did not quit our premises at once."

I allowed my astonishment to show, as truly as I felt it.

"Were you clever enough," I said, 'to affect a great sorrow for those unfortunate robbers, sent about their business?"

"I did indeed try to exhibit the signs of unaffected sorrow," she replied. "I even made them believe that I had sought to melt my husband's heart with prayers and tears, but that I found him firm as marble. I gave them some alms, and three hours ago they dislodged."

"Well done!" I exclaimed. "The affair could not have gone better than it does. Now, even if your husband asks to see the miniature, it will be easy to persuade him that they stole it. You will incur no sin of falsehood; for steal it they did, in good sooth, the arrant pair of sharpers."

"Ah!" cried she, "why cannot I enjoy the privilege of your society at home? What relief would my oppressed soul find in the company of such a friend! My sadness would assuredly be dissipated. Alas! it is impossible. My husband is too, too strict upon the point of visitors. I must abandon this desire. Yet do not cease to love me; and believe that my sentiment for you exceeds the limits of mere esteem. Be sure that I shall find occasions for our meeting, if indeed these be not irksome to yourself. Your modesty and reserve embolden me. I know my duties as a married woman, and would die sooner than prove myself disloyal to them."

The conversation which followed this effusion was both lively and tender, an interchange of sentiments diversified by sallies of wit. Our caresses journeyed from clasped hands and gentle pressure of the fingers at some *mot* which caught our fancy, to tender whispers of eternal friendship and faithfulness. We were a pair of sweethearts madly in love with one another, yet respectful, and (apparently) contented with the ecstasies of mutual affection.

Oh, that I had quitted that gondola then with a pure heart, and nevermore set eyes upon this lady! This heroine I had conjured in my mind, beautiful as an angel, had inflamed my Quixotic heart. It would be a crime, I told myself as I gazed into her bewitching green eyes, not to give myself up entirely to a Lucretia like her, so thoroughly in harmony with my own sentiments regarding love. Yes, surely, surely I had found the phœnix I was yearning for!

☙ Sunday Morning, 21 December 1879 ❧

Missing Notes and John in Distress

"GONE!" WE ECHOED GIACOMO'S CRY as he came further into the room, the empty strongbox in his hands. He placed it on the table, then sat down suddenly, his head in his hands.

"Quickly," I said, trying to sound both gentle and commanding at once. "Tell me what you remember of those notes." I pulled a pencil and a small pad of paper from one of the pockets of my jacket (I always try to keep them handy), and glancing at John to communicate to him the urgency of my request, I looked encouragingly at Giacomo.

"I remember one that you showed me, Giaco," John said quietly. He closed his eyes as if he could see the words better that way, and spoke slowly. "A nondescript hand, black ink on bad paper, like paper used to wrap meat or food…I remember there were only a few words…something about water and fire…yes, *Water will inflame life*. Rather a puzzle, that." He opened his eyes and looked at our host. "Is that right?"

Giaco nodded tersely. "That was the first one," he said.

"How many were there?" I asked. "And when did you receive them?" My pencil was again poised above the paper. A glance at *Signora* di Contadini showed me she was following the conversation very closely, although trying to appear not to as she sipped her coffee.

"There were only two," Giaco said, almost apologetically. He looked very tired, but composed. "The first one came two days after the first girl met with her…accident," he said. "Even at the time, I didn't connect the note with that event." He spread his hands, palms up, as if entreating us to believe him. "How could I? There still doesn't seem to be any connection."

I pondered this momentarily. "And the second note?" I prompted.

"This time," he said wearily. "It was two days before poor Anna…was found."

I paused, though impatiently; out of respect for the dead and the feelings of the living, I counted to ten.

"Do you recall what that note had written on it?" This was like wheedling a wayward child into eating its porridge! Not that I had ever attempted such a thing, but I saw it done once.

Giaco appeared to be thinking hard. "It looked the same as the first," he said at last. "I mean, the same hand, the same kind of paper. It said, *Oranges will bring resurrection.* Yes, I'm sure that's what it said." He looked at me, most unhappy. "It was easier to connect it to poor Anna's death, you see…"

"Because of the orange peels," I finished his sentence, not that I needed to. But I was rather thinking out loud, and not attending to tactful politeness at the moment, but I didn't miss the grimace on John's face as he was reminded of that grotesque detail of the maid's death. "But how…*resurrection?* A death is not a resurrection. And how can oranges bring that about?"

The two men, and the *Signora*, looked at me as if I were the Sphinx and they were hoping I would solve the riddles for them. Well, all in good time. I felt confident that I could break these enigmas before too long.

"Was your strongbox broken into?" I abruptly asked.

Giaco looked startled. "Why, of course, I mean, everything in it was taken…" He looked at me, uncertain, I think, if I were suddenly become feeble-minded.

"Yes, yes," I said, a trifle impatiently, "and I would like to ask you more about what other items than the two notes were in that box, but what I mean is, was the box *forced open* or had you left it unlocked, perhaps, or was it locked and if so, how many keys to it are there and who has access to them?" Gracious, I had to spell it all out—artists! They think with their fingers and their eyes, not with their brains. I instantly chided myself, knowing well that John had a first-rate mind, as did many other creative people of my acquaintance. My lack of sleep was making me less than courteous.

"I beg your pardon, *Signorina* Violet," Giaco said, passing a hand across his brow. "You must forgive me, I think my mind is muddled." He took a deep breath, and handed the box to me. "Please take a look at it yourself and see what you think."

I took up the box, it was heavy indeed, with thick metal plates on the top, sides and bottom, with an extra layer of tooled leather on the top. There were hinges on the back of the lid, and opposite them was a heavy, thick clasp, with a hole punched through the center of it, which came down from the top to cover a slightly protruding lock. It needed a key to both lock and unlock it.

"Where is the key?" I asked.

Giacomo didn't answer at first, then looking slightly shamefaced, said in a low voice, "I'm not at all sure, *Signorina*." He looked wretched. "It is usually in…another place…in my chamber," he said. "It was not there when, just now, I went to look for it."

"So you went to where the strongbox is stored, and it was already unlocked and open when you saw it just now?"

He nodded.

I puffed out a little sigh of frustration, and wrote a few notes on my pad of paper. Looking up, I couldn't help but feel sorry for my poor host, who looked as miserable as a man can look.

"Pardon me, Giaco, but I have to ask—who knows where you keep that key?"

"Only myself and…my wife," he answered, his voice barely a whisper.

"None of the servants, then?" I asked, rather sharply. I have no faith in the loyalty of servants, particularly Italian ones. I realize it is a prejudice, but one born of too much experience managing my parents' household in Florence.

He shook his head. "Not to my knowledge," he said, which seemed to me to give some room for doubt.

I tapped my pencil on the paper. The room was quiet except for the desultory sounds of cups clinking against their saucers, and silverware touching china, as servants removed plates and deposited others, refilled coffee and tea cups. John was used to my taking charge of things in matters like this, but I was surprised that the *Signora* chose not to interfere.

"Please, can you tell me," I asked, "what other things were in the strongbox, that are now, I presume, missing as well?"

Giaco closed his eyes to think. "Not that much," he said. "Our marriage certificate, of course, some receipts for paintings I recently sold…." He paused.

"The deed for this palazzo?" I queried.

He shook his head. "No, that is in the bank vault," he said firmly. "But, there was in our strongbox the original architectural plans for the palazzo—I had obtained them from the Archives when we started the renovations here, a year ago. It would be a pity if they were lost for good."

I nodded my agreement, and it struck me as very interesting that someone would take the building's plans as well as a marriage certificate, in addition to the mysterious notes. Which of these was most important to the thief, and why?

As we all sat pondering these imponderables, a female servant came into the room, a lady's maid by her dress, I gathered. She curtsied deferentially to *Signora*—a shrewd move on her part, I thought—then approached Giacomo and spoke to him in a low voice, meant only for him to hear. He nodded, wearily, it seemed to me, then stood and excused himself.

"You will pardon me," he said, bowing his head slightly. "It seems my wife is in need of my company." He turned to John with a sad smile. "My dear John, I'm sure you know that everyone and every resource in my command are at your service. You have only to ask."

Before he could leave the table, the *Signora* also signalled she was ready to rise from her seat; a servant sprang forward to assist with her chair.

"Perhaps my daughter may also find her mother's presence of some comfort," she said, addressing Giacomo. He merely bowed his head, and then led the way to the door.

John and I, therefore, found ourselves alone in the breakfast room, the servants having withdrawn with their master. I maintained a thoughtful silence for a few moments, watching him.

He was nervous about something—and John was rarely nervous. Restless, yes, sometimes, and occasionally impulsive. But I had come to know well his thorough good nature, his calm acceptance—no, embrace!—of the oddest things and people. An artist does that sort of thing, by nature—looks at everything and everyone with a keen, untroubled, non-judgemental directness—and then appraises. I, as a writer and by my nature, am much more given to judgement and drama, seeking out folly and vice, pretension and vanity, in order to understand what I believe is behind most human behaviour.

But I digress, rather. I watched John carefully. He tapped his fingers. He pulled at his mustache. He drank several cups of coffee, one after another, with hardly a pause. I had never seen him like this—he was not only nervous, he was worried.

The absence of others in the ornate breakfast room spurred me to try opening the oyster shell of my friend's usual reticence.

"John," I said, stirring sugar into my coffee, "I'm feeling a little nervous this morning—something's bothering me and I can't quite put my finger on it."

He looked up, attentive as always, but also as if welcoming a distraction from his own brooding.

"Why, Vi," he said, a glimmer of humour in his dark brown eyes, "It's odd to hear you admit you don't quite know something."

I stuck out my tongue at him—heavens, it felt like we were ten-year-olds again, playing in the dirty streets of Rome!—but smiled, too.

"Sometimes, I admit," I said, attempting to look pensive, "I find myself affected by an atmosphere, my surroundings—as when Mama and my brother Eugene are having a tiff and either barely speaking to each other or engaging in the most annoying conversations—I positively want to jump out the window into the Arno." I glanced at my friend. "Do you ever feel like that?"

That was, apparently, too direct, and John deftly turned my question aside. "Perhaps you are feeling the tension in this house, between Giacomo and his mother-in-law."

"And between said mother-in-law and dear Giaco's wife," I added, musingly. I looked at John with some intensity, suddenly impatient with tiptoeing around.

"My dear Twin," I said. "Something has you deeply worried. You cannot hide it from me, I know you too well."

John looked straight at me, a tiny smile on his lips, but only shook his head. "It's true, I am worried, dear Vi," he said. "But there's nothing I can say to you."

"You mean there is something," I insisted, "but you don't want to say it aloud. What could be so awful?"

John's neck flushed red, and his answer was halting, stammering as he often did when overwhelmed with emotion. "You...you r-r-really don't want t-t-to know, Vi," he said, throwing his napkin on the table as he rose. "I pray you, do not question me again."

He practically ran from the room, leaving me in utter astonishment and dismay. Given that murder was what I was there to investigate, his reluctance to speak suggested volumes to my fertile imagination. Was he protecting his friend?

Was he protecting himself?

† December 1739 †

Two Days before Christmas

—Memoirs of Count Carlo Gozzi

I FOUND I COULD NOT DISMISS THE INSIDIOUS WARNING of the Masked Woman (as I referred to her in my mind) about my fair neighbor and lady-love, despite my entrancement with *Signora* Caterina del Rosso. The rational side of my nature had long held sway over my more sensual instincts, and determined scholar that I was, I knew that deep inside I was ultimately guided by the precepts and greater wisdom of the ancients and yes, the Saints, as to what course of action in my life it was best for me to choose.

But, and here is the flaw in all the rationality of the mind! I was young, and hot-blooded, and I dreamed of amorous adventures, of gallantry and romance, with a perfect mistress worthy to be my soul-mate! Of marriage I had only the utmost disdain and fear—the results of my own parents' sad relationship, and my brother Gasparo's domineering, ungenerous wife, and my two sisters, married off to greedy, petty small aristocrats! Unhappy unions all around me—no, it was not a state to which I aspired. I would be free, free to write and publish, to keep my own hours and my own mind and body as I saw fit. And besides, I had come to realize that a great part of the burden of keeping my family's fortune and well-being in a reasonable state had fallen upon my shoulders.

But that did not necessarily exclude a platonic (or nearly so) relation with a well-bred, well-educated, virtuous woman with like principles and interests.

Beware your fair neighbor, Carlo Gozzi. She is not who she seems to be.

The Masked Woman's words came back to me, relentlessly. What could I do?

What any self-respecting Venetian would do in such a case. Seek out the gossips and find out what I could about my adorable beloved!

I started with my own housekeeper, a native Venetian, who had been in my family's employ for some five years, hired after I had gone into the service. She, I quickly learned from her comments and her behaviour, had not been well-inclined toward her mistresses in our family household, and therefore, when I kept her on in my own employ once my family decamped for Friulia, she had easily and happily transferred her loyalties to me, and served me well. Her name was Giulia; she was a widow, somewhere in her mid-forties; a well-looking woman, and seemingly happy with her independent life as my housekeeper. As far as I knew, she had no children, though she often spoke of this or that nephew or niece, so I knew she had some family in town. I decided to saunter down to the kitchen, her principal domain, and see what my youthful charms could winkle out of her.

"Giulia, dear lady," I began, lounging in the doorway to the low-ceilinged, somewhat smoky kitchen; the air positively shimmered with the aromas of tomatoes and garlic, emanating from a large pot on the hearth. "I'm absolutely famished!" I continued. "Is there a crust of bread to spare for this poor scholar's stomach?"

"You nonsensical boy!" she returned, stirring the pot and not even turning to look at me. "Where do you think I would get bread at this hour of the day? Do you think I have

THE LOVE FOR THREE ORANGES

already been outdoors to the market, just to get you your precious bread?"

Her gruff manner never put me off, as I had discovered her heart of gold beneath the irascibility. And I had spied two loaves of bread peeking out of a basket in the corner.

"What!" I cried, pretending to be faint, and collapsing into a chair. "You would have me starve, right here in my own home?" I could tell she was enjoying this act immensely. She turned and looked fiercely at me, shaking a long wooden spoon at me, and trying not to smile.

"You would deserve no less," she said. "Coming in at all hours of the night, on such a night we had! Goings-on all over town, masks and drinking and bad behaviour!" She continued grumbling, but I saw that she was heading for the bread basket. She took out one of the loaves, tore off a sizeable piece, put it on a plate and, carrying it over to the hearth, splashed a great dollop of sauce on it.

She set it down in front of me, pretending to be greatly put off. "There you are, you great simpleton," she said. "Never let it be said that a young man didn't get his fill in Giulia's kitchen." At this salacious *double-entendre*, she whooped with laughter as I fell back in mock dismay, shaking my head, then falling with great gusto upon the bread and tomato sauce.

After a few minutes' grateful munching, I spoke aloud, trying to sound casual.

"Giulia, my dear," I said. "What do you know about our next-door neighbors? Does anyone actually live in that palazzo? It seems empty and yet, it looks like it's been recently painted and fixed up."

With one question, the floodgates opened! I saw immediately that Giulia was filled to the brim with facts and speculations about the palazzo next door, and couldn't wait to spill it all to me. But she took her time, savoring, I believe, the juicy gossip she was about to impart.

"That palazzo was under renovation until about ten years ago," was the first thing she said. "I know your family has lived here"—she pointed with her spoon to the ceiling—"for many decades, but I expect you were too young to pay any attention to it."

I nodded. Most of my early childhood was spent in Friulia, in the country, and when my family visited Venice, we often stayed in a different palazzo, in Dorsoduro—it was currently leased out to strangers, a fact which struck my heart every time I thought of it. The family had been coming more often to this house, San Cassiano, in the last eight years or so, but my time in the army had taken me away from the area. I mused on these changes of fortune, then realized Guilia was speaking again.

"I used to work for a family about three streets over from here, and heard a lot about it from a cousin of mine who was working on one of the renovating crews." She sniffed and raised a shoulder in the general direction of the palazzo next door. "You may know that the ruins underneath the current palazzo are the remains of the residence of the great Caterina Corner, she who was once queen of Cyprus…"

"But that was more than three hundred years ago!" I interrupted her. "And the Corner family, are they still on the List—and weren't they originally part of the Black Families?"

Giulia crossed herself and kissed her thumb. "Best not to speak of that, even though I know they served the Popes way back in the old days." She looked around as if fearful of being overheard. "But no, some part of the family is still around, but diminished, you know what I mean?" She made a crude sign as if chopping off the male member, which I took to mean that the family had ceased to be fruitful.

"Anyway," she continued, "there are so few of them that they have leased out the *piani nobili*, the second and the third floors, to those who can pay—you know, merchants and rich farmers, like your family." Here she smiled knowingly but not unkindly—well aware that my family was rich in land only.

"Ah, I see," I said, letting her know I didn't take offense. "So what kind of people are living on those two floors? I never see them." I tossed this off innocently, with indifference, but I swear Guilia gave me a sharp glance as she turned away again to stir the sauce. I'd better watch my step, I thought, she probably knows all about me and *Signora* Caterina del Rosso next door. Oh, well, I thought, there's no harm if she does.

My housekeeper stirred the sauce a moment longer, then leaving the long wooden spoon to rest on top of the pot, she sat down across from me at the broad wooden table, and leaned forward over the assembly of onions, carrots and greens that filled the space. A knowing gleam in her eyes told me she had something of interest to say.

"The old man who leased the place, *Signore* del Rosso, he made his money in the cloth trade," she started out. "Couple of generations back, actually, so there's enough money that he could probably live like a lord, but he prefers to work, old as he is." She nodded approvingly, and looked to see my reaction.

"Nothing wrong with good honest merchanting," I said, nodding also to keep her talking. "We Venetians have it in our blood." I paused. "How old is he?"

She shrugged. "Old enough to know better," she said with a smirk. "He upped and took a wife—forty years younger than him—in the last year, and she looks like she's barely out of the convent school."

"Really?" I said, showing both disdain and interest. "I suppose she was handed over to him by an indigent father? The usual thing, you know, youth instead of a dowry?" I paused again. "I suppose she's very beautiful, and, what with the convent education, well-mannered and educated?"

Giulia gave me another one of her sharp looks. "I haven't seen her myself, but that's what I've heard said about her."

"Well," I said, shrugging my shoulders and leaning back. "That all sounds very proper and boring."

Giulia barked a harsh laugh, and leaned forward a little more. "But that's not all I've heard about her." Again she looked around as if fearful of being overheard.

"They say," she whispered, "that all her airs of being the daughter of a shiftless, no-good count who's beggared the family are all a fabrication! That she's nothing more than a sharp *putana* who's made her way into a certain level of society with her fine clothes and manners, and now she's hooked a big fish and is set for life."

"No, really?" It was easy for me to look astonished, for astonished I was at this base calumny—though my heart misgave me when I considered that it might possibly be true. "But she is so young, that is, you said she is very young."

"Yes, well, looks are deceiving," my housekeeper said with a sniff. "Apparently she was married before, for a short time, to another old man." She watched me carefully. "And he conveniently died, leaving her his entire fortune, which, it is said, was middling, but enough to set her up as a lady, so she could trap another idiot into marrying her."

I thought about what my amour had told me about her previous marriage; those facts, on the face of it, seemed true.

"But what about her education? She wouldn't be able to fake that, around people who really are educated."

"Pah!" said Giulia, waving her hand in dismissal. "Any clever woman can read a few books and easily fake it, especially if she looks adoringly at the men who are talking, and just asks them questions, and parrots back to them their own ideas. Men are such fools." She snorted in contempt, and placing her hands firmly on the table, boosted herself up from the chair. "But enough gossip for now, I've got work to do," she said. But she turned to give me a penetrating look, and said in a stern voice. "You must decide now for yourself whether our fair neighbor is a person worth knowing or not, *Signore* Carlo."

I sat dumbfounded and distressed for several moments, then roused myself to get up and leave the room. I was shaken to the core of my being over this new information, and I desperately re-played all my conversations with my lady, trying to remember whether she actually had been an equal partner in those conversations, or had she just smiled and laughed, echoing the high-minded principles and ideas that I—vain, love-struck fool—had incessantly talked about?

I didn't know whether to rush over to confront her immediately, or throw myself in the Grand Canal and hide my shame! But after a few hours' contemplation, anger overtook my shame, and it seemed to me that exposing her for the fraud she was might be the best revenge.

☙ Sunday, 21 December 1879 ❧
A Visit to the Biblioteca is Delayed.

I DEPARTED THE BREAKFAST ROOM in thoughtful dismay at John's sudden and unusual, for him, display of emotion. I wish I had not pressed him, but then, what was a good friend to do? I climbed the grand staircase to my room, noting that the dreary, lowering clouds had departed this morning, and the sun, though pale and thin at this time of year, was doing its best to lighten the interior of the old palazzo. Giacomo's renovations to the place were all that was modern and beautiful—and expensive—and I noted with approval the many framed paintings of his own and other artists that adorned the walls of the staircase—including one of John's, a lovely watercolor of St. Mark's Square. Looking at it, I was reminded of my planned destination today—the *Biblioteca Nazionale Marciana*, housed now for some decades in the Doge's Palace, as it had outgrown its original home across the square. Surely it would have a copy of Gozzi's *Memoirs* I could peruse, or if need be, I expected I could find a cheap set in one of the many small bookstores between here and St. Mark's, perhaps in Bettinelli's, one of the most popular bookshops in Venice, just behind the Square.

Hoping to reconcile with John, and also enlist him as an escort to the library, I tapped on his chamber door, which was at the end of the hall from my own, but received no answer from within. A passing housemaid spoke timidly as she curtsied to me.

"*Signorina*, he is gone out," she said in heavily accented English, and she waved her hand, in the way that Italians do, to indicate his whereabouts were now somewhere in the depths of the watery city.

"*Grazie*," I murmured as I turned away. Well, there was nothing for it, I would go to the *Biblioteca* on my own. After all, it is 1879, I thought to myself, not 1779, and a lady doesn't need an escort in Venice in broad daylight anymore. But should I walk? It seemed more than likely that Ca' Favretto had its own gondoliere, and I rather fancied a ride along the Grand Canal, floating by under the *Ponto Rialto* and right up to the steps of the Doge's Palace. I felt sure that the hospitality of Ca' Favretto extended to its guests making use of the family conveyance.

As I readied myself in my room, I thought perhaps I ought to at least make a polite inquiry of my host and hostess about their welfare, if not their permission to utilize their gondoliere. Wrapped in my long cloak and scarf, I stepped lightly down the staircase to the first floor, where I presumed the Favretto's chambers were situated, and turned to my right from the staircase, where I saw a door partly opened. As I approached, I heard voices, one raised in excited urgency—Caterina's—and the other responding gently, Giacomo I presumed. I am not ashamed to say I drew nearer, halted, and listened.

"You have no idea what is upsetting me!" Caterina's voice was high and tense. A mumbled response, too low to hear, from her husband. It appeared that the formidable mother-in-law was not with them—surely I would have heard her voice above all!

"Oh dear Lord, what I have done?" Caterina wailed, and I heard a burst of tears and sobbing. Then, "No, nothing can help me, just go, please, Giaco, leave me alone, I just need to be alone."

I took this as a warning to make myself scarce, and I turned to tiptoe away—only to see the *Signora* watching me from another doorway further down the other end of the hall. Her rapid steps toward me gave me only a few moments to collect myself and prepare for an interrogation.

"*Signorina* Paget," she said severely. I had walked toward her myself, and we met at the top of the stairs.

"*Signora*," I said, smiling pleasantly, "perhaps you can help me? I had thought to ask your son-in-law about possibly making use of his gondoliere, but he and your daughter are—" I hesitated delicately, "otherwise engaged, and I did not wish to disturb them."

Signora looked at me with veiled fierceness mixed with doubt, then shrugged. "If you ask one of the footmen, he will call the gondoliere to the canal door."

I nodded, and she stepped aside to let me pass to the stairway.

A few minutes later, I was safely seated in a shining black gondola at the water door of Ca' Favretto, and soon was on my way. The footman had tucked a lovely warm rug across my lap and also handed me a flask of "something warming" for the journey. These Venetians know how to travel! Ancient palazzos—some whose dark green walls were crumbling into the canal, while others made a braver face with new, pastel-tinted washes on their old stones—slipped by as I leaned back, sipping at what turned out to be a mulled, spicy wine with a lovely orange fragrance—well-watered, though, which was good, as I wanted to be alert for my researches. The aroma of orange brought to my mind the second mysterious note—*Oranges will bring resurrection*—as well as the first, *Water will inflame Life*. Very puzzling, indeed.

The sun did its best to warm the damp and mossy stones in those few spots where its light actually penetrated. Venice is a city of piquant contrasts—brilliant light on the water, in season, that dazzles one's eyes, then the next moment, plunging into dank, unlighted *sotoportegos* to get from one cramped *campo* to the next, with twisting, narrow alleys like stone rivulets carving a thin way between buildings four stories high, blocking out all but the tiny patch of blue or grey sky straight above one's head. I shivered at the thought of becoming lost in that labyrinth, especially after dark. I glanced up at the pale morning sky and was glad I had got an early start.

"*Signorina*," said the boatman, as we rounded the last curve and he prepared to draw up at the water steps to the Square. "Do you wish me to wait for you here?"

"Oh, no, I think not," I said. "Thank you, I shall return to Ca' Favretto on my own." I had no idea how long I would be at the library, and if my quest was unfulfilled there, how much time I might spend searching through various bookstores. I was familiar enough, I thought, with Venice's greater areas, even beyond where the tourists usually go, and felt I would easily find my way back to Ca' Favretto, either in a hired gondola or perhaps, if I felt adventurous and it was still light out, I might walk!

The boatman dexterously ported and steadied the gondola, and helped me debark easily. He tipped his hat to me and turned to ply his pole through the murky waters.

I looked around at the great Square of St. Mark's that lay before me. It was nearing mid-day, but long before the typical Venetian luncheon time, so there was a large number of men and women hurrying by on business or shopping, or just standing about enjoying the mild sunshine, a gift on a wintery day. I gazed at the seemingly endless arcade of pointed Gothic arches that ran along the three sides of the Doge's palace, pillared on the squat Corinthian-topped columns, an impressive sight even with the time-blackened stones dimming their glory somewhat. Launching myself into the crowd, I tried to recall which of the many doors was the entrance to the library; it had been some time since I had visited the *Biblioteca*. I knew it was one *not* facing the Square directly, and not on the water side, so I made my way through the crowd to the western façade, confident I would find the entrance, and deploring the lack of signage for such things. The English were finally, to my mind, beginning to be so obliging as to erect signs in front of institutional buildings, well, *some* of them, such as buildings to which the general public had access, though not, of course, the British Museum, or Parliament. Apparently one should know which buildings were which all on one's own, and naturally, private institutions such as the many gentlemen's clubs, disdained to advertise their presence. If you had to ask, you clearly didn't belong there. It seemed as if that principle still held true in Venice.

There was quite a large assembly of people at the main entrance to the Doge's Palace, maybe some fifty or so—perhaps there was a special exhibition there today. I suddenly found myself caught up in a rush of passing vendors of some sort, waving their arms and speaking unintelligible Venetan—had I landed in a riot or a strike? I felt someone push at me from behind, so that I almost lost my footing, but then another hand, firmly clasping my elbow, righted me before I had tottered more than a step or two. I looked up to see a man's face under a black beaver top hat, his eyes some eight inches above my own gaze, an Englishman by his looks, and proved, shortly, by his words to me.

"Pardon me, miss, I hope you understand my taking the liberty just now of grabbing your elbow so roughly," he said. His hazel eyes looked merry, and his voice and manner were quite correct but also friendly. He looked to be a few years older than I, but not by much—perhaps twenty-five?

"Not at all, sir," I replied promptly. "This crowd had nearly swept me away, and I am grateful that you acted promptly as you did," I added, looking briefly at the dirty ground, "or I would have fallen and possibly been trampled, like an unlucky matador in Barcelona."

My rescuer grinned widely at this and, seeing that the crowd was pressing both of us again, he took my arm once more and led us to a relatively unpopulated spot under the arcade. There he removed his hat and bowed.

"If I may take the additional liberty of introducing myself," he said, straightening up, and taking a card from his vest pocket, he handed it to me. It read, "Charles Wilkinson, Esq." Under that, in smaller letters, "Consular Consultant."

Much amused, I looked at the card and then its owner. "What on earth is a Consular Consultant, Mr. Wilkinson?" I realized I had not replied with my own name—but that could wait.

"Oh, he is a variable animal, indeed! A man of many parts," said Mr. Wilkinson, with a charming smile. "Part advisor, part protocol expert, part confidante…and part detective," he finished, his left brow arched a little defiantly.

I leaned back a bit and surveyed his features, which were good—straight nose, medium-full lips (I have always mistrusted men with very thin lips, I have to say), good strong chin, thick brown hair cut rather short, as was beginning to be the fashion, no facial hair at all, not even the ghost of a mustache, which surprised me somewhat—and the cut of his clothes was excellent. That he admitted to being a detective—not a career held in very high esteem by those who, of course, did not have to work for their living and therefore, disdained those who did—was the most intriguing point about him. I made up my mind and held out my hand, American-style, to shake his hand. He took it and shook heartily, but not too fiercely as to injure my much smaller appendage.

"I am happy to meet you, Mr. Wilkinson," I said. I reached into my reticule and brought forth my own card—my literary persona—and observed him carefully as he perused it.

"Vernon Lee!" He gave out a low whistle—maybe, I thought, he's younger than twenty-five after all—then caught himself. "You mean to say that you, you as you stand here, are the author Vernon Lee, he who has written so knowingly about…well, about so many things, cultural and artistic and aesthetic… that is, *she* who has written…Well, I say!" He stared at me in wonder, and smiled even more charmingly.

"Miss Lee," he said, "for I do not ask your real name, the author is enough for me! Is it possible I might induce you to take some tea or luncheon with me? I just recently read your wonderful essay *Tuscan Peasant Plays* in Fraser's—wonderful! I have many questions." He looked at me so very hopefully, full of literary enthusiasm and reverence for me as an author—what was I to do? Perhaps I should have had more misgivings, but my instincts and intuition were quite silent.

"I should be delighted," I said, putting aside all thoughts of Carlo Gozzi's *Memoirs* for an hour—surely such a short delay wouldn't be harmful? "Shall we repair to Caffé Florian?"

My gallant rescuer held out his arm for me to hold, and we strode through the remains of the crowd toward a table—indoors—at the famous, beloved institution on the Square.

† December 1739 †

Two Days before Christmas

—Memoirs of Count Carlo Gozzi

A THICK, DARK FOG ENVELOPED THE WHOLE CITY as I set out late that morning, determined to find a way to expose my (formerly) fair neighbor for the fraud she was. But an hour or so's somber reflection led me to feel that I needed solid proof, not just the gossip of the neighborhood. But how to find it? My moods alternated between sorrowful brooding over the betrayal of my hopes and beliefs about Caterina, shame that I should even give credibility to such gossip, and anger rising to rage that I had been so tricked, cozened and fooled. As I made my way through the dense fog, hearing muffled footsteps and unearthly voices emanating from alleyways and windows, I began to be aware of a strangeness in the very air, an other-worldly miasma of sorts—it is so difficult to describe! One might call it a fragrance detectible only by the mind—or a color only perceived by tasting it. I believe this is an actual condition, described by the ancient Greeks as *synesthesia*, the replacing of one sense for another—hearing flavors, touching colors, tasting sounds.

I felt I was in danger of losing my reason altogether!

As I rounded a very narrow corner at the end of a particularly dark *sotoportego*, I ran full-on into a man, a gentleman by his dress, who—when we both stepped back and began to apologize—turned out to be a dear acquaintance of mine from my early military service, whom I had not seen for some years. We embraced as brothers.

"Carlo, you look fit as ever," he said, then peered at me more closely. "However, there is something, I can tell, that is troubling you right now. A lady, perhaps?"

"Bruno," I said, for that was his name, "I see you are the same as you always were! So like you to suspect that any trouble at all is founded on something involving the fair sex!" I laughed and clapped him on the back.

He laughed in his turn, readily admitting it. "Let us go to some warm place and talk over old times, my friend," he said, and I gladly complied. It would be a relief to my tormented feelings to be distracted by someone who knew nothing of my current life and troubles.

We turned into a small *campo* nearby and found a tiny restaurant just opening up for lunch. We ordered pasta with sausages and bread, and a large flask of the house red wine, and settled into a cozy corner to renew our acquaintance. I will not bore my readers with the tedious recounting of our reminiscences, but will readily relate the significant, almost impossible coincidence that occurred as we departed the restaurant some three hours later.

Bruno and I were standing in the tiny *campo*; the fog had lifted slightly, enough to allow one to see other people at some distance, and there, emerging from the *sotoportegos* across the way, was my fair neighbor Caterina, accompanied by a female companion. They were dressed elegantly, with voluminous furs and wraps to keep out the cold, and wore small black eye masks, as was fitting during the Solstice Days, but I knew her immediately, and realized that while I had recognized her, she had not as yet spied me out. I was seized with a strong desire to turn away and run down the opposite alley, to avoid having to greet her and, especially, to introduce her to my friend. But alas, I was not quick enough off the mark.

I saw her give a slight start as she and her friend approached the spot where I stood with Bruno, who himself had ceased chatting to me when he noticed the two—I must say, both of them—very beautiful women coming near us.

"*Signore* Gozzi," said my Caterina, giving a slight and graceful curtsey. I bowed, stiffly, in return. Despite the mask, I could see a somewhat puzzled look cross her face, but she continued to speak to me. "May I introduce my dear friend, Countess Maria del Uffizi?" The other lady, less restrained than Caterina, smiled broadly and nodded at us, glancing at Bruno with interest. My friend was a tall and handsome man, with courtly manners, full of good cheer and gallantry toward women. He poked his elbow into me, reminding me of my manners, and I hastily introduced him to the ladies, albeit with a poor grace, I admit.

We four stood awkwardly for a few moments, then my lady Caterina informed us that she had been forced to come out, and her good friend was kind enough to accompany her, to try to lighten her spirits and distract her worried mind. I did not feel inclined to ask her any questions about this, but Bruno jumped in and queried her most amiably. It turned out that her husband, old and sick as he was, had been called away, most unaccountably at this time of year, she said, to Verona, where there were business problems at his cloth manufactory there that required his presence particularly. Her husband, given his natural kindness and solicitude, had insisted she not be put to the trouble of such a journey, and had insisted that she stay in Venice and try to enjoy herself. She was distressed for his health, and was so lonely in the house by herself, that she couldn't resist coming out into the town in search of some amusement and distraction.

After a few more comments back and forth, Caterina announced that she must be on her way, and locking arms with her friend the Countess, they both curtsied and hurried off across the *campo*, with only the Countess del Uffizi looking back once or twice, to smile at me but especially at Bruno.

Bruno immediately began to banter me, loudly praising my good taste. I played the part of a prudish youngster, exaggerated the virtues of my neighbour, and protested that I had never so much as set foot in her house—which was indeed, the truth. It was not easy to deceive my friend in anything regarding the fair sex. He positively refused to believe me, swearing he was sure I was the favoured lover of the beauty, and that he had read our secret in the eyes of both.

"You are a loyal friend to me," he added, "but in the matter of your love affairs, I have always found you too reserved. Between comrades there ought to be perfect confidence, and you insult me by making a mystery of such trifles."

"I can boast of no intimacy whatever with that respectable lady," I replied, "but in order to prove my sincerity toward a friend, I will inform you that even if I enjoyed such an intimacy as you suspect, I would rather cut my tongue out than reveal it to any man alive. For me the honour of women is like a sanctuary. Nothing can convince me that men are bound by friendship to expose the frailty and the shame of a mistress who has sacrificed her virtue, trusting that the man she loves will keep the secret of her fault; nor do I believe that such honourable reticence can be wounding to a friend." We argued a little on this point, I maintaining my position, he treating it with ridicule, and twitting me with holding the opinions found in musty Spanish romances.

I had invited him already to take up his abode in my house, while he was visiting the city, and as soon as we were there, I began to regret it. Over the next day or two, he was always hanging about in my little writing room, on the watch to catch sight of my fair neighbor, and to exchange conversation with her at the window. He drenched her with fulsome compliments upon her beauty, her elegance and her discretion, artfully interweaving his flatteries with references to the close friendship which had united himself and me for many years. To hear him, one would have thought that we were more than brothers! She soon began to listen with pleasure, I could see, entering deeper and deeper into the spirit of these dialogues. Though ready to die of irritation, I forced myself to appear indifferent. I knew Bruno to be an honourable and cordial friend; but with regard to women, I knew that he was one of the most redoubtable pirates, the most energetic, the most fertile in resources, who ever ploughed the seas of Venus. He was older than I, a fine man, however, eloquent, sharp-witted, lively, resolute and expeditious.

Two days went by in these preliminaries, and the date of his departure was approaching. In other circumstances I should have been sorry at the prospect of parting from him. Now I looked forward to it with impatience. One morning I heard him telling Caterina that he had taken a box at the theatre of San Luca—for that night, being Christmas Eve—and that he was going there with his beloved friend (that is, me). He added that it would cheer her up to join our party, breathe the air, and divert her spirits at the play. She declined the invitation with civility. He insisted, and called on me to back him up. She looked me in the face, as though to say: "What do you think of the project?" My friend kept his eyes firmly fixed on mine, waiting to detect any sign which might suggest a *No*.

I did not like to betray my uneasiness, and felt embarrassed. I thought it sufficient to remark that the lady knew her own mind best; she had refused; therefore she must have good reasons for refusing. I could only approve her decision.

"How!" cried my friend, "Are you so barbarous as not to give this lady courage to escape for once from her sad solitude? Do you mean to say that we are not persons of honour, to whose protection she can safely confide herself? Answer me that question." Bruno looked at me intently, daring me to deny him.

"I cannot deny that we are," said I, most reluctantly.

"Well, then," interposed Caterina upon the moment, much to my surprise, "As you may recall, my friend the Countess del Uffizi, whom you met the other day, comes every evening to keep me company, and to sleep with me, during the absence of my husband. We will join you together, masked. Wait for us about two hours after nightfall at the opening of this *calle*."

"Excellent!" exclaimed my friend with exultation. "We will pass a merry evening. After the comedy we will go to sup at a restaurant. It will not be my fault if we do not shine to-night."

I was more dead than alive at this horrendous plan, yet I tried to keep up the appearance of indifference. Can it be possible, I said in my own heart, that these few hours have sufficed to pervert a young lady whom I have so long known as virtuous? Or is it, rather, proof that she whom I esteemed so highly, and who professed to love me, is nothing more than a pleasure-seeking, wanton woman of little virtue and no integrity after all?

The bargain was concluded, and at the hour appointed we found the two women in masks at the opening of the *calle*. My friend swooped like a falcon on my mistress. I remained to man the Countess, (if indeed she was a Countess at all!) who was a blonde, well in flesh, and far from ugly; but at that moment I did not take thought whether she was male or female. My friend in front kept pouring out a deluge of fine sentiments in whispers, without stopping to draw breath, except when he drew a long sigh. I sighed deeper than he did, and with better reason. Can it be possible, I thought, that yonder heroine will fall into his snare so lightly, and thus prove once for all that she is the fraud the gossips say she is? Then I would have the proof I had longed to find, but my heart was heavy with the prospect, and I did not relish either knowing the truth, or exposing her for it.

☙ Sunday, 21 December 1879 ❧

Coffee at Florian's, and then some

ALTHOUGH IT WAS, RELATIVELY SPEAKING, A FINE DAY for winter, it was still too chilly and damp for anyone but the most hardened caffé devotee to sit outside—there were, indeed, chairs and tables set out under the arcade fronting Florian's, but we, along with everyone else, preferred to go indoors and enjoy our repast under the crystal chandeliers and lighted candles, huddled over tiny baroque tables with inlaid wood or marble surfaces. My companion and I were seated immediately, at a window facing the square—I saw a nod and smile of recognition on the waiter's face as we approached, and assumed that Mr. Wilkinson, as could be expected, was a known entity in Venice—or at least, at Florian's.

My deductions were further bolstered by the flattering attention we were given, and by Mr. Wilkinson's subsequent interactions with the waiter. Mr. Wilkinson, unlike many a gentleman of my acquaintance, did not take it upon himself to order on my behalf, a detail of his character and manners which impressed me immensely. Instead, he first directed a question to me.

"Miss Lee," he said, as the waiter hovered nearby, "may I recommend to you some of the creations of Florian's pastry chef which I have come to enjoy with some regularity, but which you will not find on the regular menu?" When I nodded my head in agreement, he informed the waiter in rapid and perfect Italian what those choices were, and again, deferring to me first, ordered coffee for two.

I have to admit I was close to being enchanted by the man—although my innately suspicious nature kept a handhold on my, shall I say, feminine flutterings? We would see what we would see. I have never been one to ignore the oft-said warning, "If it is too good to be true, then it probably isn't."

We were served our selections—incredibly light, flaky pastries as only the Italians can make them—and began to sip our coffees; then it was time for conversation. I decided to take charge and direct it in my own way.

"You are interested in the eighteenth century in Italy?" I started in a general place, so as not to assume that my previously published essays on the subject were to be the only focus of our discussion.

"Not really," said Mr. Wilkinson, smiling and leaning back in the little chair. He seemed amused at the (no doubt) slightly nonplussed look on my face. But I would not protest, only waited for him to continue.

"I had never given it a thought," he admitted, still smiling, "that is, until I happened across your article on the origins of the Tuscan peasant play, the *Maggio* I believe it is called?" He leaned in to take a bite of his pastry, then neatly wiped his lips with the snowy white napkin. "Your description of the countryside, the colorful people, the lanes and walkways, and the picturesque towns—I must say, it was all presented so artistically and with such admirable emotion that I have to admit, I hired a coach and went there myself, not two months ago, in the autumn, and had a dashed delightful time." He settled back in his chair again, his coffee cup held up in salute. "You are an excellent and perceptive writer." He mused thoughtfully a moment, then spoke again.

"There was one description, of the bluish shadows on the round green hills, and the yellow afternoon light on the mulberry trees, that stuck with me, you see." He seemed to be gazing far off, then returned to the present and looked at me. "I saw it all, just as you had written it," he said.

I was struck at the accuracy of his recounting the scene, and his deep appreciation for my writing.

"I thank you for the compliment, and I marvel at your good memory," I said, a little awkwardly. I was not used to such praise—nay, hardly any praise at all! For Mama barely read the essays I wrote, and Eugene, my poet-brother, typically found too many words of mine to which he took a virulent dislike to spare any thought for enjoyment of my prose.

"But beyond the merely scenic," I said, "what did you think of the cultural aspects of my essay—the plays themselves, or the chanting that is the method the actors use to speak their lines?"

There followed an intense discussion between us of the remarkable aspects of these Tuscan plays—he showed that he had read my article closely, and that he was in no way an unschooled amateur in regard to the origins of theatre in general, and the Italian theatre in particular. We spent a good hour exchanging opinions, arguing for our own views and against the other's, and generally enjoying ourselves immensely, downing cup after cup of coffee and (it must be said) several more pastries.

"And to what then," my interlocutor wound up our discussion, "will all these researches and essays lead? Surely you must be planning a book!"

I laughed, heady with the pleasure of such a conversation, and such a companion. "Nay," I said, "it is about to go to press, the moment I return to Florence!"

"Indeed!" Mr. Wilkinson looked surprised and pleased, but then solicitous. "I do hope your return isn't anytime too soon," he said. "My dear Miss Lee, such delightful discussions as we have had just now must be renewed, again and again. Do tell me your departure is not imminent."

I shook my head, and took the last sip of coffee. "That I cannot say for sure, but I intend, I sincerely hope, to leave before Christmas Day," I said.

"Why are you not staying in Venice for the holidays?" He protested, then changed complexion as he realized the question bordered on the impertinent. "Pardon me, Miss Lee," he said, "in my zeal for more of your conversation, I overstep the bounds of politeness."

"No offense taken, sir," I said with a gracious nod. But the glance at impropriety brought back to me with renewed force that here I was, sitting *tête-à-tête* with a complete stranger at Florian's, drinking coffee and carrying on in a worldly, sophisticated manner quite beyond my usual deportment. I felt indeed it was time to end the undoubtedly pleasurable, but somewhat unconventional encounter. Therefore, as I took a peek at the decorative watch pinned to my dress, I spoke in a more detached manner.

"The time has slipped away, I see," I said as I began to feel about for my gloves and reticule. "I'm afraid I have an errand to run—I am seeking a copy of Carlo Gozzi's *Memoirs* which I find I need to consult, one which can no longer be delayed." It struck me then, with considerable force, that here I was light-heartedly and frivolously enjoying myself while my dear John and his friends were suffering under the most dire distress and worry.

"You were not, I hope, thinking to obtain a copy at the *Biblioteca*?" he said, knitting his brows.

"Why yes, as a matter of fact I was," I returned.

"It happens that I attempted to gain entrance there this morning," said Mr. Wilkinson, "and was unceremoniously turned away. It seems they have already closed for the Christmas holidays."

I looked at him in dismay, and then thought about my options.

"Do you suppose that Bettinelli's is still open?" I asked him, as he seemed to know so much about the goings-on in the town.

"Absolutely!" he said. "And I'm sure you will be able to find Gozzi's *Memoirs* in that estimable establishment."

I nodded my head, pleased, and rose from my chair to take my leave. "Well then, I must thank you, Mr. Wilkinson...." I started to say, but he interrupted me.

"Oh, but you must allow me to accompany you!" cried my companion, also making ready to go. "It would not do at all for a lady to range about the city, especially now, as the day has turned dark." He looked at me most sincerely, and I saw through the window, that indeed the sun had retreated behind very threatening clouds. He persisted, seeing my glance at the sky. "Truly, you must, I beg you, take advantage of my protection, Miss Lee. I know this city, and its ways, and I could never forgive myself if you were to come to even the slightest harm that my presence could have avoided."

I did feel a shiver of apprehension at this words, and the thought of traversing the shadowy *calles* and *sotoportegos* unaccompanied gave me pause.

"Very well," I said, trying my best to sound cool yet gracious. "Extraordinary as it may seem, I accept your offer to accompany me to Bettinelli's. Thank you."

We were both standing by then; he cast some coins on the table, then offered me his arm to escort me out the door. Unaccountable as it seemed to me—even risqué!—I found myself walking across St. Mark's Square with this charming, interesting, well-read stranger—and wondering what would happen next.

† December 1739 †

Christmas Eve / Christmas Day

—Memoirs of Count Carlo Gozzi

WE ARRIVED AT THE THEATRE IN GOOD TIME, and seated ourselves in the excellently-situated box my friend Bruno had acquired for the evening. It being Christmas Eve, with a lively comedy on the stage, the theatre was filled with happy families, lovers, would-be lovers and party-goers, all intent on seeing and being seen in their festive apparel. Our two female companions were sumptuously dressed, with daring décolletage, feathers in their hair, and sparkling jewels. My neighbor retained her slight eye-mask, perhaps in deference to her absent husband, but anyone who knew her would have immediately recognized her anyway. Her blonde friend, the Countess, was bold and haughty, and showed off her jewels and her dress by frequently standing and looking over the railing of our box, peering into the audience below. Needless to say, we were at the center of a great deal of attention and, I thought to myself, probably a great deal of speculation as well. Even I had to admit, however, that we were a handsome quartet—young, fashionable, well-dressed, and well-mannered enough to draw everyone's eyes repeatedly to our location.

My friend had seated himself directly to the right of my fair Caterina, who was at the far end of the box; the Countess sat to his right, which left me to sit next to her, the farthest

I could be from Caterina. With youthful indignation and stupidity, I muttered within myself that it was just as well, I didn't want to sit near her anyway, but it raised my ire to overhear Bruno's constant whispering his sweet nothings into her ear. And she looked for all the world as if she were enjoying herself immensely! What it was all about I knew not, though I saw her turning red and losing self-control; she employed her fan continually, and if I leaned forward enough, I could see the quick rise and fall of her rounded breasts above her elegant gown, as she reacted to whatever my friend was suggesting to her. I chafed with rage internally, but pretended to follow the comedy, of which I remember nothing but that it seemed to be interminable.

When it was over, we repaired to a nearby restaurant, the Luna—as before, in couples—my friend with my mistress, I with the blonde Countess. Supper was ordered; a room was placed at our disposal, and candles lighted. My friend, meanwhile, never interrupted his flood of eloquence, while I sat or walked around, moody and discontented. The Countess—I felt more and more certain this was a falsely assumed title!—tried to engage me in conversation, but after several failed attempts, turned her attention to the flask of wine the waiter had brought in, and to the platter of antipasto set on the table to amuse our appetites while we waited for dinner. Caterina and Bruno were seated in a somewhat secluded alcove near a window with heavy draperies, an already half-empty bottle of wine on a table close by—it looked to me as if he had her backed into the corner, and was pressing ever closer. I could hear her murmurs of polite protest, which grew fainter as he began to offer her kisses—first only on her hands, then her bare arms, then on her neck. I tried not to look but it was impossible not to notice what was going on.

Abruptly I turned to the Countess, sat down next to her, and began an intense conversation—a monologue, rather, as

I rarely gave her the opportunity to speak herself, and I have no idea what I was even talking about—and I began drinking heavily, pouring glass after glass of the potent red wine and swallowing it down without tasting it. This went on for several long moments, my own voice drowning out the increasingly passionate sounds I could hear from the alcove, until finally the waiters began bringing in the various dishes for the first course, and we were all obliged to assemble at the small, square table to begin our repast.

Slightly disheveled and with a high colour in her cheeks, my fair Caterina sat across from me, blushing and avoiding my eyes. Bruno attacked his dinner with gusto, occasionally turning to Caterina to offer her a morsel of food, which he put into her mouth with his fingers, lingering against the soft flesh of her lips and tongue. She blushed again and again, although she was smiling, and her breathing was rapid; she was liberally partaking of the wine, which gave her a dazed and unintelligent look. Suddenly I could stand it no longer, and as soon as the last waiter had left the room, I began speaking, heedless of my own sense of decorum or even the gentlemanlike behaviour I was raised to maintain, especially with women.

Raising my glass, and standing up, though unsteadily, I offered a toast.

"To my fair neighbor, Caterina del Rosso, whose virtues and attributes are no doubt a topic of general conversation throughout the town!"

"Hear, hear!" cried my friend Bruno, completely missing my double meaning, as did the Countess, who enthusiastically raised her glass and drank heartily. Caterina, I saw, though muddled by the wine and food and constant attention of Bruno's hands, caught something of the sarcasm in my voice, and hesitated a moment before she drank, glancing at me quickly, then away in some confusion of spirits.

The Countess spoke next, and her words proved her, contrary to my estimation of her, fully capable of understanding the meaning of my toast.

"And to Carlo Gozzi, my dear friend's scholarly neighbor, whose mind is the greatest attribute he can offer to a woman!" She winked at Caterina as she said this, and I felt myself growing red in the face.

Bruno laughed uproariously at this veiled insult—he was always quick to catch a sexual joke—and I thought I saw a tiny smirk move my lady's lips.

I was still standing, and I began to make my way, still a little unbalanced, over to the side of the table where Caterina sat next to Bruno. She looked up at me as I drew nearer, and on some feminine instinct or idea, she stood up and faced me, her hand held out in supplication, her eyes directed toward mine with a friendly, questioning gaze.

"My dear friend and neighbor," she addressed me, coming even closer. "How is it that you are in such a state this evening? Is there anything I can do to help calm your nerves?" At this, I saw Bruno smirk and cover his mouth to hide it, and it seemed to me there was a similar look of disdain in Caterina's eyes, towards me—although it could have been the wine and, I admit, my raging jealousy that suggested it to me.

In any event, a sudden blind impulse, impossible to control, made me raise my hand to her, and though I did not positively slap her smiling face, I gave her such a shove as sent her reeling three steps backwards. She hung her head, confused with chagrin. My friend looked on in astonishment. The blonde opened her eyes and mouth as wide as she was able. I pulled myself together, ashamed perhaps at having shown my anger; then, as though nothing had happened, I began to complain of the host— "Why did he not bring more wine, and our second course? It was getting late, and the ladies ought to be going home." I noticed that my mistress shed some furtive tears.

Just then the waiters returned with the fish and the meat courses, and we again arranged ourselves around the table. For me it was nothing better than the banquet of Thyestes. Still I set myself to abusing the comedy we had seen earlier, which I had hardly observed at all, and the host, and the viands, swallowing a morsel now and then, which tasted in my mouth like arsenic. My friend betrayed a certain perplexity of mind; yet he consumed the food without aversion. My mistress was gloomy, and scarcely raised a mouthful to her lips with trembling fingers. The blonde fell to with a good appetite, and partook of every dish. When the bill was paid, we conducted the ladies back to their house, and wished them good-night.

No sooner were we alone together, than my friend turned to me and said: "It is all your fault. You denied that you were intimate with that young woman. Had you confessed the truth to me, I would have respected your amour. It is your fault, and the loss is yours."

"What I told you was the truth," I answered, "but permit me now to tell you another truth. I am sure that she consented to join our company, relying upon me, and on my guarantee—which I gave at your request—that we were honourable men, to whom she could commit herself with safety. I cannot regard it as honourable in a friend to wheedle his comrade into playing the ignoble part which you have thrust upon me."

"What twaddle!" exclaimed he. "Between friends such things are not weighed in your romantic scales. True friendship has nothing to do with passing pleasures of this nature. You have far too sublime a conception of feminine virtue. My opinion is quite different. The most skillful arithmetician could not calculate the number of my conquests. I take my pastime, and let others take theirs." He looked at me in great indignation and confidence of his superior position.

"If a ram could talk," I answered, disgusted with him (but mainly with myself), "and if I were to question him about his love-affairs with the ewes of his flock, he would express precisely the same sentiments as yours."

"Well, well!" he retorted, still playing the man of the world with me, "you are young yet. A few years will teach you that, as regards the sex you reverence, I am a better philosopher than you are." He broke off, smiling at a thought. "That little blonde, by the way, has taken my fancy. The other woman told me where she lives. To-morrow I mean to attack the fortress, and I will duly report my victory to you."

"Go where you like," I said, "but you won't catch me again with women at the play or in a restaurant." We parted less than amicably, he to sleep and dream of the blonde, while I went to bed with thoughts gnawing and a tempest in my soul, which kept me wide-awake all night.

Early next morning—Christmas Day—I awoke to the same tormenting thoughts that had closed my eyes at last, just a few hours ago. I heard the Christmas bells ringing and announcing the joy of the birth of the Savior, but it was a bitter sound to my ears and my soul. I managed to drag my sluggish body to the church of San Cassiano, where I sat in the family pew and contemplated, to my great distress, how my late, sainted father would have looked on me with disappointment and dismay. The very statues seemed to disapprove, and the religious scenes of Christ and the saints, painted by the great Tintoretto, seared my soul with their humility and holiness, reminding me of how little I had of either virtue.

My friend had been abroad throughout the day, and I only saw him at dinner-time, when he returned to inform me with amazement that the blonde was an inhuman tigress—

all his artifices had not succeeded in subduing her. "She may thank heaven," he continued, as he ate heartily of the Christmas dinner my cook had created for us, "that I must quit Venice to-night. The prudish chatter-box has put me on my mettle. If I had more time, not two more days would pass before I stormed the citadel and made her my victim." He went away that evening, embarking on a ship headed to Greece, and leaving me to the tormenting thoughts which preyed upon my mind.

☙ Sunday, 21 December 1879 ❧

A Visit to Bettinelli's

WITH MR. WILKINSON AS MY "PROTECTOR", we easily wound our way through the crowds in St. Mark's Square and, without any alarms or delays, found ourselves at the front door of Bettinelli's, the most celebrated bookshop in all of Venice—renowned for its extensive collections of books in many languages, its comfortable chairs, and the coffee and biscuits offered to patrons. Equally famous was the proprietor himself, *Signore* Bettinelli—the latest scion of a generations-old book-selling family—as dry and sere as any of his antique scrolls, but amiable and knowledgeable beyond imagining—he knew the exact location of every book in his shop, and it was impossible to mention any title he had not yet heard of.

I asked the clerk at the front desk, in Italian, for a copy of Count Carlo Gozzi's *Memoirs*, volume one only, and I emphasized that I did not want an expensive edition, though I felt a little awkward saying this with Mr. Wilkinson standing by. I knew, as always, that I needed to economize somewhat, especially as I had all three volumes at home in Florence, so there was no need to buy another whole set. I knew that the sections about Gozzi's "loves" were all in the first volume.

As we waited for the clerk to retrieve the book, Mr. Wilkinson continued the conversation we had been having while we walked from Florian's.

"And so a good deal of your new book, on the Italian eighteenth century, is about Carlo Gozzi?" He picked up a book on the counter—a travel guide to Venice—and put it back down again without looking at it.

"Well, not really," I said, ruminating on various sections and numbers of chapters. "I believe there are probably more chapters about Metastasio than anyone else, and after him, Goldoni and Gozzi—their stories are so intertwined, they keep interrupting each other."

"I like the way you speak as if those great musicians and playwrights are alive in your book, and having a conversation to which you—and your readers, happily—are privileged bystanders."

I laughed and nodded my head. "That's exactly what it's like, writing about such things," I said, approving his insight. "They just talk, and I just write it down."

"You are too modest," Mr. Wilkinson said, inclining his head to me a little. After a pause, he said, "And what need have you of Gozzi's *Memoirs* at this very moment, when your book is all but published? Surely you have copies of them at your home?"

His question gave me pause; I felt a flicker of intuition sparking up, a little *caution* sign, making me hesitate to answer—but my more rational self intervened—why wouldn't he think it odd that I so pressingly had to have a copy of a book I already owned? But still, I dodged answering directly.

"Oh, well, as you may know, an author's nerves are tightly strung on the eve of publication," I said, trying to sound airy and uninterested, "and it occurred to me that I may have misread some information about Gozzi's youth, and got it wrong in the text—I have the proof pages with me, and this is my last opportunity to make a change." This wasn't exactly true, as the pages I carried with me were for the very end of the book, which had nothing to do with

Gozzi or his youth. But of course, Mr. Wilkinson wouldn't know that.

"Ah," he said. "I can understand how that might nag at one until it is set straight." He picked up another book from the counter, it looked to me to have a title in Cyrillic, and glanced through its pages. "Is it something to do with the time he was a soldier in Croatia?" he said, looking at the book in his hands, "or perhaps with one of his infamous lady loves?" At this he looked at me, smiling brightly.

"Upon my word," I returned, my intuitive sixth sense all alive again, "you seem to know quite a bit about the Count."

He waved a hand in deprecation. "Only what one picks up from a general education, and being part of this so interesting city herself." He continued to look at me, his question still in his face, but I was determined not to answer.

The clerk returned *at last* (it felt to my nerves) with a cheap little volume, with blue paper covers, of the *Memoirs*, and I concluded the transaction quickly. By then, I felt indeed as if I had spent an unaccountable amount of time in Mr. Wilkinson's company, and my thoughts were immediately directed toward John and his friend, how they might be faring, and how I needed to return to our investigation of this sad murder and mystery. Therefore, upon leaving Bettinelli's, I put out my hand to shake Mr. Wilkinson's and wish him a good day, with my grateful thanks for the delicious coffee and pastries at Florian's.

"My dear Miss Lee," he said (and I realized with some relief that he actually didn't know my real name), "I cannot express to you the pleasure and delight it has been for me to spend this time with you—and I hope that you will not refuse me the continued enjoyment of, perhaps, corresponding with you in future—on strictly literary matters, of course!" He added the last with a laugh, possibly because the look on my face may have struck him as surprised and taken aback.

We had been walking swiftly from the bookshop into the Square once more, and I paused momentarily, to think of something to say and also to wonder if I could attempt to return to Ca' Favretto on foot, instead of finding a gondola?

"I believe you may reach me through my publishers," I said, somewhat primly. "T. Fisher Unwin, Pater Noster Square, London." I held his gaze steadily, and he nodded graciously. I then turned to look around the square—it was very dark outside now, with lowering clouds threatening rain. Mr. Wilkinson was alert to the situation, and offering his arm, said, "You must allow me one last service, Miss Lee," he said. "The gondolas are lined up as usual, but with this rain coming, they will be in much demand. Let me escort you to the *porto* and secure a gondola for you."

I felt a drop or two splash upon my arm, and readily agreed to his proposal. In a trice, I found myself stepping into a gondola with a little compartment, perfect for avoiding the inclement weather. Before I could seat myself and turn to speak to the gondoliere, I saw Mr. Wilkinson hand the man some money, and instruct him to take me swiftly and safely to Ca' Favretto. I started to protest, but Mr. Wilkinson, retreating a few steps from the boat, bowed to me, hat off, and gave me what I took to be a very significant, serious look of some meaning I would need to spend some time on in order to decipher.

But it wasn't until we were floating under the *Ponto Rialto* that it struck me: I had never once mentioned to him that I was staying at Ca' Favretto.

† December 1739 – February 1740 †

The near conclusion of this sad affair

—Memoirs of Count Carlo Gozzi

I WAS RESOLVED TO BREAK AT ONCE AND FOR EVER with the woman who had been my one delight through the last few months. Yet the image of her beauty, her tenderness, our mutual transports, her modesty and virtue in the midst of self-abandonment to love, assailed my heart and sapped my resolution. I felt it would be some relief to cover her with reproaches. Then the remembrance of the folly to which she had stooped, almost before my very eyes, returned to my assistance, and I was on the point of hating her.

Three days passed in this contention of the spirit, which consumed my flesh. At last one morning a pebble flew into my chamber. I picked it up, without showing my head in the window, and read the scroll it carried. Among the many papers I have committed to the flames, I never had the heart to burn this. The novel and bizarre self-defence which it contains made it too precious a specimen of woman's folly, in my judgement. Here, then, I present it in full. Only the spelling has been corrected.

"You are right. I have done wrong, and do not deserve forgiveness. I cannot pretend to have wiped out my sin with days of incessant weeping. These tears, thankfully, are sufficiently explained by the sad state in which my husband has returned from Verona, reduced to the last extremity. They will therefore appear only fitting and proper in the sight of those who may observe them. Alas! would that they were simply shed for my poor dying husband! I cannot say this; and so I have a double crime to make me loathe myself.

"Your friend is a demon, who carried me beyond my senses. He persuaded me that he was so entirely your friend, that if I did not listen to his suit I should affront you. You need not believe what seems incredible; yet I swear to God that he confused me so and filled my brain with such strange thoughts that I gave way in blindness, thinking I was paying you a courtesy, knowing not what I was doing, nor that I was plunging into the horrible abyss in which I woke to find myself the moment after I had fallen.

"Leave me to my wretchedness, and shun me. I am unworthy of you; I confess it. I deserve nothing but to die in my despair. Farewell—a terrible farewell! Farewell for ever!"

I could not have conceived it possible that any one should justify such conduct on such grounds. Yet the letter, though it did not change my mind, disturbed my heart. I reflected on her painful circumstances, with her husband at the point of death. It occurred to me that I could at least intervene as a friend, without playing the part of lover any more. Yet I dared not trust myself to meet the woman who had been the object of my burning passion for so long. At the cost of my life, I was resolved to stamp out all emotions for one who had proved herself alien to my way of thinking and of feeling about love. Moreover, I suspected that she might be exaggerating the illness of her husband, in order to mollify me. I subdued my inclinations, and refrained from answering her letter or from seeing her.

But two days later, another little stone hit against my window pane, and I snatched up the missive it carried to me.

"*Signore*," went the writing, in my lady's hand, "if you retain even a drop of affection for me (respect I do not ask for), you will meet me in the *calle* between our two houses tonight, as the bells strike one. Do not fear any further indiscretion on my part, but I find you are my only friend in an hour of great need, one to whose integrity and honesty, as a gentleman, I believe I can entrust something of great value to me." Signed, *Caterina del Rosso.*

I admit, my curiosity got the better of me, and I readily prepared to meet her at the appointed hour. I arrived early, so as to keep a sharp lookout for both our safety's sake— Venice after midnight, especially during the dark hours of winter, is haunted with treachery and villainy. Thankfully, we both would be mere steps from our doors; nonetheless, I had my dagger at my hip.

Caterina arrived about ten minutes after myself, a dark shadow wrapped in a black cloak, with a veil over her shimmering hair and face. She did not remove the veil as she spoke to me, but it was transparent enough for me to see her (still, to me) bewitching face and beautiful, sad eyes.

"I have no time for niceties, *Signore*," she began immediately, in a low whisper. In her hands she held a medium-sized wooden box, which she held out to me. "I am about to become a widow for the second time—my poor husband is at Death's Door—and I must provide for myself when I find myself alone and, perhaps, once more at the mercy of my infamous, greedy father! You, you alone, I trust to help me in my hour of need! Here," and she thrust the box into my hands. "Keep this safe for me—my father the count must never know that I have such riches! I will hold you to your honour as a Venetian and a gentleman, that you will keep this box and its contents safely for me until I am able to ask for it again. And I will ask for it, someday!"

I was so astonished by this rapid, outlandish request that I was unable to speak. I stood there, in the darkness, with only a dim light from a torch high above my garden wall, and gazed at her. But I held the box in my hands and because, apparently, I did not move to hand it back to her, she decided I had accepted her charge, and she turned and swiftly disappeared back into her own house door. I sat gaping and wondering like a buffoon, and realized that I had no choice but to acquiesce to her desire, and to find some place to safely hide whatever riches the box contained.

You, reader, no doubt are instantly wondering if I opened the box, then or at any time, to discover its contents as well as the truth of the lady's assertion as to it containing riches. I am not ashamed to say that I did—though it wasn't until the next morning that I broke through my sense of decorum and opened it. The contents were indeed spectacular—necklaces and earrings of diamonds, rubies, sapphires, pearl and gold; two elegant little clocks of gold, silver and diamonds; several bejeweled golden bracelets; rings by the dozen, and in one corner, a velvet bag filled with gold ducats. A veritable treasure, indeed! I wondered anew at Caterina's just handing it over to me so trustingly! Surely in that big palazzo she lived in, there would be some hiding place—but then I thought about what she said, that she would soon be a widow, and it occurred to me that of course, she couldn't count on being allowed to stay in that palazzo; her husband didn't own it, and she might very well have to leave before long. It occurred to me, uncomfortably, that perhaps she was somehow maneuvering me into a position to become her third husband!

I mused over this thought as I picked up one precious piece of jewellery after another, examining them closely. Finally, at the very bottom of the box, underneath the bag of ducats, was another velvet bag. I opened the drawstrings, and out fell—to my astonishment—a painted miniature of my one-time love, Caterina del Rosso, set in a frame of jewels and gold—in fact, the very one (I assumed) she had asserted to me had been stolen by her perfidious servants! Had it *all* been a lie? Trickery and deceit right from the start? My blood boiled up in anger, and I flushed at the fool I had been. Well, I would avenge myself now in such a way that she would both know it and yet be unable to act upon it in retribution to me—I would take this miniature as a keepsake of our sad affair, and consider it due payment for all my besotted, misguided love for her. I pocketed the miniature in its velvet case, put all the jewellery back in the box (I had no interest whatsoever in their value or accessibility for me), and hid it quite securely in a secret, small vault behind the wall of my closet in my room at the top of the house. When she asked for the box, I would give it to her, and know that she would miss the miniature on the instant—and realize there was nothing she could do about it, and that I was aware of all her deceptions.

The fact is that only three days had elapsed when I beheld the funeral procession of her husband pass beneath my windows, with the man himself upon the bier. This revived my sympathy for the unhappy, desolate, neglected beauty. I was still hesitating about what to do, even standing outside my garden door, looking up at the neighboring palazzo a few days later, when I was hailed by a priest of my acquaintance who told me that he was going to pay a visit of condolence to the youthful widow. "You ought to come with me," said he. "It is an act of piety toward one of your neighbors." I seized the occasion offered, and joined company with the priest.

We found her plunged in affliction, pale, and weeping. No sooner did she set eyes upon me, than she bent her forehead and abandoned herself to tears. "With the escort of this minister of our religion," I began, "I have come to express my sincere sorrow for your loss, and to lay my services at your disposal." Her sobs redoubled; and without lifting her eyes to mine, she broke into these words: "I deserve nothing at your hands." Then a storm of crying and of sobs interrupted her utterance. My heart was touched. But reason, or hardness, came to my aid. After expressing a few commonplaces, such as are usually employed about the dead, and renewing my proffer of assistance, I departed with the priest.

❧ Sunday, 21 December 1879 ☙

Upon Arriving Back at Ca' Favretto

WHILE I MUSED WITH INCREASING ALARM over Mr. Wilkinson's startling knowledge of my residence in Venice, I also pondered that serious look on his face. It did not seem to me to be menacing, or threatening, or otherwise indicative of harm toward me; rather, I thought I could read actual, live concern for me, for my well-being—as if he knew about something that threatened me, and wanted to warn me of it, and also wanted to relay to me his willingness and obligation, even, to protect me. As these thoughts passed through my mind, I alternately laughed at my imagination—my vanity!—in supposing such a protective motive on his part, and shivered to think that somehow, there was something I should rightly fear—and he knew it. But how? And why? These were questions to which I had to find answers, and quickly.

My gondoliere safely deposited me at the water door of Ca' Favretto, although it took several minutes of his calling out before someone answered the door, flinging it open rather recklessly. It was one of the maids, which was quite odd, that not being a maid's duty, and she seemed about to berate the boatman when she caught sight of me, clambering out of the gondola and up the steps. Then she hurriedly curtsied, held the door for me, nodded her apologies to the gondoliere, with whom it appeared she was acquainted, based on the subsequent rapid exchange of Venetan between the two, and then hastened after me, closing the door and asking if she could take my cloak.

As she did so, I could see that she was in a highly nervous state, and that there were tear-stains on her cheeks. I did not think it fair or kind in me to ask her what was wrong—probably some scolding by the housekeeper—but when I asked her if Mr. Sargent and *Signore* Favretto were at home, she burst into tears and began wailing most alarmingly. I led her to a chair and made her sit down, but she continued weeping and pointing to the drawing room, whose doors were closed. She repeated the word "polizia" several times, and it sent a chill to my heart. Had another body been found?

I moved away from the maid toward the drawing room doors, through which I now heard raised voices, men's voices, loudly asserting themselves in Italian. I opened one of the doors quietly, and entered the room unnoticed by anyone save John, who was facing the doorway and, immediately catching my eye, communicated distress and caution in one glance.

Here was the sight presented to my eyes: three *Carabinieri* stood in the center of the room, their backs to me, and filling the space with their military presence. These were not just the local police constables (as we call them in England), but the national military guard, who managed local police forces. These three were resplendent in their severe navy uniforms, with the dashing scarlet stripe down the outside of their trousers, the white criss-cross of their pack belts across their chests, white shoulder pads trimmed with gold tassels, and gleaming brass helmets topped off by a brilliant black feather towering above their heads. As it was winter, a scarlet cloak also adorned these military gentlemen's shoulders. In my estimation and experience, the bravado of their uniforms vastly outshone the integrity of intellect to be found in this hybrid guardsmen force.

The three of them stood mostly facing away from me, but confronting *Signore* Favretto and John—the raised voices I had heard moments before were quieted now, and Giacomo was just getting to his feet. I caught his speech mid-sentence.

"...no reason to think that there is any substance to this 'tip' as you call it," my host was stating, very politely but with an agitated air. "But I have nothing to hide, and you may search Anna's room—you may search the whole house!—if it helps solve this dreadful crime!" His voice cracked as he said these last words, and he put his hand to his forehead, deeply distressed.

The *Carabinieri* clicked their heels and bowed, and Giacomo led the way out of the drawing room, presumably to the stairway and up to Anna's room. I had stepped aside before they reached the door, and immediately closing it after them, I rushed over to John, who was pouring a glass of wine from the sideboard and downing it in one great gulp.

"What on earth is going on?" I demanded. I could see John was trying to steady himself.

"Someone—an anonymous tipster—has told the *Carabinieri* that there is incriminating evidence of the murderer to be found in Anna's room," he said, slowly and quite precisely. He drank the last of the wine in the glass and began to pour another.

"But you and I searched her room very thoroughly," I protested. "I cannot imagine anyone—much less the *Carabinieri!*—finding something *we* missed!"

"They said they were provided with a clue as to where this...," he paused to drink some wine, "where this evidence was to be found."

I just looked at him, incredulous.

John shrugged, as perplexed, seemingly, as I was myself.

"Well, I'm going up there to see what they're doing," I declared. "If they find something, I'd like to know exactly where they find it—I want to *see* them find it!" I nearly ran to the door, opening it and heading for the grand staircase; after a moment, John followed me, and caught up with me on the second floor. I could hear the voices of the *Carabinieri* and Giacomo drifting down to us from the third floor, which they had just attained. They were standing before the open door of the room, Anna's tiny chamber, when we arrived on the landing.

It would have been comical, if it hadn't been so serious. There was no way all three officers could be in the room, and searching it, at the same time—they just took up too much space, with their helmets and feathers, and capes and swords and heavy boots. After a seemingly endless consultation, during which Giacomo insisted he be present in the room during the search, and I stood clamping my mouth shut to keep from screaming in frustration at the dilatory policemen, the senior officer (so I took him to be, from his greying hair) finally decided he would go in first, with *Signore* Favretto, and if the others wanted to look around too, they would take turns, one after another.

This plan satisfied everyone, and the two men entered the bare little room. I wondered anew what they could possibly think to find—and what was the nature of the "clue" John said they had from the anonymous informant? I used my feminine prerogative—and my diminutive size—to slip in front of the other two *Carabinieri* and stand in the doorway, where I had the scene in full view.

After considerable stepping around, peering under the bedframe (I noted the officer did not get down on the floor to look, and almost sniffed in contempt), and examining the window and chair, the lead *Carabinieri* approached the wardrobe. He opened it, and I could see him as he surveyed the interior of the cabinet. One of Anna's two black dresses no longer hung where I had seen it the day before—it took me a moment, but I inferred from its absence that it had probably been taken away to be used as her burial garment. What a sad thought! Another glance told me that the medallion of the holy saint on its thin pink ribbon, was also gone.

My attention was claimed by a knocking sound I heard, loud and impertinent, and I realized it was the officer sounding his knuckles against the inside walls of the wardrobe. I too had searched for hidden panels, and although I had found one, it was empty. I leaned forward slightly, wondering if he would be able to detect the slight indentation I had found, which released the panel on the floor. He wore very thick gloves, I noted, so I didn't think the odds were good.

Then he took off his gloves, and felt around the floor again. A moment later, with a slight grunt of satisfaction, he had the panel open and was feeling around inside.

To my utter astonishment, he brought forth—with no little triumph, I might add—what looked to be two or three charcoal drawings: a female form, draped, was the very most I could discern from a very brief glance. At this point the other two *Carabinieri* shoved past me into the doorway of the room; I could no longer see what was happening, but I could hear the exchange among the men very easily.

"*Signore*, are these your drawings?"

I assumed the chief officer was addressing Giacomo. There was silence, I heard the rustle of paper, and presumed he had handed them to Giacomo to look at.

"Why, I...don't know, for certain...the light is not good."

Even to me that sounded evasive—I could only imagine what the officers were thinking.

"Surely, *Signore*," the chief said in a reproachful, unbelieving tone, "surely you would recognize your own drawings—and the lovely young woman depicted here—tell me, do you recognize this woman?"

Another silence drawn out. Giacomo must have nodded his head, and the officer pressed him for an answer.

"If you know her, you must tell me her name, *Signore*," he said, almost gently. "It is...it is our Anna," Giacomo said, his voice so low I almost didn't hear him.

"And these are your drawings of her," the officer made it a statement.

"No, no, I, that is," Giacomo once again equivocated in his answer. "I don't think so, I don't think I recognize them at all." He sounded very frightened.

Suddenly one of the two *Carabinieri* in the doorway turned and looked appraisingly at John. "We have two artists here, sir," he said to his senior officer. "Show it to him, too."

Both officers at the door stepped aside for their comrade to exit and confront John with the drawings. I could see them clearly now: two pages, one with a full-sized charcoal rendering of Anna (as I had heard Giacomo attest), somewhat immodestly draped in some fabric that fell from one shoulder to the floor, but revealing a soft, round breast and a considerable length of thigh. The other page, which I took in as quickly, were smaller variations of the same pose, and partial drawings of her face and hands—an artist's sketches, trying to find the right pose or line.

The senior officer held out the drawings to John, who took them in his own hands, almost unconsciously. He was dreadfully pale, but calm.

"These are my drawings," he said after a long moment.

The effect on the *Carabinieri* officer was instantaneous—he took the papers back from John and laid a heavy hand on his arm. He was nearly as tall as my friend, and was an imposing personage.

"Then by the authority given to me by the government of His Majesty King Umberto," he said sternly, "I arrest you, *Signore* Sargent, for the murder of the maidservant, Anna."

✝ March 1740 ✝

The Epilogue to the Love Affair
—*Memoirs of Count Carlo Gozzi*—

A FULL MONTH ELAPSED BEFORE I SET EYES on Caterina again. It chanced that I had commissioned a certain tailoress to make me a waistcoat. Meeting me in the road one afternoon, this woman said that she had lost my measure, and asked whether I would come that evening and let her measure me again. I went, and on entering a room to which she had conducted me, was stupefied to find my mistress sitting there in mourning raiment of black silk. I swear that Andromache, the widow of Hector, was not so lovely as she looked.

She rose on my approach, and began to speak.

"I know that you have a right to be surprised at my boldness in seeking an occasion to meet with you," she said, although her look was calm and confident. "I have every reason to trust in your integrity and honesty, and I pray and hope that I may also be somehow deserving of your compassion. You remember what I told you about my father; and now he is moving heaven and earth to get me under his protection with my little property. However, I feel that I owe it to you to tell you myself, in person, that I have received offers of marriage from an honest merchant, and that as soon as we are married, I will be able to relieve you of the burden I placed upon you, just before my husband died."

Here she looked away, becomingly, but I saw her glance at me from the corner of her eye, to see my reaction.

"I congratulate you most sincerely for your good fortune," I said, really and truly trying hard to sound sincere. "And of course, the moment you require your possessions to be returned to you, be assured I shall do it most promptly."

Her face clouded over, and tears sprang to her eyes. "In truth," she cried, "I sought this opportunity of speaking with you, merely that I might be able to swear to you by all that is most sacred, that I would gladly refuse any happiness in this life for the felicity of dying in the arms of such a friend as you are!" She clutched her hands at her bosom, and looked the very picture of remorse and holy passion. "I am well aware that I have forfeited this good fortune; how I hardly know, and by whose fault I could not say. I do not wish to affront you, nor yet the intriguer whom you call your friend; I am ready to take all the blame on my own shoulders. Accept, at any rate, the candid oath which I have uttered, and leave me to my remorseful reflections."

Having spoken these words, she resumed her seat and wept. Armed as I was with reason, I confess that she almost made me yield to her seductive graces. I sat down beside her, and taking one of her fair hands in mine, spoke as follows, with perfect kindness.

"Think not, dear lady, that I am not deeply moved by your affliction. I am grateful to you for the stratagem by which you contrived this interview. What you have communicated to me with so much feeling not only lays down your line of action; it also suggests my answer." She let me continue holding her hand, but her face was turned from me. I spoke again.

"Let us relegate to the chapter of accidental mishaps that fatal occurrence to which you allude, which will cause me lasting pain, and which remains fixed in my memory. Yet

I must tell you that I cannot regard you, after what then happened, as I did formerly. Our union would only make two persons miserable for life. Your good repute with me is in a sanctuary. Accept this advice then from a young man who will be your good friend to his dying day. Strengthen your mind, and be upon your guard against seducers. The opportunity now offered is excellent; accept at once the proposals of the honest merchant you named to me, and place yourself in safety under his protection."

    I did not wait for an answer, but kissed her hand, and took my leave, without speaking about my waistcoat to the tailoress. A few months after this interview, I received a letter requesting the return of her jewel box; I was to give it to the servant who brought the note. I presumed it meant that she was now married again, and safe from her conniving father. I handed over the box, with no return note, and that was the end of the matter. She and her husband moved to a different *sestiere* in Venice after that, and I never saw them in society. I disdained to listen to any gossip or rumors that my cook tried to tell me, about what may or may not have happened to Caterina del Rosso, the one-time love of my life.

For the next few months, I would take out and gaze longingly at the miniature portrait of my lost love, but ultimately calling forth a resolute courage against such self-indulgence, I stayed my hand every time I thought to take it up, and after a while, I ceased to think of it, and eventually forgot all about it. As I write these memoirs—an old man with many trials and adventures behind me, having long ago sold the palazzo in Venice, and living at last in the countryside of my youth—I have no idea where that miniature portrait may be.

Sunday, 21 December 1879

What is to be done?

"Nonsense!" I loudly spoke the word and was gratified when all those large soldiers turned to look at me. "Those drawings are no evidence of murder, and besides, they weren't even there in the wardrobe yesterday when I looked!"

"When *you* looked, *Signorina*?" The lead officer addressed me politely but sternly. "And what business of yours was it to be looking in that wardrobe?"

"Miss Paget is here at my invitation, officer," said Giacomo, in a voice of unanswerable dignity. "She is my guest, as is Mr. Sargent—they are helping me with the investigation of Anna's death—and I find your actions exceedingly precipitous and outrageous."

The officer inclined his head slightly, in Giacomo's direction, but kept his penetrating gaze on me. "And were you alone when you were in this room—investigating, *Signorina*?" His disdain was clear in his brown eyes.

"I was with her," John spoke up. He had shrugged off the officer's grip on his arm, and looked wretched. "I, too, saw that the hiding place was completely empty."

I have to give the officer credit, he was fast off the mark. "So, you helped to discover this secret hiding place," he said, turning to John, "and came back later to place the drawings in there, thinking that of course no one would look there again!"

I drew breath to speak, but he held up his hand imperiously. "No, *Signorina*, *Signore* Favretto"—this as he bowed to Giacomo—"this gentleman is under arrest, and we must take him to the station." At that, the other two *Carabinieri* took hold of John by both his arms and escorted him down the staircase.

Exchanging hurried but despairing looks, Giacomo and I followed after them. Giacomo was calling loudly for Samuel, who met us at the bottom of the staircase, his master's cloak and hat, as well as John's coat, held out in his arms. Giacomo rattled off instructions about calling lawyers, and Samuel nodded and made reassuring noises as he helped his master with his cloak. I stood a few steps up on the staircase, which allowed me an overview of the incredible scene—John being led off by the two burly *Carabinieri* while Giacomo poured earnest and threatening imprecations into the ear of the chief officer. Samuel followed them to the door—they were going to the station through the streets, not via the Canal—and closed it solemnly behind them. I waited for him to come back to the main hallway, when I descended another step or two, to be on eye-level with him, and gestured that I wished to speak with him.

"Where are they taking Mr. Sargent?" I said, commanding as much calm as I was able.

"To the police station, *Signorina*," he said, and looked as if he was prepared to move on. I could have slapped him!

"I am aware of that much, Samuel," I said icily. "*Where* is the police station located?"

With a face utterly impenetrable as to his emotions, Samuel replied most succinctly.

"Campo San Polo," he said.

I was not as familiar with this *sestiere* as I was with those closer to St. Mark's Square; it was already dark, and I didn't have enough confidence in my sense of direction in this treacherously mapped city to attempt getting there on my own.

"Is there a footman or other servant available to accompany me to the station, and who would know the way there?" I don't know what it was about this man, but I detested having to ask him for what seemed like a favour; his disdain for me was palpable!

He shook his head. "*Sono così dispiaciuto,*" he said, although he didn't seem a bit sincere in his sorrow. "There is no one available," he continued, and he actually took a step away, when he stopped and looked at me with a most severe eye. "And if I may take the liberty, the *Signorina* would not be at all welcome at the station, and in all likelihood would not be permitted to see the prisoner."

I was shocked at the word "prisoner," so much that I was unable even to reply with the strength of the contempt I felt for this cold-hearted man. I stood there seething as he walked down the hall and through the door that led to the kitchen and work rooms downstairs. I realized in a dazed way that I still had on my outdoor cloak and hat, still carried the bag which held the copy of Gozzi's *Memoirs* I had purchased at Bettinelli's earlier this afternoon—a lifetime ago, it seemed!—in the company of the charming and mysterious Mr. Wilkinson.

Mr. Wilkinson! Suddenly I knew that I had to contact him—somehow, I felt this very strongly, he would be able to help in this situation. I looked around, to see if I could spy out a servant who might be able to assist me in this matter, and I descended the remaining steps of the grand staircase. The intolerable episode with the police had clearly thrown the household into a state of insensibility, as the lamps in the hallway had not yet been lighted, and no servant was to be found. The pale, waning light of the late winter afternoon was barely sufficient to illuminate my way to the little sitting room where I had met with John on my first night here. But the water door to the Canal afforded some light, and as I entered the small room, I was heartened to see the maid who had opened the door for me earlier, leaning into the fireplace and lighting the kindling. She had also lighted the oil lamps in that room, and their soft glow and flickering were rather comforting. How welcome a glass of wine and some cheese and bread would be, and to simply sit and think, gather my thoughts, there before the fire. But I had to get word to Mr. Wilkinson first. I composed myself to address the maid, and realized I didn't know her name.

"*Scusami, bambina,*" I said gently, not wanting to startle her. She turned a still tear-stained face up to me, and hastily arose. "*Per favoure, dimmi il tuo nome, cara.*"

"Maria," she said shyly.

"So, Maria," I said, taking her hand and gently sitting down with her on the sofa. "You know that the *Carabinieri* have taken Mr. Sargent away to the police station, the one in Campo San Polo?"

She nodded, unable to speak.

"I must help him, of course," I said, and she nodded again. "I need to get a message, right away, to a gentleman who can help." I dug around in my reticule for Mr. Wilkinson's card. There was no address on the front, but I turned it over and saw to my relief that he had written *Hotel Barbesi* on the back. I knew of it—one of the most expensive hotels that catered to Europeans and British visitors, particularly—and remembered it was not far from St. Mark's Square. I turned back to Maria.

"Do you know someone who can take a message, now, to this gentleman? He is at the Hotel Barbesi. And possibly bring him back here?" The girl thought a moment, then nodded.

"My brother," she said. "He is nearby, and I know he can get away whenever he wants to." She rolled her eyes slightly at this. "I just have to whistle down the *calle* and he will come."

"Excellent!" I cried. I dug again in my reticule for a few coins, and pressed them into her hand. "One for you, and one for him—but only when he comes back with the gentleman, or with a message from him!" She nodded at this, approving my wisdom when it came to the ways of boys, and gathered herself together to fetch him.

"One more thing, Maria," I called her back. "Is your mistress at home, and her mother?"

There was a quick flash of what looked like relief in the poor girl's face as she responded. "*Signora* di Contadini has returned to her home," she said, and then looked up at the ceiling. "*Signora* Caterina keeps to her room, for now."

"Then she is not aware of what has happened—with John and the police?"

Maria shook her head. "I do not think so, *Signorina*."

I nodded, and sent her on her way to fetch her brother.

I sank back on the sofa, momentarily exhausted and overcome. The fire flickered and greedily consumed the kindling and the small logs Maria had piled on top. Yes, a glass of wine would do very well, and I could proceed to think about this monstrous situation, until Mr. Wilkinson put in an appearance. I found it amusing that I didn't have a doubt but that he would, indeed, show up, and that he would turn out to be very helpful.

I straightened up after a moment, though, realizing that I needed to compose the message to send to Mr. Wilkinson. The warming fire made it seem possible for me to remove my cloak and hat and gloves without feeling unduly chilly, so I proceeded to do just that, carefully placing them on one of the comfortable chairs. I shook out my skirts, smoothed my hair, and looked around the room—yes, a desk in the corner! Surely that would have the writing materials that I sought for my task.

I sat down at the *escritoire* and looked in the cubbyholes and drawers for a blank piece of paper. I found crisp linen stationery with "Ca' Favretto" engraved in black at the top, and with a pen and inkstand ready to hand on the desk, I began to write.

My dear Mr. Wilkinson,

You must forgive the impertinence of my writing to you,...

Here I paused—how should this be phrased? *But I am in great need....? But I am hoping that you....?* I didn't want to sound like a desperate female. And, now that I was on the verge of asking for his assistance, what was it I thought he could actually do? I looked at his card again, and his title, *Consular Consultant*, reminded me that he had said he was "part detective." I put pen to paper once more.

but I find myself in a situation of great urgency and some delicacy, taking place at the home of my host, Giacomo Favretto. If you would be so good as to call upon me here, at Ca' Favretto, at your earliest convenience, I would greatly appreciate the counsel of the detective part of your consulting brain. Please send word by this messenger if you cannot meet with me.

Yours sincerely, Vernon Lee

I threw a little fine-grained sand upon the page, to dry the ink, then searched for an envelope. After a moment, I folded the paper, put it in the envelope and addressed it to Mr. Charles Wilkinson, c/o The Hotel Barbesi.

The door opened and in slipped Maria and, I assumed, her brother—younger brother, given his smaller stature and mischievous eyes, whom she introduced to me with the extraordinary name (as these inventive Italians do) of Archangelo. I explained to him in reasonably correct Venetan what his task was; he seemed to know exactly where to go, and I asked him to wait for an answer, or to escort the gentleman here. He nodded, and practically dashed for the door, so eager was he (I assumed again) to earn his penny.

Maria curtsied to me and seemed about to leave, but I asked her first if she could have some refreshment brought to me in this room, and second if someone could take my things upstairs to my room. She immediately gathered them up herself, curtsied again, and left the room with a quiet step.

I sank gratefully into the soft cushions of the sofa, and began thinking about what use I could make of Mr. Wilkinson.

† March 1750 †

*On the absurdities and contrarieties to which
my star has made me subject*

—*Memoirs of Count Carlo Gozzi*

THE YEARS SINCE THAT SAD AND DRAMATIC LOVE-AFFAIR, which I have related in all its detail, and possibly with indiscreet minuteness, taught me some lessons in life. I experienced them before I had completed my twenty-second year. They transformed me into an Argus, all vigilance in regard to the fair sex. Meanwhile I possessed a heart in some ways differing from the ordinary; it had suffered by the repeated discovery of faithlessness in women—how much I will not say; it had suffered also by the brusque acts of disengagement, which my solid, resolute, and decided nature forced upon me. The result was that I took good care to keep myself free in the future from any such entanglements, and ever after looked upon life and love with the eyes and heart, and resignation, of a philosopher.

I must say, however, that the varieties of reversals and trying situations that I have had to endure in my life were such that even the most stoic and indifferent of philosophers would find it hard not to rail at the stars or the gods whose whimsicalities and ill-will were continually raining upon my poor head.

If I were to narrate all the absurdities and untoward accidents to which my luckless star exposed me, I should have a lengthy business on my hands. They were of almost daily occurrence! Those alone which I meekly endured through the behaviour of servants in my employ, would be enough to fill a volume, and the anecdotes would furnish matter for laughter—or madness.

    I will content myself with mentioning one singularity, which was annoying, dangerous, and absurd at the same time. Over and over again have I been mistaken by all sorts of people for someone not myself; and the drollest point is that, in spite of their obstinate persistence, I did not in the least look anything like the persons they took me for! One day I met an old artisan at *San Pavolo*, who ran to meet me, bent down and kissed the hem of my garment with tears, thanking me with all his heart for having been the cause of liberating his son from prison through my influence. I told him firmly that he did not know me, and that he was mistaking me for someone else. He maintained with great warmth and assurance that he knew me, and that I was his kind master Paruta. I perceived that he took me for a Venetian patrician of that name, but I vainly strove to disabuse him. The good man, thinking perhaps that I denied the title of Paruta in order to escape his thanks, followed me a long way with a perfect storm of blessings, vowing to pray to God until his dying day for my happiness and for that of the whole Paruta family. I asked a friend who knew the nobleman in question if I resembled him. He replied that Paruta was lean, tall, very lightly built, with thin legs and a pale face, and that he had not the least similarity to me.

    This kind of mistaken identity occurred on a monthly basis, with people insisting I was someone I was not. But even more than this absurd annoyance, I was continually subject to the vagaries of weather and circumstance—for instance, no matter how long I would stand under an awning, waiting for a rain shower to pass, I would ultimately be obliged to dash home, arriving soaked through, only to have the sun burst through the clouds, and the rain cease, the moment I stepped inside my door. If I had to answer an urgent call of nature, and duck into a dark, deserted alley to relieve myself, inevitably a door would open right before me, and forth would issue two or more well-dressed ladies, requiring me to scramble and run as best I could, to avoid exposing myself (literally) or at the least, to escape their horrified laughter. Eight times out of ten, through the whole course of my life, when I hoped to be alone, and to occupy my leisure with reading or writing for my own distraction and amusement, letters or unexpected visitors, more tiresome even than worrying thoughts or importunate letters, would come to interrupt me and put my patience on the rack.

I believe that even the fortitude of a sainted philosopher would be tried by a lifetime of such petty, constant, annoying trivialities and inconveniences. Through those years, I made do with living in simplicity and, sometimes near penury, in the palazzo at San Cassiano, with one or two servants, and occasionally the company of some of my family, if they were fit or able to make the journey from our farm in Friuli. I did, indeed, spend many happy visits in the country, where time and old age had worn down my mother to a sort of querulous affection, and my sister-in-law into a less imposing martinet than she had been in younger days.

But all in all, despite these petty mischances of daily life, my existence in Venice was lightened, illuminated and blessed—and ultimately, crowned with achievement—by the pursuit of literature and drama, which I undertook constantly, in my little room at the top of the palazzo, and which, when I became a creator of plays for the stage, earned me not money but a famous name in Venice for reviving the *Commedia dell'Arte*, a feat that won over the hearts of the theatre-going public, and also brought me some very wicked and dire enemies. It all began with *The Love for Three Oranges*.

❦ Sunday, 21 December 1879 ❧

A Consultation with Mr. Wilkinson

THE FIRE FLICKERED QUIETLY AS IT WARMED the comfortably small sitting room, and I felt myself relax under the influence of a glass of red wine, which a servant had brought in a short time before. A plate of cheese and bread lay so far mostly untouched on a little table next to my chair (the effect of all those pastries perhaps), and I felt at last that my mind was clearing away the chaos of the untoward events of the last few hours—indeed, the whole day, starting with John's strange behaviour at breakfast, my odd yet interesting encounter with Charles Wilkinson, and the ghastly scene of the discovery of the drawings of Anna, and the arrest of John by the *Carabinieri*.

I needed to lay things out in some kind of order, especially if I were to have the opportunity to consult Mr. Wilkinson. Setting my wine glass aside, I rose, walked over to the *escritoire* and sat down, reaching for another sheet of paper and the pen. I wanted to write down all the facts and speculations or questions I had so far, in close order.

FACTS – *(and Questions)*
- *First maidservant fell into the canal, recovered, left. (Accident? Deliberate?)*
- *First mysterious note received, "Water will inflame life."*

- *Second mysterious note received, "Oranges will bring resurrection."*
- *Second maidservant fell into the canal, deceased. (Pushed? Murdered? Above all, WHY?)*
- *Police suspected Giacomo but only questioned him, let him go.*
- *Orange peels in mouth of deceased maidservant, clearly the work of another person. (WHY? What is the meaning of this? Any connection to Gozzi's Love for Three Oranges?)*
- *Mysterious notes stolen from Giacomo's (unlocked) lock box—along with other items: architectural plans to the palazzo, marriage certificate. (Who stole these items? Query: what use is the marriage certificate? Plans to palazzo to help discover treasure?)*
- *First search of Anna's wardrobe—hidden compartment empty; second search, one day later, drawings of Anna found there. (Who obtained them, and from whom? Who put them there? Does this indicate an insider? Someone trying to shift blame to JSS? Did the person who did this also call in the "hint" to the police?)*

I paused to consider this issue: I realized I didn't know if the drawings had been in Anna's possession, or if John had them in a portfolio? Either way, someone else had gotten hold of them somehow, and placed them in the hidden compartment in the wardrobe. There hadn't been time for John to say much of anything before his arrest—but I wondered if they were drawings he had done recently, rendered since Giacomo had invited him here after the incident with the first maidservant? Or had he sketched them the previous year, when he had visited Giacomo? Were they related to his distraught condition this morning? These were home questions, but it made me uneasy even to think about them. What *had* John been thinking, making such sketches of a maid? I shook my head and returned to making my list.

- *Signora's story of her ancestress's ghost and the "stolen" bejeweled miniature, perhaps other jewellery. (Is it still hidden somewhere in the palazzo? Is someone pretending to be the ghost in order to look around?)*
- *Ca' Favretto is former Gozzi family palazzo. (Which room(s) did Gozzi use? Could he have hidden something somewhere which remains hidden?) N.B. must look at Gozzi's Memoirs right away.*
- *Suspects:*

I paused again, and realized that unless I were willing to write down the name of nearly everyone in the palazzo, from the cook to the *Signora*, and also include John's name, there wasn't much point to think about suspects just yet. Something about this household was off, I felt it intuitively—yes, this was complicated, but somehow, in too many ways.

After a few moments' thought, looking over the list, I rose again from the desk and looked around for the sack from Bettinelli's, which held the copy of Gozzi's *Memoirs*. I remembered I had put it on the chair along with my cloak and hat earlier, and that Maria had taken those items up to my room. The chair was empty—the maid must have scooped up the sack along with the coat. I let out an exasperated sigh—I didn't particularly feel like climbing the two stories up to my room to retrieve the book.

The door opened, and I turned, hoping it might be Mr. Wilkinson—but surely he must have flown here to be coming so quickly! So I was rather surprised when Caterina entered the room, and from the slight start she gave upon seeing me, she had not expected me to be there either. But she composed herself quickly, and smiled.

"Ah, *Signorina*," she said, coming further into the room. "I had understood you had gone out into the city." She walked over to be nearer the fire, and I saw her glance at the slight repast on the table, then look more intently at the paper on the *escritoire* on which I had been taking notes. She then seated herself abruptly, on the sofa near the fire. I discerned with some amusement that she seemed to feel she was intruding, but after all, it was her house, and she had every right to be in any room she wanted to be.

"You were correctly informed, *Signora*," I said, walking back to the chair I had been sitting on, and bending over, I picked up the paper from the desk, folded it, and put it in my pocket. "But I have returned, and availed myself of your gracious hospitality in this most comfortable room." I hoped that by complimenting her house, she would feel more at ease with me. I wasn't far wrong.

"This is a favourite room for me and my husband," she said simply, looking around with a slight smile. "We have already spent many happy hours here—" She broke off, as if some memory or thought intruded to belie her words. Her calm demeanour indicated to me that no one had told her what had happened to John; and apparently her husband's absence did not disturb her. Perhaps Giaco had bidden the servants to be silent, for fear of distressing his wife. I was brashly about to address the issue, regardless, when Caterina spoke.

"Miss Paget," she said, speaking entirely in English, albeit with a charming accent. "May I speak to you with candour?"

"Of course you may," I rejoined, turning to her with an open, eager look.

She sighed. "I know my mother has told you about the ghost of our ancestress who, she imagines, haunts this palazzo of Carlo Gozzi." She looked at me questioningly, and she seemed only mildly agitated, unlike her response the day before.

"Yes," I said. "And I will be as candid in turn—did she tell you that I saw—something—that could have been that very ghost?"

A small, sad smile played across Caterina's lips, and she nodded. "She told me. A trick of the light, yes? upon—" She stopped, looking a little embarrassed.

"Upon an already heated imagination, previously disposed to think about ghosts?" I said it with a big smile.

She smiled in return, looking all at once like an intelligent young woman of some strength, not a fainting, fragile blossom dependent on her husband and mother.

"I should not tell you this," she continued, looking conflicted, "but I have reason to believe that my mama, and—"

The door opened, interrupting her likely very interesting revelation, and we looked up to see Samuel advance slightly into the room, whereupon he announced, in a disapproving tone, "*Signore* Charles Wilkinson, for the *Signorina*."

The next moment Mr. Wilkinson stood before me, bowed quickly, then turned when he saw me look elsewhere, in short, at Caterina, who had gone completely white, and was rising from the sofa in apparent consternation. But even before Mr. Wilkinson could bow his acknowledgement to her, she recovered her complexion and her composure, though not without effort.

"*Signora* Favretto," I said, "may I have the pleasure of introducing a friend to you, Mr. Charles Wilkinson, of the British Consulate here in Venice?"

Mr. Wilkinson, easy and correct in his manners, bowed and murmured something about it being an honour.

"*Signorina* Paget," Caterina said, after nodding her acknowledgement of this new guest, "I shall leave you to visit with your friend. I have some matters to attend to in my room." Without waiting for a reply, she nodded to both of us and left the room quickly.

I was too astonished to say anything—I wondered if she was affronted by my having invited someone—and a gentleman at that—for a private meeting in her home? It made me think—perhaps it *was* a bit indecorous, and perhaps *Society* might have many negative things to say about it, but good heavens! What was there to suspect about poor little me?

Mr. Wilkinson took my hand and led me to a chair, then seated himself. He didn't seem the least bit cognizant of any strange behaviour on Caterina's part, nor of any possible impropriety of our meeting in such private conditions.

"My dear Miss Lee," he said, looking even more handsome for the kind and considerate tone he used. "Please tell me what distress you find yourself in, and I will do my utmost to help or advise you, in any way, I assure you."

What a prepossessing character this man had! By this time, I had become composed enough after Caterina's oddness, and his charming ministrations, to notice that Samuel had not left the room, but was lingering near the table on which stood my glass of wine and small repast. I looked up at him inquiringly.

"Does the *Signorina* wish more wine and food to be brought?" said Samuel, inclining his head slightly toward Mr. Wilkinson.

"Please, nothing on my account, I thank you," that gentleman said, addressing the servant but still with his eyes on me, as I had turned to look at him again, inquiringly.

"You may go then, Samuel, thank you," I said, happy to dismiss him quickly.

When the *major d'omo* had left the room and closed the door once more, I took a deep breath and smiled a little at Mr. Wilkinson.

"Sir," I said, "let me first thank you for such promptness in reply to my rather mysterious note, and also for your generosity in…"

He interrupted with a gentle pressure of his hand on mine. "Say nothing of that," he said. "I am only to happy to be of assistance to a fellow compatriot, and more, to Vernon Lee."

I smiled and nodded slightly. What a sensation this man's presence was creating in my mind and, I had to admit, my feelings. But then I sternly told myself to get back in control—these flutterings and sighings would do no one any good, least of all myself! I gently pulled my hand out from underneath Mr. Wilkinson's, and leaned back in my chair.

"You may have heard, given your official capacity in Venice, sir," I said, assuming a serious air, "of the death a few days ago, here at this palazzo, of a young maidservant. Her body was found in the *rio* next to the house."

Mr. Wilkinson looked solemn, and nodded his head once, affirming my statement. "A terrible tragedy," he said. "Has it been determined in what manner she died?"

I thought this a curious question, but then realized I did not know what the local newspapers had said about the girl's death, nor what information would or would not have been divulged by the police.

"Although it seemed at first this was an accident, or possibly a suicide," I said, "the police now appear to consider it murder."

Mr. Wilkinson's eyes widened at this news. "Murder!" he repeated. He reached out his hand again to lightly touch mine. "Surely I hope this does not put you in danger, Miss Lee!"

This startled me a bit, as it hadn't occurred to me; I considered a moment, then spoke. "I have no reason to consider that I am in any danger, Mr. Wilkinson," I said, although thinking to myself, *not yet*. "Though I do thank you for your concern." I continued. "What you may *not* know, is that another young maidservant, about six weeks ago, was also fished out of the *rio*—but fortunately, she was rescued in time."

Mr. Wilkinson uttered a low cry of consternation, but remained silent, waiting for me to go on. We sat there for a moment, looking at each other, all at once like strange cats facing each other in an alley—I, admittedly, much more wary of him than he appeared to be of me; I couldn't help thinking of *how* he knew I was staying at Ca' Favretto. I searched my inmost feelings for that intuitive sense that had rarely failed me in times past, and realized that while there were questions, there was no sense of danger. I decided then that I would trust him.

"Prepare yourself for an odd and complicated story," I said, smiling a little, and waved my hand at the carafe of wine on the table. "I expect you may want to fortify yourself for the telling." An amused gleam flashed in his eyes, and he leaned forward to pour himself a glass.

I proceeded to bring him up to date on the complete story, leaving out nothing. But the whole time, I still had a sneaking feeling that I wasn't telling him anything he didn't already know.

✝ March 1757 ✝

A review of the origin and progress of
the literary quarrels in which I was engaged

—*Memoirs of Count Carlo Gozzi*

I MUST BEGIN BY CONFESSING THREE WEAKNESSES, which pertained to my way of looking upon literature, as both I and my elder brother gained reputations for our literary contributions to the cultural life of Venice, and Italy in general.

In the first place, I resented the ruin of Italian poetry—established in the thirteenth century, fortified and strengthened in the fourteenth, somewhat shaken in the fifteenth, revived and consolidated in the sixteenth by so many noble writers, spoiled in the seventeenth, rehabilitated at the end of the last and at the beginning of the present eighteenth century, then given over to the dogs and utterly corrupted by a band of blustering fanatics during the period which we are doomed to live in. You may say, strong words! But I have ever been known for my honest ways.

In the second place, I resented the decadence of our Italian language and the usurpations of sheer ignorance upon its purity. Purity of diction I regard as indispensable to plain harmonious beauty of expression, to felicitous development of thought, to just illumination of ideas, and to the proper colouring of sentiment, especially in works of wit and genius in our idiom.

In the third place, I resented the extinction of all sense for proportion and propriety in style, that sense which prompts us to treat matters sublime, familiar, and facetious upon various planes and in different keys of feeling, whether the vehicle employed be verse or prose. Instead of this, one monstrous style, now bombastically turgid, now stupidly commonplace, has become the fashion for everything which is written or sent to press, from the weightiest of arguments down to the daily letter which a fellow scribbles to his mistress. It is insupportable that every idea or whim must now be presented in such a way that the least common denominator of "the public mind" can be presented with something that it thinks it understands, merely because it is dressed up in the clothing of the latest fashion and trend.

You may call me passionate, you may say that I flame with outrage against the mere usage of words—and so what is the harm in that, you say? Words are just words—but alas, words are the face and hands, the arms, the sword and shield of intellect, of ideas! If words themselves become meaningless, and truth is interchangeable with dishonesty and dissembling, if hatred is touted as virtue and love as weakness, then all is chaos, and humankind falls from its divine calling to Reason as well as Faith.

You must excuse an old man, fierce as ever in the defense of what is good and just, who has had the misfortune to live through decadent times, and felt helpless before it. However, I will rouse my spirit from its doldrums, swallow my bitterness, and try again to recount in these memoirs of mine, some of the lighter and happier jousting among the literary lights of my day, which ultimately ended with a dare and a wager that I was fool enough—and wise enough!—to enter into, one day at Bettinelli's bookshop—but we will get to that presently.

The last three years of the decade of the 1750's were a time when I came into my own as a writer and a literary critic. Unlike others who penned Dedications and Odes to wealthy merchants or politicians—for reward or pay—I never took a sequin for any of my work, all of it dedicated only to the Muse and *La Serenissima*, my beloved city. It was in the year 1757 then that I composed a little book in verse, closely following the style of good old Tuscan masters, and giving it the title of *La Tartana degl'influssi per l'anno bisestile 1757 (The ship of coming trends for the Leap Year of 1757)*. This little work contained a gay critique in abstract on the literary uses and abuses of the times. It was composed upon certain verses of an obscure Florentine poet Burchiello, which I selected as prophetic texts for my own disquisitions. It took the humour of the literary club of which I was a founding member (the *Granelleschi*, a group of clever and talented young men), and I dedicated it to a patrician of Venice, Daniele Farsetti, to whom I also gave the autograph, without retaining any copy for my own use. This Cavaliere, a man of excellent culture, and a Mecænas of the Granelleschi, wishing to give me an agreeable surprise, and thinking perhaps that he would meet with difficulty in getting the poem printed at Venice, sent it to Paris to be put in type, and distributed the few copies which were struck off among his friends in Venice.

This trifling volume might have gone the round of many hands, affording innocent amusement by its broad and humourous survey over characters and customs, if a few drops of somewhat pungent ink, employed in lashing the bad writers of those days—particularly Carlo Goldoni and Pietro Chiari, both playwriters—had not played the part of venomous and sacrilegious asps. Goldoni, besides being a regular deluge of dramatic works, had in him I know not what diuretic medicine for composing little things in verse, songs, rhyming diatribes, and other such-like poems of a very muddy order. This gift he now exercised in one of his commonplace *terza-rima* rigmaroles against my innocent little pamphlet. He abused the book as a stale piece of mustiness, an inept and insufferable scarecrow; treating its author as an angry man who deserved compassion, because (he chose to say) I had wooed fortune in vain. Many other polite expressions of the same stamp adorned these triplets.

Meanwhile, the famous *Signor* Lami, who at that time wrote *the* literary paper of Florence, thought my *Tartana* worthy of notice in his journal, and extracted some of its stanzas on the decadence and corruption of the language. Padre Calogerà, too, who was then editing the *Giornale de' Letterati d'Italia,* composed and published praises on it, which were certainly above its merits. I flatter myself that my readers will not think I record these facts out of vanity. I was not personally acquainted with either Lami or Calogerà. It is not my habit to correspond with celebrated men of letters in order to manufacture testimonials out of their civil and flattering replies. I do not condescend to wheedle journalists and reviewers into imposing on the credulity of the public by calling bad things good and good things bad in my behoof. I have always been so far sensible as to check self-esteem, and to appreciate my literary toys at their due worthlessness. Writers who by tricks of this kind, extortions, canvassings, and subterfuges, seek to gratify their thirst for fame, and to found a reputation upon bought or begged for attestations, are the objects of my scorn and loathing. For Lami and Calogerà I cherished sentiments of gratitude. I seemed to find in them a spirit kindred to my own, and a conviction that I had uttered what was useful in the cause of culture.

In short, my funny little book obtained a rapid and wide success. The partisans of Goldoni and Chiari took it for a gross malignant satire. The next four years were spent in lively back-and-forths between what grew to be two fierce and partisan armies—the "reformers" led by Goldoni and Chiari, and the "purists" (if you will), led by myself and other prominent members of the Granelleschi literary club. It was great fun indeed, and the populace of Venice, avid as always to cheer on or abuse one side of anything or the other, given the smallest provocation, joined in the battle, with arguments leading to not a few knocks on the head in cafés and taverns throughout the town.

Finally, in 1761, there was a confrontation in Bettinelli's bookshop—and how the sparks did fly!

☙ Sunday, 21 December 1879 ☙

Mr. Wilkinson lends his aid to resolving the mystery.

"So you see, Mr. Wilkinson," I wound up my long narrative, "we have murder, theft, ghosts, mysterious notes, possible references to events some one hundred-fifty years past, and an attempt to frame my friend John for some or all of these things." I shook my head, and then said in a firm voice, "There is no doubt in my mind that someone stole those drawings from John's possession—or Anna's—and placed them in that wardrobe compartment, to point an accusing finger at my poor friend." I did not, however, say aloud my own opinion of John having made the drawings in the first place, and what that might possibly mean. Mr. Wilkinson was not slow; he would work that out for himself, no doubt, and quickly.

My patient listener had leaned forward all during the time I told the eerie tale, but now he frowned and leaned back in his chair. After a moment, he looked at me thoughtfully, his eyes clear and piercing.

"Where is the copy of Gozzi's *Memoirs* you purchased earlier today?" he asked.

I smiled. "You go right to the heart of the matter, I see." I rose, feeling my limbs to be stiff and knotted after sitting so long, and in rather a tense state. "I believe the maid took it up to my chamber with my cloak and things, so I will go now to retrieve it." He nodded, and I left the room quickly. Once outside the door, I leaned against the panel, feeling a kind of relief, almost to exhaustion, and yet—there was tension still. I hurried to the staircase, quickly stepped up to the floor my room was on, and found the book in its sack from the bookshop right where I expected it to be. I realized at that point how fearful I had been that it would have disappeared! I chuckled to myself, thinking that the wandering ghost of Caterina (or whoever) wasn't a reader. I nearly ran back down the stairs to rejoin my new-found friend.

Mr. Wilkinson was standing at the mantle when I entered the sitting room, a glass of wine in his hand, which he quickly quaffed and set on the table by the fireplace. We proceeded to sit side by side on the little velvet-covered divan, which was close to a large oil lamp, giving us adequate light to peruse the *Memoirs*. It was, of course, in Italian, but as we were both proficients in the language, that was not an insuperable barrier. I paged through the early parts of the book, and found the chapter I had remembered skipping during my researches.

"*The history of a brief love affair which, though true, may be considered as fiction,*" I read aloud. "Interesting," I mused. "Gozzi himself brings his own writing into question as to whether it's true or not."

Mr. Wilkinson shrugged—I would term it a *French* shrug rather than an Italian one, based on the skepticism it conveyed; Italian shrugs typically telegraph indifference—but I digress.

"Do you recall the gist of this story?" he asked me, and glanced my way. We were sitting, perforce, very near each other, as the divan was sized for the intimacy of two persons, and I felt the warmth of his body even through our respective sets of clothing. Heavens! I imagined I could sympathize with ladies who swoon, after all!

"Actually," I confessed, "I did not read this chapter, nor any of those relating his various youthful love affairs—I was more focused on his literary affairs." I shifted my position on the divan slightly further from Mr. Wilkinson, adjusting the book in my lap as I did so, as if I were trying to give him a better view of the pages. "Shall we read it together, and compare our understanding of this *amour* and how it may be connected to our present researches?"

The passage was long, but we sat in silence as we skimmed through the pages, a silence broken occasionally by one of us murmuring "hmmmm" or "oh!" as we read. Twenty minutes passed, during which I felt under a most pleasing yet nerve-wracking spell, sitting so close as we were, with our hands occasionally touching as we both moved to turn a page at the same time. All in all, however, I was glad when we reached the end, and could be released to sit back and take a deep breath. I was the first to rise, taking the book with me, and I sat down on the chair opposite to the divan. With distance came calm, and a cooler disposition—better, I thought, to more rationally canvass our thinking about what Gozzi had revealed.

"On the matter of the grievance that our present-day *Signora* feels on behalf of her ancestress," I began, "it appears to me that naturally, with Gozzi having depicted the original Caterina as a wanton, scheming, greedy social climber, subsequent generations to that lady might have just cause for offence." I tapped my finger on the book for a moment. "But still, he doesn't seem to have exposed her so very dreadfully, at least not for many years. This *Memoir* was published only after Gozzi's death, when he was very old."

Mr. Wilkinson shook his head. "As you know, Italian grudges go on for centuries. But," he said, "as to the much more pertinent matter of the missing bejeweled miniature, and the other items of jewellery which he describes, he states clearly that she asked for them back, and he gave them all back to her. That is," he corrected himself, "the miniature he declares was lost to the ruffian servant and his wife, if we can believe Caterina's story about that in the first place."

"Yes, well, that's at least what he wrote in his *Memoirs*," I said, thinking at the same time that I was betraying Gozzi by deeming him untrustworthy. "Perhaps we should search the palazzo next door," I said, treating it lightly, "and we might find the cache of jewels hidden by *Signora* Caterina—or her brazen servants—left there in haste after the death of the master of the house?"

Mr. Wilkinson gave me a sharp, amused glance. "I think it highly unlikely that the lady would leave anything so precious behind her in her flight." He appeared to muse on this, then shook his head. "Perhaps, if Gozzi did take them, the jewels are hidden somewhere in *this* palazzo? And the ghost of Caterina is more human than spirit, using the legend as a cover for seeking the treasure?"

I shook my head. "The *Signora*, that is, *Signore* Favrettos' mother-in-law, insists that a thorough search has already been made, and nothing was found."

He gave this some thought. "And so, are you inclined to believe the worst of *Signora* Caterina, the ancestress? That she made everything up out of whole cloth? Or perhaps Gozzi tells the story as he does to actually cover up his *own* acquisition of the jewels?"

I gave a little shrug of my shoulders, in my own best French style. "Gozzi himself warns us he may not be telling the truth, and after all, when an old man writes his memoirs of his youthful love affairs," I paused, an eyebrow lifting slightly, "it seems only natural that he would present it in the light most flattering to himself—especially given Gozzi's clearly misogynist leanings in his later years."

At this, Mr. Wilkinson laughed aloud.

"You are an admirable woman," he declared. "I'm glad I'm your friend and not your enemy!" He checked himself, and added, with a becoming smile, "I hope, that is, that I may call myself your friend?"

I smiled. "As to that, Mr. Wilkinson," I said, with my best façade of *insouciance*, "it remains to be seen how useful you will be." At that, he looked serious again, and rose from the divan.

"Then let me show my usefulness at once," he said. "I will go directly to the *Questore*, and see what can be done about extracting poor Mr. Sargent from the hands of the *Carabinieri*." He took a step or two nearer, and reached down for my hand, which I gave up willingly. He bent over it with a most graceful bow, and spoke his parting words. "I want you to know that I believe you when you say that Mr. Sargent is innocent, and I will do everything in my power to prove it so."

With that, he turned and departed, leaving me with heightened feelings and a growing perplexity about who this man was, and how it was that he had turned up so propitiously at this moment of our great need?

† March 1761 †

*I resolve to amuse my fellow-citizens with
fantastic dramatic pieces on the stage.*

—Memoirs of Count Carlo Gozzi

THE WINDS OF MARCH WERE BLOWING IN FROM THE EAST, causing all travelers abroad in the late afternoon to seek the comfort of a café or restaurant or, in my case, the warmth and fraternity of Bettinelli's bookshop. It was situated in a tiny alley behind the north façade of the Doge's Palace, with an old, time-worn wooden door of ample breadth and height—and thickness—to ward off invading barbarians by the score from entering its hallowed literary precincts. Small windows set high in the outside walls reinforced the feeling of a fortress, and a roaring fire in an over-sized fireplace at the far end of the main room gave forth not only heat but light that threw friendly shadows on the ranks of shelves and tables that held more books than seemed possible to gather in any one place.

And *Signor* Bettinelli knew where every single book resided—long-time customers would laughingly test the old man (he was *never* a young man, I swear it), calling out an obscure title—and shake their heads in amazement as he would ponder a moment, then walk directly to some stack or other of books, and pull out the title with a flourish!

As I say, I was sitting in an old, stuffed chair by the fire there one afternoon, surrounded by my colleagues from our literary club, the *Granelleschi*, and I believe we were discussing the latest screed from the supporters of Goldoni, which castigated my own writing and several others' as well—when in walked the man himself, Goldoni, followed closely by his pale shadow, Chiari, and a small crowd of their own ill-educated creatures. Chiari and Goldoni, formerly, had been at war with each other over their differing styles of theatre and poetry, but they had recently joined forces, as it were, to battle more effectively the growing popularity and influence of my own *Granelleschi*, with our emphasis on purity, clarity and harmony above all.

I was in a good humour, though, and inclined to be polite and gentlemanly—after all, I was of the nobility (though, I admit, of the poorer ranks), but I felt generous, and had a reputation to uphold, for civility *in person*, if not necessarily in print. I therefore rose and addressed the newcomers.

"My dear *signores*," I said, bowing to them. "We the *Granelleschi* would be pleased to share the warmth of Bettinelli's fire with our literary colleagues, however oddly assorted we all may be as to talents and success."

The slightly obscured sting of my words did not seem to penetrate the thick heads of our opposing force; Goldoni was, after all, a good-hearted fellow, just monumentally vain and lacking in talent (he started his career as a lawyer, and not a very successful one, but the aggressive manners and legal language he learned there frequently imbued his prose and poetry), so after a moment's pause, he graciously acceded, and my fellows and I re-arranged the stools and benches to provide room for our rivals to sit amongst us. Chiari was more surly, even less well-educated than Goldoni, and he sat to the side with an unbecoming glower on his face.

Bettinelli, merchant that he was, sent over his shop assistant to see if we wanted to order any food or drink, which could be easily obtained from the tavern *Pellegrino* next door;

I believe Bettinelli took a cut for these referrals. We placed our orders and sat back with polite smiles.

But alas, the cordiality of our greeting soon gave way to sarcasm, blustering and outright accusations between the two forces meeting on this literary ground. One of my very young colleagues, Pietro, lobbed the first volley; he was a cherubic, long-haired fellow whose look of innocence hid behind it the bite of an asp.

"Signore Goldoni, if I may," he began, politely lifting his cup in Goldoni's direction, "I would like to present a little offering of words in your honour."

Goldoni and his followers looked wary of this, but took up their cups accordingly.

"Standing before the Court of Literature, in the Civil Complaint of Poetry versus Goldoni," young Pietro intoned solemnly, "The Petitioner presents her case: That whereas the Party of the First Part (hereinafter known as The Muse) has been used in such a manner by the Party of the Second Part (hereinafter known as Goldoni) as to reduce The Muse to a disgraced and bedraggled shadow of her former self through lack of theme, cadence, harmony, grace, proper diction and correct spelling..." At this point, several of Goldoni's colleagues began to mutter and call out imprecations on Pietro, but Goldoni held up his hand, as if to say, *patience, let us hear him out.* Pietro continued, "She humbly begs the Court that upon submission of appropriate evidence, that is, any or all of said Goldoni's scribblings, that the Court will disbar Goldoni from practice at the Literary Bar, and revoke his Poetic License for whatever period of years it pleases the Court to set."

Immediately a young gentleman of Goldoni's persuasion rose and took the floor.

"Be it submitted to the Court," he said, "that a second Respondent should be added to this Complaint, namely, one Count Carlo Gozzi, in light of his insufferable moralizing, his self-righteous attitude of literary martyrdom, his antiquated and anti-modern loathing of personal freedom and independent speech, and his insatiable lust for fame, poorly disguised in his satirical writings that are no more than *ad hominem* attacks on the most popular writers of our day, devoid of literary merit or rational ideas—in short, a pure case of sour grapes if ever there was one."

And so it went back and forth, with one side and then the other, posturing, attacking, expostulating, while the maidservant from the tavern next door kept us well supplied with wine and possets, cheese and meat and bread—all in good fun, I have to say, as neither Goldoni nor I stood to defend ourselves, and he and I exchanged several good-humoured glances as we watched our young defenders plead our respective cases.

But then it was time for we two elders, finally, to speak our minds—that is, Goldoni and I, as Chiari wasn't much given to public debate. The afternoon had long waned into dusk, and dusk into evening, and all of us had had a little too much to drink, and were looking to find our way back to our homes and families. I, alas, had no family to return to in my desolate palazzo of San Cassiano, but no more of that here.

Goldoni stood, cleared his throat, and looked around the room. "Gentlemen," he said, his voice raspy with wine and the chill of early Spring. "Colleagues, friends, opponents...but lovers of The Muse, all of us. I have a proposition."

I wondered what path he was treading. In the past months, our two partisan groups had been waging a battle about the theatre in particular. Both Goldoni and Chiari professed themselves the champions of theatrical reform, to bring a more "realistic" kind of theatre to Venice, such as had been for some time popularized in Paris and other European cities—dull dramas (to my thinking) about the *bourgeoisie*, the merchant class and their mistresses, wives and business partners. The "realism" of the everyday! Didn't we all live in that soup all day and all night, in our own private lives? Did we have to see it on the stage as well, when we might hope to be relieved of the tedium and weariness of the *quotidienne*? With their love of "realism," part of Goldoni's and Chiari's programme was to cut the throat of the innocent *Commedia dell'Arte*, which had been so well received, indeed beloved, in Venice, with several deservedly popular comedic plays some decades ago. It had seemed to me that I could not castigate the arrogance of my "reforming" opponents better than by taking our old stock-theatre characters Truffaldino, Tartaglia, Brighella, Pantalone, and Smeraldina under my protection.

Accordingly, I had opened fire with a dithyrambic poem, praising the *extempore* comedies of old in question, and comparing their gay farces favourably with the dull and heavy pieces of the reformers. Chiari and Goldoni had replied to my attacks and those of my associates with vigour. Goldoni, in particular, called me a verbose word-monger, and kept asserting that the enormous crowds which flocked together to enjoy his plays constituted a convincing proof of their essential merit.

"It is one thing," Goldoni was now saying, pulling me from my reverie. "It is one thing to write subtle verbal criticisms, but it is quite another thing to compose dramas and comedies which fill the public theatres with enthusiastic audiences." He bowed to his friend Chiari, who lifted his cup in reply, smiling malignantly. Goldoni spoke again.

"Therefore, I challenge Count Carlo Gozzi with this proposition: he shall attempt to write a play, a comedy in particular, as he is so inflamed against the form of drama as I and my esteemed colleague Pietro Chiari produce, and get it staged here in Venice, and we shall see what kind of audience will come to see a comedy without topical humour, without sophistication, without style and form, in short, without all the things that the populace of Venice loves to see on their stages."

There was silence in the room; even Bettinelli, I could see, had come close and was watching the proceedings with awed amusement. Goldoni was staring at me with a challenging, arrogant look. His insult to my creative ability, and to Comedy, required a swift and lethal response.

I rose from my seat, looked around the room, and spoke. I had anticipated this challenge some time ago, and I was ready with my answer. "I am, first, of the opinion that crowded theatres prove nothing with regard to the goodness or the badness of the plays which people come to see." Goldoni smirked at this, and Chiari leaned forward and said in a stage whisper, so all could hear, "Sour grapes indeed!"

I continued. "I nonetheless accept this challenge, and I hereby stake my reputation as a member of the Venetian *literati,* on drawing more folk together than either *Signor* Goldoni or *Signor* Chiari can do with all their immodesty and modernity and scenic tricks, by simply putting the old wives' fairy-story of *The Love for Three Oranges* upon the boards."

The room erupted in acclamations and protests of derision.

"Bring back Pantalone and Smeraldina? No one will show up for that old saw!"

"Brilliant! Everyone loves a fairy-tale!"

"What! Magic and witches and fairies…pah! Our Venetians are too sophisticated for that!"

"Good for you, Count! I for one will attend every performance!"

Goldoni and I exchanged looks across the space of the small room, and I believe I detected a hint of trepidation in his watery eyes. Well, I thought to myself, I had better get busy making good on my boast!

☙ Late Sunday, 21 December 1879 ❧

I learn more about those drawings, and we conduct a search.

THE DREARY WINTER EVENING CLOSED IN, and although I had little appetite, I thought it best to consider some dinner, even though I imagined I would be dining quite alone. As far as I knew, *Signora* Caterina was still keeping to her room, and I expected that Giacomo was still at the *Questura* with John. Dear John! It was misery to think that he was alone in some damp, ill-lighted cell, forlorn and worried. I wanted to be with him, but Mr. Wilkinson had been adamant about my not attempting it—he knew, he said, for a fact that I would not be allowed to see my friend. I tried to take heart in thinking Mr. Wilkinson was, perhaps at that very moment, securing John's release; certainly, I felt sure he was doing everything in his power to make it happen.

The housekeeper Jocasta came to the sitting room to announce that dinner was being served; I wondered briefly why Samuel had not come to announce this, but perhaps he was about some other business of the household. It didn't really matter. I felt as if she were watching me narrowly, but I imagine it was mere nerves on my part. She departed after delivering her announcement. After a few minutes, as I rose and went to the door, I heard some noises echoing off the high marble entryway at the other end of the great hall, and with a heart beating fast, I walked rapidly to the street-side door and saw, much to my delight, that John was standing there, handing over his coat and umbrella to a footman. I ran to him and threw my arms around him, and I felt a great shudder go through his whole frame.

"My dear Twin!" I cried, rejoicing in the simple fact of him being alive and whole. He held me fast for a few moments, then kissed the top of my head. When I stepped back at last, I nearly gasped at how wretched he looked. "Oh, John, you look absolutely terrible!" Although he had been in the keeping of the police a relatively short time, perhaps some six hours, his clothes were wrinkled, with spots of grime on his trousers, and his hair was mussed, as from his running his hands through it continually. I shuddered to think of the cell he had been put in.

He grimaced in a lop-sided way, and tucking my arm into his, walked further into the hall. "I daresay I do," he agreed, and with an effort, tried to shake off all gloom. "But after a bath and a change of clothes, I shall be right as rain once again!"

"Of course, of course," I said, gripping his arm in reassurance. "There is dinner all prepared, and I shall tell the servants to wait a bit until you are ready—you must be so hungry!"

John nodded, but his face indicated his thoughts were far from dinner. "The police kept my passport—they have instructed me to stay in this palazzo until they give it back to me."

I felt a little quiver of fear at this; of course, he would still be under suspicion.

"I have so many questions," I said, as we walked toward the staircase, "and so many things to tell you about what has occurred this day—" I broke off quickly, seeing the weariness in his eyes. "But that will all come later, it's enough that you are free and well."

He nodded again, and saying no more than "I'll be back down shortly," he left me at the foot of the staircase to go to his own room. I watched him climb the stairs, with a slower tread than I'd ever seen John employ, and then I turned away with a sigh. I went in search of Maria, or Samuel, or Jocasta, to let them know John would be coming down to dine soon, and to set another place.

I roused up Jocasta by knocking on the door that, I presumed, led to the kitchen and servants' quarters downstairs. I turned the handle, preparing to descend if need be, and opened the door to find Jocasta hastily making her way upstairs. I stepped back to allow her into the foyer, and she quite firmly closed the door behind her. I had the distinct feeling I would not be welcome down there.

"What may I do for you, *Signorina*?" I could tell she was trying to be polite and calm, but her hands were moving nervously under her apron, and her eyes looked tense and worried.

"*Signore* Sargent has returned from the *Questore*," I said, watching her carefully, but she had become more composed than at first, and showed no reaction other than a nod of her head. "He will be ready to dine soon, so please have a place set for him." I started to turn away, then thought of Caterina. "Is your mistress—can you send someone to see if she would like to join us for dinner?"

Jocasta shook her head. "*Signora* Caterina has told us that she will not leave her room for the rest of the evening, and begs your indulgence, and wishes to not be disturbed by anyone." This made me wonder even more about the mental and emotional state of my hostess, but what could I say? I thanked Jocasta and allowed her to go on her way.

I was soon seated at the dining table, feeling quite diminutive in the high-ceilinged room, and ruminating about Mr. Wilkinson—had it been by his hand that John was free? And so quickly! If so, did John know this, had they met? Should I tell John about this strange but wonderful gentleman? Oddly, I felt conflicted about this—on the one hand, why shouldn't I relay to John all that had occurred on my outing to find a copy of the *Memoirs*? On the other, something nagged at me about Mr. Wilkinson, there was too much mystery there, and I didn't feel comfortable talking about him until I had sorted it to my satisfaction.

The door opened and John entered the room, some twenty minutes after he had gone upstairs. He looked all the better for what must have been a hasty bath, and a change of clothes. He seemed calmer, although he still looked weary and worried. The servants entered a moment later and began offering us plates of pasta and vegetables, fish and potatoes. A footman poured wine into our glasses—John immediately drank his whole glass—and left the carafe of wine on the table. He and a maid went dutifully to the sideboard to wait on us further, but I was anxious to talk to John alone.

"You may go now," I said to them, quite the mistress of the situation. "We shall ring the bell if we need anything more." I paused a fraction of a second. "Thank you so very much for your kind attention to us, in the absence of your master and mistress." The two servants, both of whom were rather young, looked astonished at my thanking them, but bowed and curtsied their way out of the room, and we were alone at last.

We ate in silence for a few moments. I was the first to speak, and I was proud of my diplomatic patience in beginning the conversation.

"My dear John," I said. "Do you feel quite up to discussing the situation we find ourselves in? Can you give me an account of what happened to you after you left this house in the company of the *Carabinieri*?"

John took another long draught of wine before he answered, and it gave me time to see what an effort it was taking for him to pull himself together. He shook his head, and at first I took it to mean he wasn't going to say anything, but then he began speaking. He didn't look at me, but stared at the plate of food in front of him, stirring it occasionally with his fork, but not attempting a single bite.

"This is all my fault," he began, in a low, wretched voice. I quashed my first impulse, which was to soothe and contradict him, but I schooled myself to hold my tongue and let him talk. "Anna...those drawings..." he shot me a quick glance, quickly withdrawn. "You saw them, you saw what they were..." It seemed for a moment he couldn't go on.

"Were they...done recently, John? Or when you were here last year?" I asked the question gently, in a non-committal tone—I was not in the least sitting in judgement here, and I wanted him to know that.

He nodded. "Yes, you see it, they were done last year, when I was visiting in the summer," he said, and took another gulp of wine. "There wasn't anything...there wasn't much, that is, between us, between Anna and me," he said, turning the glass by its stem in his sensitive artist's fingers. He nearly shrugged, but stopped himself. "We exchanged a few kisses, that's all...there was nothing...she wanted to learn how to be an artist's model, you see," he said, one hand turned upward toward me in explanation. He gave a low, choked laugh. "She said she could earn a good deal more money doing that, than she could as a housemaid," he said. "And she was very interested in earning more." He fell silent.

I thought for a moment, then spoke. "Did she have the sketches in her possession?"

He looked up at that, and nodded. "I gave them to her when I left, last year." He shrugged fully then. "She wanted them to show other artists how she could pose, and how good a model she could be. I was happy to help." He drank the rest of the wine in his glass and reached for the decanter. "You see that I didn't sign them...." He trailed off, and I nodded, understanding his point.

"So tell me how this is 'all your fault'," I said, a trifle sternly. I wondered what irrational thoughts were driving his deep wretchedness. He looked up at me, and I could the color rising from his throat to his face.

"I...I'm assuming that Anna's..." he stumbled for the word, "*fidanzanto*? Her *amore*? Perhaps he found the drawings, and they quarreled, and he..." John turned his head away from me, so I finished his sentence.

"And he, this *amore*, killed her in a fit of passion? Stuffed the orange peels in her mouth and threw her into the *rio*?" I disliked speaking so plainly but I felt that John needed to be thinking more clearly. "Do you even know if she had such a man in her life? And what about the orange peels, doesn't it seem they are more closely tied to the note that Giacomo received than some unexplainable and grotesque act on the part of a lover? If it was a crime of passion, why would he have oranges with him? And if it took place in this house, surely someone would have seen him—someone would know that he even exists, and what his relationship with Anna was."

John had turned his attention back to me, and was looking more like himself, calmer and more rational. He nodded slowly. "I see your points, Vi, I guess I haven't been thinking very clearly."

"Of course you haven't," I rejoined briskly. "You've been manhandled by the *Carabinieri*, you've been in jail! For the love God, how ill did they treat you there?" I raised my hand. "Never mind, you probably don't want to relive that!"

John smiled faintly. "Actually, other than the jail cell being very cold and rather grimy, they treated me well enough—even gave me some coffee and a roll."

I eyed him closely; he was regaining his sense of himself. I steeled myself—why would I have to do that, I wondered—to ask my next question.

"And how is it they let you go, so soon after dragging you off? And where is Giacomo? Did he leave you there?"

My indignation flared at the thought, but John quickly quelled that fire.

"No, no, not at all! Giaco was with me every second until I was released, when I begged him to go to his wife at her mother's house rather than escort me home. I could see that's where he felt he should be, and wanted to be." He shrugged again. "And I, though shaken, was perfectly fine, and able to find my way back here—the police station is not far, a ten minutes' walk."

"But Caterina is here!" I said, startled. "Why did Giacomo think she would be at her mother's house?"

John looked puzzled. "I'm not sure, but I believe he may have said she told him she was going to be there—this morning, before all this happened."

I remembered the couple's distressed exchange I had overheard earlier in the day, and thought perhaps Giacomo was saving face before his friend John. He was, perhaps, granting his wife's wish to be left alone. Maybe he was staying, not at his mother-in-law's, but at some hotel? I decided to leave that issue for later, and not bother John with it. "And why," I asked again, "did they let you go? Did they tell you anything?"

John looked thoughtful for a moment, taking up his fork with some pasta on it, at last, and hesitated before he brought it up to his mouth.

"Actually, they did say one thing, that it was lucky for me that I had 'friends in high places'," he said, shaking his head. "I asked them what they meant, but they just shrugged and muttered something about it being too high up for it to be worth their jobs to ask any more questions."

"So you didn't see…no one came to you, or the police, and asked them to release you?" I was very puzzled at this turn of events; I had been certain that Mr. Wilkinson would himself had gone to the *Questore* to assist John, as he'd said he was going to do. But perhaps, he just notified his contacts with the diplomatic corps? Other Italian contacts as well?

"No one," John said. He started to dig in to his plate of food with renewed gusto—ah, the ability of a young man to recover from misadventures of a certain type! I myself did not feel my appetite returning, but I was glad to see John restoring his energy.

"Italy—and Venice especially—is always a mystery to me," he said, reaching for a piece of bread, and more wine. "I just assumed that Giacomo sent some notes, although he said he did not. Who knows how, or why, things happen as they do? I'm just glad there were some 'friends' of mine in whatever places they were in who were able to effect my release."

"But, I presume," I said, with an increase of worry I tried to hide from John, "the police still consider you a suspect. John, we must find out who took those drawings from Anna—where she kept them, who knew about them, how they got into that hidden compartment in her wardrobe! We must find out these things, and so much more!"

John nodded his agreement, but I could see from the exhausted look on his face, despite his returning appetite, that he would soon be fit for nothing but a good night's sleep, and it would be the better part of friendship for me to urge him to it.

I, on the other hand, never felt more awake, and as I sat there, waiting for John to finish, a plan began to form in my mind.

† April 1761 †

The Fairy-Story of the Love for Three Oranges, slightly adjusted for satirical purposes

—Memoirs of Count Carlo Gozzi

ONCE UPON A TIME, THERE WAS A KING who was impatient for his only son and heir to finally marry and therefore secure the succession of the kingdom. This son, lazy and stubborn, refused to hear his father's entreaties until suddenly, one day, while eating some white cheese, he cut his finger and two drops of blood fell on the cheese. As if struck by the arrow of Cupid, the Prince declared that he would only marry a woman whose skin was as white as the cheese, and whose lips and hair were as red as the blood. So off he went wandering, much to his father's dismay, meeting up with witches and ogresses, dragons and fortresses closed against him, until he finally lit upon an old crone who handed him three oranges, saying only that he must be sure to have water ready to hand upon opening the oranges.

So sure enough, being a lazy, rather unintelligent Prince, he sat down a little way from a brook, and unpeeled the first orange. Out sprang a fairy lady, as white and red as he could wish, as beautiful as the dawn! But she was choking on the pith and peels of the orange, and pleaded with him to give her some water; the Prince, mindlessly gawking at this lovely vision, couldn't get his feet to move fast enough, and so the fairy disappeared in a puff of cloud. Cursing himself for an idiot, he opened the second orange—the same result and the same consequences as the first time, with the second beautiful fairy fading into a cloud. By this time, having at last learned his lesson, the Prince went down to the brook and put some water in a cup, then unpeeled the third and last orange. Voila! The water was ready to give to the poor choking fairy, and she survived her ordeal. They swore eternal love to each other, and were determined to be very happy.

Dear Reader, this is as much of the original fairy tale as you may want to know, especially as my own version of it was changed rather drastically, for my own purposes of satire and parody. Although I expect that many of you may remember this tale as told to you by your mothers or grandmothers? How the servant girl betrayed the fairy, who turned herself into a bird to escape, and how the servant girl convinced the Prince that *she* was indeed the fairy, only changed by a spell to look like a much less beautiful servant girl; how it all came to its tragi-comic ending at the wedding feast, when the fairy-bird was roasted in the fire by the despicable servant girl, but then the old woman appeared again with more oranges, by which means the Prince (after stupidly letting the first two orange-fairies die of suffocation *again* from the orange peels in their mouths), manages to get back the very same fairy from the third orange! So they throw the servant girl into the fire, and everyone lives happily ever after.

While I kept many of the same characters, and the most basic story line of the old fairy tale, I very cleverly (if I do say so myself), altered a number of things to press home the points I wanted to make about theatre, style, diction, plot, humour—and the vile shortcomings of Goldoni and Chiari in all these respects.

I am sorry to say that there is not, at this time when I write my *Memoirs*, any extant copy of this earliest of my many *fabula* plays, so the exact words are no longer available. And this is also due to the style of acting that was used to perform these plays, which was primarily improvisation—the highly talented acting troupe I engaged at the time only needed an outline and some direction from time to time as to what the story line was, and their genius for comedy and improvisation would carry the rest. Of course, there were some very particular lines of dialogue that I insisted they were to speak, otherwise my satire would be missed. But they were very well able to learn the specifics, and as time went on, they very thoroughly became as invested in the project as even I could have wished them to be.

But at the time of which I write, when this challenge had been proposed and accepted, I sat at my poor little wooden desk high up in the attic of my family's crumbling palazzo of San Cassiano, pen in hand, waiting for inspiration to strike. The soft winds of Spring had begun to blow away the Winter chill, and the whole of the summer was before me to create my satirical play, with time enough before the opening of the theatre season in the early Fall, for rehearsals and revisions. I had received pledges of support from my colleagues of the *Granelleschi*, to help pay the actors and lease the theatre—the play would be performed at the *Teatre di San Cassiano*, right in my own *sestiere*—and how proud I thought my brother Gasparo would be to share in the success and glory of a Gozzi production in San Polo!

My mind and spirit strengthened by the thought of the triumph before me, I lifted my pen and a theme struck me: it would be a contest between Tragedy and Comedy, nay, all of the various kinds of drama, Farce and Romance too! I would use the stock characters—the Masks—of the *Commedia del'Arte*, and add some magicians and witches and giants to enchant the populace with fairy-tale magic, all the while excoriating and decimating my rivals with pointed satire.

I began to write a synopsis for the play.

↳ Even Later on Sunday ↲
21 December 1879

A late night adventure with the help of a young friend

JOHN HAD LEFT ME IN THE DINING ROOM to make his way to bed and sleep, but I sat there even after the servants had removed all traces of dinner. I noted that Samuel had not made an appearance throughout the evening. The younger staff had behaved perfectly respectably; in fact, they were more cordial and attentive than when under the severe eye of their *major d'omo*. I was startled from my musings when the ormolu clock on the sideboard struck the hour—and was not amazed to see it was ten o'clock. I felt as if I'd been awake and scrambling about for at least two days, so much had occurred in this one day.

On a sudden, I rose from the table—I needed to take some kind of action, and the place I wanted to begin was at the top of the house—Carlo Gozzi's writing retreat, with the window that faced the palazzo next door; this much I had refreshed my memory with upon reading the chapter about his love affair with the lady Caterina, his fair neighbor. The palazzo next door was also an open question in my mind, though perhaps not in anyone else's. I just felt...*something*...about it, and wanted to pursue my intuition.

As I approached the door to the hallway, it opened and my little friendly maid, Maria, appeared. She curtsied prettily, and asked if there were anything more the *signorina* might require before retiring for the night?

"Yes, *cara*," I said, smiling at her. "I would like a lamp to carry with me, and I would also greatly appreciate it if you could call up your little brother again—I have an errand for him!"

Maria, though looking a little puzzled, curtsied again and said she would get her brother right away. We walked into the hall together, where she asked me to wait a moment; she opened a door that I believe led to a storage room, and brought out a small oil lantern. She stopped at a table in the hall, opened the lantern, and taking a match from a drawer in the table, proceeded to light the wick and settle it to a soft glow.

"*Grazie mille, cara,*" I said, taking the lantern from her. "When your brother comes, please send him upstairs to the top floor, the penthouse."

"But, *signorina,*" Maria protested. "That is where Anna, poor Anna...." She looked stricken at the thought of my going to that floor. A thought occurred to me. "Isn't your own room on that floor, too, Maria?" I asked. The girl nodded, tears starting in her eyes.

"I am sleeping downstairs now, *Signorina,*" she said, "ever since..."

"Of course," I said, soothingly. "It's all right. I must have another look around, though. No harm will come to me, I'm sure of it."

Maria looked doubtingly, but nodded her head.

I started up the stairs with my lantern, and my thoughts were full of the description of the old palazzo in Gozzi's *Memoirs* on that long-ago night when he and his comrade returned from the wars in Dalmatia, expecting warmth and plenty, and instead experiencing the shock of a home destitute, broken and empty of family joy. I reached the top floor before many minutes passed, despite my musings, and found myself on the tiny landing which let into three doors: the one on the left being the dead Anna's room, overlooking the *rio*; the one to the right being Maria's room, with no window, but facing the direction of the Grand Canal; and the one in the middle, of which I had no knowledge. Previously, when John and I had been up here to look at Anna's room, we had not thought to look into it. But it faced the palazzo next door, and so it surely must be the writing room of Carlo Gozzi. I recalled that the *Signora,* Giacomo's formidable mother-in-law, had said it was now a storage closet, and that they had searched it previously.

I stepped forward, my hopes high, and turned the handle of the door. To my surprise, it opened readily! I laughed at myself for imagining all the usual insuperable (or almost) difficulties that Gothic mysteries always throw in the face of the curious heroine, intent on uncovering ghosts or murder or ancient skeletons in chains. The room was small, perhaps some ten feet by six, but with a high ceiling, and seemed indeed to be a storage place for old and useless pieces of bric-a-brac, boxes, and some clothing, although not simply in a jumble but more or less neatly stowed on shelves to the left and the right. Without the shelves, I could easily imagine how it could have been used as a little study, especially if there were a window.

This did not, at first, seem to be the case. The wall straight in front of me was blank, but there was a small wooden desk placed up against it. I carefully placed my oil lamp on a shelf, and turned it up to give me more light. The desk looked as if it could easily be more than a hundred years old, very worn on the edges, and with old stains, probably ink, here and there on its weathered surface. It was more a table than a desk, as it had only one little center drawer under the flat part of the table. Of course, my heart beat fast as I touched my fingers to the broken handle, thinking that naturally the drawer must contain some relic of Gozzi, some half-page remnant of an original manuscript of a poem or a letter. And equally of course, when I opened the drawer, I saw that it was completely empty. I even felt around it for hidden compartments, but there was nothing.

I closed the drawer and turned my attention to the blank wall above it. Gozzi was very clear about the window; after all, that was how he first met his lady love, and conversed with her all those days and weeks. I touched the wall, and the feel of it was soft—there was wall paper on it! Perhaps the window had been boarded up and then papered over by residents who lived in the palazzo long after the Gozzi family left it behind. I scratched with a fingernail against the paper, and though it yielded a bit, as it was old and soft, I needed some kind of implement to tear into it.

I admit it did not occur to me that I about to destroy Giacomo Favretto's property, so eager was I to find the window and whatever it might reveal. I looked around on the shelves to see if I could spy some household article I could make use of—a knife, a fork, even a spoon! Alas, everything I touched was soft and pliant. I muttered to myself that here was, again, another reason why I should carry a pocket knife—a notion that had occurred to me on many other occasions, and which, of course, I forgot about in the intervening times. I promised myself I would procure one the first time I was out in the marketplace again.

At that moment I heard footsteps on the marble staircase, and whispers of excited voices—Maria and her little brother. I felt cheered at the thought—surely an enterprising little boy would have a pocket knife about him!

I stepped out of the closet and awaited the two at the landing. Their pale faces came into view as I held the lantern up so they could see me there. Maria's face, indeed, looked cautious and sad, but her brother, little Archangelo, was eager and full of boyish energy for an adventure. I must confess that I had a moment's scrupulous pause about asking the boy to perform the task I had in mind for him, but dismissed it immediately with the thought, *oh, he won't get into any harm by it!*

I motioned to the two to come forward, but as I noted Maria's increasingly fearful look, I decided it would be just as well to send her back downstairs—I didn't want anyone to become suspicious of her absence, and start asking questions. She didn't seem to me to be the type to be a very good liar—unlike her brother, whom I sized up instantly as able to tell the most bald-faced, outrageous stories without turning a hair. Consequently, I laid a comforting hand on Maria's shoulder, and spoke to her in a low voice.

"*Cara*, please go back downstairs and take up whatever duties you have for the rest of the evening, or retire to bed if you will," I said, trying to sound reassuring. "Archangelo and I will get on perfectly well by ourselves."

She traded looks with her little brother, which seemed to be asking him whether that was a good plan for him, at which he shrugged and smiled, which I took to be affirmative. She gave him a little peck on the cheek, and a little shake of his shoulders, and made her way back downstairs.

"So, *Signore* Archangelo," I said, turning to the boy and, seeing a small chair on the landing, I sat on it so I could talk to him eye-to-eye. "You know the religious house next door, the Cavini, is that it?"

He nodded. "It is their mother house," he said, with no prompting. "Most of the monks live elsewhere, but a few of the important ones are in Palazzo Cornaro from time to time." He called it by its ancient name, *Cornaro*, when in the 15th century it had housed the illustrious Caterina Cornaro (why were they all named Caterina, I wondered idly) who became the Queen of Cyprus for a time and was, I recall, the daughter of a famous Doge of Venice.

"You have a sharp mind," I complimented the boy, and eyed him speculatively. I thought it best to waste no time and get right to the point. "And what are the chances that you can gain access to that palazzo without anyone knowing about it?"

He looked thoughtful and, I thought, a bit wary. "To-night?" he said. He shrugged, as if to say, *not too hard*. "And what is it I am to do there once I get in?"

"So you *can* get inside," I confirmed, and was gratified when he nodded solemnly. "But first," I said, recollecting my primary mission, "Do you have a pocket knife I can borrow for a few moments?"

He sniffed, as if to say, *how not?* and produced a sharp little implement, placing it in my outstretched hand. I rose from my chair and walked over to the closet.

"Now," I said, holding my hand over my heart, "do you swear to me that you will tell no one what you are about to see and do—at least, not until I tell you that you may do so?"

He too held his hand over his heart, and swore by the Blessed Virgin and all the saints, which I took to be a fairly definite sign that he would hold his tongue.

"Good," I said, "Let us see what we can find."

We entered the closet, taking the oil lamp with us, and again I placed it carefully on a shelf. I opened the knife so the blade was extended, and made a careful cut into the wall-paper above the little wooden desk. It came away easily from the wall, and I continued to carve away a space about two feet across and three feet high. It was as I had thought, the window had been boarded up and wall-papered over.

But on closer inspection—both Archangelo and I eagerly had leaned into the shallow space of the window frame—I could see that it wasn't simply boards placed across the window—first, there was no glass, which I supposed made sense, given the age of the palazzo—and second, there was an old, rusted iron latch, of the hook and ring variety, that indicated someone had merely closed the ancient wooden shutters, and not really boarded up the window at all.

"Why is this of interest to you, *Signorina?*" Archangelo asked.

I didn't answer, as my heart was beating fast to think that here I was, in Carlo Gozzi's own writing room, about to touch the very window shutters that possibly may not have been touched since he himself closed them, a century ago, when he finally left Ca' San Cassiano to its fate. With a few strong tugs, I forced the rusted hook to loose its hold on the iron ring, and, glancing at my little companion, who understood my meaning instantly, we both pushed on the shutters which gave out with a creak and a groan, falling open to the winter night sky above, and the looming wall of the palazzo across the *calle*.

And just slightly below the level of our own window, there was the window at which the lady Caterina had sat and sewed her linen, looking up demurely at poor smitten Carlo Gozzi all those decades ago! It, too, was shuttered, but looked to be in more frequent use than its papered-over counterpart on our side.

"*Alora*," I said to Archangelo, my hand on his shoulder. "This is what I want you to do."

He nodded at my whispered instructions, asked an intelligent question or two, and was off in a flash down the stairs to start his *avventura*.

I put out the flame in my oil lamp, and sat at Gozzi's desk, staring across at the shuttered window, and waited for what would come next.

† April 1761 †

*The Love for Three Oranges—I Begin to Write
A Comedy in Five Acts*

—*Memoirs of Count Carlo Gozzi*

L'AMORE DELLE TRE MELARANCE

Act 1

THE KING OF CLUBS AND HIS ADVISOR Pantalone lament the "incurable hypochondria" of the Prince, brought on by an indulgence in tragic poetry. Doctors inform the King that his son's ailment can only be cured with laughter, so Pantalone summons the jester Truffaldino (that is, Chiari) to arrange a grand entertainment, together with the (secretly inimical and dire) prime minister, Leandro (that is, Goldoni).

The full outline of the plot, alas, took more than a few weeks to construct, but my brain was so brimming over with sly satires and character assassinations of my enemies and their pompous, "realistic" theatre, that I felt as if I barely ate or drank or slept during those weeks. I worked in a tornado of paper and ink, and the walls of the small writing room at the top of my family's palazzo of San Cassiano absorbed many a long night's worth of tears of both delight and anguish. I found I had to greatly alter the original fairy-story of the *Three Oranges* to suit my satirical purposes, but once I had lighted upon the initial structure in the Prologue of making the whole thing a battle for ascendancy between the different forms of theatre, it became easier. I could see it clearly in my mind's eye, how the play would open....

> The curtain rises on the Advocates of Tragedy, Comedy, Lyric Drama and Farce, who argue for their favourite form before the curtain goes up for a play. Dressed in clearly recognizable costumery, the four Advocates would quickly go from polite debate to raucous baiting and cat-calling.
> *To hell with Tragedy, you ghouls and hypocrites! You pompous stuffed shirts!*
> *Silence! We want wit and laughter, jokes and fun!*
> *We want kisses and moonlight! We want romance and poetry and sentimentality!*
> *Enough, you vulgar loud-mouths, you empty-headed layabouts and buffoons!*
> The free-for-all is broken up by the actors themselves, not in Mask, but dressed in their street clothes. They persuade the Advocates to calm down, and sit in the audience, and the actors will perform for them the best kind of theatre—with intrigue and action, with romance and magic, wit and laughter, philosophy and beauty—and the Advocates can judge its worthiness. And so we move into the actual play of *The Love for Three Oranges.*

Once I had achieved this overarching structure, and the synopsis was written down, I was ready to spring into action. First, I had to find actors! In the long course of my observations upon human nature and the different sorts of men, I had not as yet enjoyed an opportunity of studying the race of actors. I was curious to do so, and the time had come.

With the view of attacking my two poet adversaries in the theatre, I made choice of the comic troupe of Antonio Sacchi, the actor who was famous for his portrayal of the ancient jester Mask, Truffaldino. Sacchi's troupe was composed for the most part of close relatives, and bore the reputation of being better behaved and more honest than any others. Professionally, they sustained our old national comedy of improvisation with the greatest spirit. This type of drama, as I have said above, Goldoni and Chiari, under the mask of zeal for culture, but really with an eager eye to gain, had set themselves to ruin and abolish.

The four leading men of the troupe were Antonio Sacchi, Agostino Fiorelli, Atanagio Zannoni, and Cesare Derbes, all of them excellent players in their several lines, and they represented the four principal "Masks", or characters:

- Truffaldino, the jester/fool (sometimes known as Arlequino), canny but also foolish;
- Tartaglia, a foppish statesman (with weak eyes, a long sword and a big cape, ineffectual and stuttering);
- Brighella, the top servant or *major d'omo* (cunning, often malicious, always out for himself, tricking others and getting everyone but himself into trouble); and
- Pantalone, the pompous, naïve advisor (or sometimes a wealthy merchant, often the gull of tricksters who take advantage of his greedy nature).

Each of these actors could boast of perfect practice in their art, readiness of wit, grace, fertility of ideas, variety of sallies, bye-play, drollery, naturalness, and even some philosophy. The *soubrette* (or the stock maidservant character) of the company, Andriana Sacchi-Zannoni, possessed the same qualities, and had perfected the role of the saucy maidservant, Smeraldina.

A decade or so earlier, the Sacchi troupe had been extremely well-to-do and popular in Italy. But the two playwrights in question, (my enemies) after having lived in partnership with them, had turned round and taken the bread out of their mouths by dismissing the Masks as old-fashioned and unsophisticated. Sacchi, in these circumstances, withdrew his company to the Court of Portugal, where they prospered, until a far more formidable enemy than a brace of poets assailed them. The terrible earthquake of Lisbon put a stop to all amusements in that capital; and our poor players, having lost their occupation, returned to Venice after an absence of some four years, and encamped in the theatre of San Samuele.

Upon their arrival, they met with a temporary success. Many amateurs of the old drama, who were bored to death with Martellian verses and such plays as the *Filosofi Inglesi, Pamelas, Pastorelle Fedeli, Plautuses, Molières, Terences,* and *Torquato Tassos,* then in vogue, hailed them with enthusiasm. During the first year the four Masks and the *soubrette*, with some other actors of merit in the extempore style, took the wind out of Goldoni's and Chiari's sails. Little by little, however, the novelties poured forth by these two fertile writers, who kept on treating the clever fellows as contemptible mountebanks and insipid buffoons, prevailed, and reduced them to almost total neglect.

It seemed to me that I should be able to indulge my penchant for laughter, and also learn a great deal of the acting type, if I made myself the colonel of this regiment. I also hoped to score a victory for the insulted Granelleschi by drawing crowds to the theatre with my dramatic allegories based on nursery-tales, a kind of theatre exactly suited to this troupe of *improvosati*. The fable of *L'Amore delle Tre Melarancie* would make a good beginning. I set myself to learning assiduously how to work with my actors.

I had formed the habit of conversing with my family of players in our hours of leisure; and very racy did I find the recreation of their society. In a short space of time I learned to understand and see into the characters and talents of my soldiers, with insight so perfect that all the parts I wrote for them and fitted, so to speak, upon their mental frames, were represented on the stage as though they issued naturally from their hearts and tempers. This added hugely to the attraction of the spectacle. The gift of writing for particular actors, which does not seem to be possessed or put in use by every dramatist, is almost indispensable while dealing with the comic troupes of Italy. To the accident of my possessing this gift, and the ability with which I exercised it, must be ascribed a large part of my success. Goldoni alone devoted himself with patience to the study of the players who put his premeditated pieces on the boards; but I defy Goldoni and all the writers for our stage to compose, as I did, parts differing in character, containing jokes, witticisms, drolleries, moral satire, and discourses in soliloquy or dialogue, adapted to the native genius of my five principal actors, without lapsing into languor and frigidity, and with the same result of reiterated applause.

In all, and over the next twenty-five or so years, I was to write and stage some ten *fabulae* based on fairy-tales, and other plays as well. At this point in time, however, the first one, *The Love for Three Oranges*, had yet to be tried before the public. I had penned my outline, and made the acquaintance and procured the trust and commitment of a talented troupe of actors. All that remained now was to produce the play!

☙ Very Late Sunday, 21 December 1879 ❧

The palazzo next door yields an alarming surprise.

AFTER WHAT SEEMED AN INTERMINABLE AMOUNT OF TIME, my intent gaze on the shuttered window of the palazzo next door was rewarded by seeing a slight movement of the panels of wood. My eyes had grown quite accustomed to the darkness, and it was therefore almost a shock to see quite clearly the flare of a match inside the room through slight cracks and unevennesses in the shutters, before they opened. As I had noticed, the shutters looked to be in recent use, and thus as they were unhooked from the inside and slowly opened by Archangelo's hand, they made no noise at all. Intelligent lad! He took great care not to fling open the shutters, keeping them from even touching the outside walls when they were extended. I leaned forward from Gozzi's little room into the space between the two palazzos.

We did not speak, but nodded knowingly at each other, suppressing our mutual excitement, which I could read clearly in his shining eyes. He looked around the room he was in, disappeared from my view for a moment, then returned, having lighted a small candle in a hand-held candlestick. I nodded my approval. As I watched from my slightly elevated perch, I saw the candle's wavering light move slowly around the room, stopping and remaining still for some minutes as my young charge searched the chamber as I had instructed him. I shook my head, however, at the thought that there would really be anything to be found—after all, the Cornaro palazzo had undergone extensive renovations decades after Gozzi's association with it, at least on the lower floors, and it was highly unlikely that any remaining relics of his fair lady would have been overlooked. But my intuition insisted that there was *something* about this neighboring palazzo that required investigation, however cursory.

The candle's reflected light moved along the walls, from corner to corner. It felt as if hours had passed by the time Archangelo appeared once more at the window, but it couldn't have been more than thirty minutes. His disappointed face told me the story without him having to speak, but he held out both hands, empty, to show me the sad results of his search. I nodded glumly, and motioned to him to close the shutters and leave the place. We had arranged to meet at the house door on the *calle*, so I could give him his well-earned penny and bid him good night.

I carefully pulled the shutters closed on Gozzi's writing room, and turned to re-light the oil lamp prior to my descending the stairs once again. I looked in wry chagrin at the torn bits of wallpaper, some shreds still hanging, others on the floor. I would have to come back up and clean this up, and prepare some sort of explanation for my host and hostess for this destruction of their property. But I couldn't help feeling pleased that I had uncovered—literally—a physical link with the lifetime of the personage who was so shining an example of eighteenth century Italian culture, and who played such a large part in my forthcoming book about that interesting age.

I wondered then about the real story of Gozzi and his fair neighbor—and how the tale told in his *Memoirs*, admitted by himself to be at least partly fiction—squared with the *Signora's* contention of his having ruined her ancestress and stolen her jewels. If Gozzi had really, somehow, gotten hold of those jewels—if he hadn't, as he wrote, actually handed them back to her, where were they? He died poverty-stricken and brain-addled, but surely he would have been better off if he'd had a hoard of expensive jewellery to sell?

I gazed around the small storage room one more time, realizing that I was probably keeping Archangelo waiting at the door, when a strong sense of a *presence*—I can think of no better word than that—seemed to fill the space. I held my breath. Oddly, I did not feel afraid, and it occurred to me that somehow Carlo Gozzi was making his ghostly soul known to me at that moment. The flame of the oil lamp flickered once, twice, thrice—and a sudden rustling noise drew my attention to the wallpaper I had torn away. One long strip still hung, curling downward, and as I watched, it silently tore away, falling of its own weight (perhaps) and slid from the wall with a soft flutter, revealing a small, inset panel, next to but lower than the window.

I stepped forward and bent down eagerly to examine it more closely—a somewhat discolored rectangle of wood, some ten inches high by eight or so across, stood out against the slightly darker surrounding wood. I traced the outside edges with my fingers but could see no indentation meant to pry it forth; I pushed against it, hoping for some spring that would make it pop open; to no avail. It was getting late; I had to leave to meet my young co-conspirator at the door and remunerate him for his efforts. But I would come back up, perhaps as soon as daylight would give me a better view of this mysterious panel. I quit the room, closing the door carefully, and half-ran down the stairs to meet Archangelo at the door.

He was there waiting, leaning against the courtyard wall, but he instantly came to attention when I opened the door. He seemed excited, and was clearly bursting with something to say. I put a finger to my lips and walked a little way outside the courtyard door into the *calle*, where we could stand under an overhanging half-trellis sort of thing—this way, I thought, our voices would not carry upwards. I handed him a couple of pennies; he took them and shoved them in his pocket without regarding them. He was trembling with nervous energy.

"What is it, my young friend?" I whispered, placing a stilling hand on his shoulder. We spoke in Italian, and I tried for as much *Venetan* as I could muster.

"As I was coming down the back stairs, inside the palazzo," he whispered back. "A door suddenly opened from one of the hallways into the stairs, and I heard voices, two people talking."

Alarmed, I said quickly, "Were you seen?"

He shook his head. "I was on the landing just above the door, in the shadows," he said. "No one saw me." He hesitated, and I felt a *frisson* of fear.

He continued. "A man stepped into the stairway, and because they left the door open, there was light to see him." He paused. "He spoke to another person, inside the room still, so I do not know who it was."

"But you did recognize the man on the stairs?" I felt another thrill course through me. *What was it I feared to hear?*

He nodded solemnly. "It was the man you bade me find at the Hotel, the one I brought here earlier today."

"Charles Wilkinson?" In my astonishment, I spoke louder than I should have. Both of us immediately looked around, to see if there were anyone nearby. No lights shone from windows in the surrounding houses.

"Did you hear...did they say anything?" I tightened my grip on the boy's shoulder.

"Si, *Signorina*, I heard him, *Signore* Wilkinson, say something, but it was in English, not Italian." The boy looked embarrassed. "My English is not very good, but I can repeat what it sounded like."

"Dear boy," I said, "Do, do try, *per favore*."

He pursed his lips and said, parrot-like, "*Is notyer faut, you mustay steronga. Fannything, I am tblama. I t'ink shela finem forus.*"

I repeated the words a few times until I hit upon its meaning: *It's not your fault, you must stay strong. If anything, I am to blame. I think she'll find him for us*—or find *them* for us.

And I had the dreadful sinking feeling that the "she" he was referring to was me.

After I had sent Archangelo to his home, with a stern reminder of his promise of silence—*not even to Maria!*—I slowly made my way back to the foot of the central marble staircase. I had asked the boy a second time if he was sure he had not been seen, and his previous hesitation became clearer to me when he admitted that he *may* have made a tiny noise, and that Mr. Wilkinson *may* have heard something, as he had lifted his head as if to hear better—but as to being seen, or found out, he swore that had not happened. Well, it couldn't be helped, one way or the other. I couldn't possibly be put more on my guard than I already was, now, with this unfathomable revelation of Mr. Wilkinson being somehow, however unbelievably, involved in the mysteries and events at Ca' Favretto.

My blood ran cold as I thought, *and the murder, too.*

My foot was on the lowest stair as I paused, deliberating with as much objectivity as I could manage—could Charles Wilkinson, with all his charm and literary interest and gentlemanly ways—could he actually be a murderer? And if so, why? And how? That he knew more than he had told me was, at the very least, clear as day—starting from the fact that he knew where I was staying while in Venice, though I had not told him. I took another step up, and paused again. I had told him everything, this very day, every detail of the maddening puzzle that permeated this palazzo, and had hinted at the possibility of the jewellery of Lady Caterina being secreted somewhere in Giacomo's lovely, ancient house.

Is that what I was expected to "find" for them? And who was his partner—a man or a woman? Could the fact that he spoke English instead of Italian to this partner suggest another English person, a colleague or fellow conspirator? Or was it an abundance of caution in a place where Italian could be more easily understood, if overheard?

I was about to take a third step, when all around me arose the strong scent of oranges, and a gust of wind from somewhere caught at my skirts, and blew out the flame of my oil lamp. In dismay, I cried out and stepped back down the stairs just in time to miss being crushed by one of the large marble vases, set squarely upon the flat finial of the staircase at the first landing, which came tumbling out of the darkness straight at me! I had flattened myself against the curved wall of the stairway entrance, and gazed in astonishment as the marble vase shattered on the floor of the hallway, scattering flowers and leaves and water in every direction. But a stray piece of marble had caught my elbow, and I tumbled down the few steps and fell flat to the floor, momentarily stunned.

When I opened my eyes, the first person I saw was the housekeeper, Jocasta, who was bent over me, looking closely in my face. Within moments, the servants' door in the hallway burst open, and two footmen came running out, all in their nightclothes, aghast at the sight that met their eyes.

"*Signorina* Paget has fallen!" Jocasta exclaimed to the footmen, and signalled to them to help me sit up, then addressing me again, "Are you hurt? What has happened?"

"I don't really know," I said, attempting to gather my wits quickly, wincing as I put a tentative hand to my elbow, and pointing to the next landing up. "But I do believe someone may have pushed that vase down the stairs, in order to injure me!" I watched my horror mirrored in their faces. "And that scent—of oranges, can you discern it?" The three servants looked puzzled, sniffed the air, and shook their heads.

The two footmen looked up into the dimness of the staircase, then valiantly ran up the stairs in pursuit of whomever they could find. Jocasta and I stayed below; I realized my knees were trembling beneath me, and she, seeing what a shock I'd had, gently led me over to a chair in the hallway, where I sat and contemplated the narrowness of my escape.

The footmen hallooed from the top of the staircase. "There is no one, there is nothing we can see that has been disturbed!" Along with their voices, I soon heard another—of course, they had awakened John. A rapid exchange of Italian could be heard as the footmen and my friend descended the staircase.

"Vi!" John came immediately to my side, kneeling down, and put his arms around me. His hair was disheveled, and his shirt and trousers were wrinkled, as if he had attempted sleeping without changing into his nightclothes. "You are all right, yes?"

"Yes, yes, I'm fine, John, just a little shaken," I said, beginning to feel calmer. Jocasta had lighted the sconces in the hallway, and motioned to the footmen to start cleaning up the clutter.

"What were you doing down here, at this time of night?" John said, looking concerned. "It's gone half past eleven, I just heard the church bells."

"Then you weren't asleep? Oh, John," I said, trying to divert his query from my wanderings. "Haven't you been able to rest, after your ordeal?"

He shook his head, but smiled a little. "I'll be fine, I will recover fully very soon, don't worry about me." Then he took another, closer look at me.

"What have you been up to, dear Vi?" he asked.

I felt very uncomfortable, and cast about furiously in my mind for some way to answer him. John was no fool, and besides that, he knew me very well—and I am not very good at telling fibs. But to tell him the whole truth now—about having met Charles Wilkinson—*by chance?*—in the Square, having had tea with him, having actually spent most of the day walking about in his company and then calling upon him to intervene in John's arrest and finally, telling him everything relative to the murderous and mysterious events in Ca' Favretto—even just reviewing all this in my own mind made me feel extremely foolhardy and *jejeune*—how could I possibly reveal all that to John—what would he think of me? And particularly, I thought with a great surge of guilt, as I had already withheld it all from him in the first place. I quickly decided my salvation would lie in telling a partial truth.

"I admit," I said, trying to look contrite—and I wasn't far from really feeling it—"that I indulged my curiosity about the palazzo next door…" I broke off as John interrupted me.

"What? You don't mean that you went over there yourself?" He looked incredulous.

"No, no, I didn't do anything so rash," I said, although I realized what I did do was certainly equally as rash. "I got one of the servant's little brothers to, well, kind of look around over there for me."

John leaned back, stood up slowly, and walked around a moment, as if to calm himself.

"And did he find anything to satisfy your infernal curiosity?" he said, looking sternly at me. I squirmed in my seat; I wasn't used to John being so severe, so judging.

I shook my head, not looking at him. "No," I almost whispered. "He found nothing." Which was true! I thought of the small wood panel I had discovered in the room upstairs, but decided this was not the time to mention it. I stood up and moved closer to him.

John looked worried, and he shook his head at me. "I know I asked you here for your help, Vi," he said, and cast a glance at the broken pieces of the vase. "But once again, you are in danger! Perhaps we ought not to pursue this—"

I cut him off, placing my hand with some urgency on his arm. "It's only because clearly I am getting close—we are getting close to the heart of this matter, John." I pleaded with him. "We cannot desert your friend now," I insisted. "Besides, if we catch the murderer, then the police will not suspect you—or Giacomo—and they are quite capable of marching back here in the morning and putting you in jail again!"

He nodded, reluctantly, at that, and looked at me seriously. "You must solemnly promise me," he said, placing his hand on top of my own, "that you will take every precaution to stay out of danger yourself."

I nodded, moved at his concern. "I promise," I said. He smiled at me at last and suddenly, gave a huge yawn. Despite myself, I was infected by it, and raised my hand to my lips to stifle my own yawn.

The housekeeper and the footmen had finished their tasks, and bidding us good night, though with worried looks on the part of Jocasta, they retreated to their rooms below. John and I trudged up the stairs and made our way to our respective chambers, John escorting me to my door, and depositing a light kiss on the top of my head.

"Sleep well, dear Twin," he said, and smiled tiredly. "Don't get into any trouble in your dreams."

I laughed softly. "I'll do my best," I said. "Good night, then."

† October 1761 †

Final Rehearsals and Opening Night

—Memoirs of Count Carlo Gozzi

MY PATIENCE WAS NEARLY AT AN END, but I forebore chastising the hard-working actors who were diligently attempting to follow my, I admit it now, rather detailed directions. After all, they were improvisationalists, and I was continually giving them specific words to say, author and writer that I was—I simply couldn't help myself.

"No, no, no, no, no," I urged softly but pointedly to Cesare Derbes, who was playing the part of Pantalone, the king's pompous yet naïve advisor and *consiglieri*. "Pantalone, for all his self-righteousness and high opinion of himself, truly sympathizes with the King. Remember," I said with utmost gentleness, "The King and the Prince together represent the people, the theatre-goers who are confused and misled by the two chief antagonists here—the jester Truffaldino whose bald and buffoonish comedies fail to make the Prince laugh, and the dour, grave and cold prime minister Leandro, who would be content to let the Prince perish of melancholy and despair."

The actor nodded, grimaced, and tried his role again in the scene we were rehearsing. As keen as their minds often were, in recognizing nuances and subtleties, at times I despaired of their truly grasping the satirical nature of my characterizations of Goldoni and Chiari—but as it turned out, I vastly underestimated this acting troupe.

We all were nervous as opening night drew near. I had, as I would continue to do, freely given my play to the Sacchi troupe—unlike my opponents, who sold their works to the highest bidder as well as bargaining for a percentage of the nightly earnings—so failure did not have the same economic consequences for me as it would have for the actors, all of whom had families to support. But the effect of failure on my reputation, both as a Venetian and a poet, would be catastrophic! I would be laughed out of the city, despite my noble ancestry; and my literary society, the *Granelleschi*, would likewise bear the burden of ignominy and ridicule. Therefore, I said to myself, we shall not fail—in fact, we shall succeed beyond our wildest dreams! I spoke in this manner to the actors, as we rehearsed endlessly, and encouraged them with humour and affection.

Talk of the feud between me and my two enemies had fueled the populace with eager curiosity, so we confidently expected a large audience—but to see a runaway success or an abject failure would be all the same to them! They only wanted to view the battle, and would be happy to cheer for the winner, whomsoever it turned out to be. But I knew that I was held in no little esteem among my townsmen, from the nobles even down to the tradespeople and beggars, such was my family's renown, and my own unfailingly polite, honest and gentlemanly presence in the city, if I do say so myself. It was only in the words I wrote that I could be scathingly satirical, and inflict wounds upon the vain, the gross, the hypocritical and the immoral. So I hoped for the best, and that scattered among the *hoi poloi* of the general Venetian populace, there would be some true friends who wished me well.

Opening night arrived, and all the last-minute vexations and harassments arose in due form to plague each of us, from missing wigs and belts to sore feet and sudden coughing spells; scenery that refused to budge as planned, and paralyzing fits of nerves, particularly among the younger players, whose first appearances would be on the stage this night. I peeked out from the side curtain to see the great hall of *Teatro di San Cassiano* filled to the rafters with the high and the low from throughout the town. The noise the audience made was thunderous, and the numbers so overwhelming that I was not able to discern any particular individual in the throng. I especially wanted to see if I could spy out either of my two rivals, but it was impossible to do so. I had to content myself with assuming they could hardly absent themselves from opening night, so as to be on the spot in case (as I'm sure they heartily said to each other) my play should be a disastrous calamity.

Finally, I heard the gong sounding its thrice three tolls to announce the beginning of the play, and the audience took their seats; the ladies plied their voluminous fans (it was a warm night), their jewels and bracelets sparkling and twinkling in the light from the candelabras; the gentleman drank surreptitiously (or not) from flasks hidden in their pockets, and quiet settled over the theatre. I held my breath as the curtains parted, and the four Advocates of Theatrical Form sauntered out. It had begun.

After that, it all became a blur of bursts of laughter, delighted gasps of wonder, cheering for the Prince and booing for Leandro and Clarice, howls of mirth when Fata Morgana tripped and fell, revealing her undergarments and thus, causing the Prince to laugh at long last. I was gratified, deeply so, to see my actors (as I always called them henceforth, with great affection) profoundly inhabiting the roles I had so carefully crafted for them, and creating new barbs and witticisms by the handfuls—as *improvisateurs*, of course, are skilled at doing, but these surpassed anything I had ever seen—and making it clear as day, though gently, that Goldoni and

Chiari were the objects of their critical remarks, and buffoonery, and tricks and taunts—and the audience applauded every trick, every scathing remark, as if it too had discerned the humbuggery of those two playwrights.

In short, a wild success! I was fortunate to witness, as we all trod the boards at the end of the play to receive the standing ovations from the crowd, and bowed and bowed repeatedly, gathering up the bouquets and ribbons tossed up to us, I was fortunate, I say, to witness both of my rivals rising from their box seats and scarpering for the door in utter humiliation and anger. The following days, in the papers, were to reveal much of their sense of revenge and outrage, their vituperative dismissals of the actors and my play, but it was but a trickle to the raging rivers of praise and delight that the people and the critics alike poured upon my *Three Oranges*.

The delightful, magical, humourous *fabula* I had created from the old fairy-tale ran for twenty consecutive nights—an unheard-of success for that time! I was to repeat this success with nine more *fabuli*, such as *The Raven, Turandot, The Serpent Woman, The Blue Monster* and *The Green Bird* among them—all based on children's fairy tales, and all winningly capable of yielding up the most stinging satire on modern morals, theatre, literature and manners of the day. Chiari, after a few faltering years, retired to the countryside, and Goldoni, my arch rival, fled to Paris, where his insipid realistic plays found some purchase among the fatuous of that city.

Ah, Venice! How you reward your sons and daughters for entertaining you—until you grow tired of them, and wish for something new, and turn your back and let them languish. Such is the fate of all who seek fame and glory.

ﻌ Monday, 22 December 1879 ﻌ

Violet has some explaining to do.

JOHN AND I WERE SEATED IN THE BREAKFAST ROOM the next morning, quietly consuming eggs and cheese, pastries and coffee, when one of the footmen entered, bowed and came over to where I sat. Again, it flitted through my mind to wonder where Samuel, the *major d'omo*, had taken himself. Perhaps he had been allowed to go home for the Christmas holidays? I hadn't expected to see Caterina, her late rising habits being well explained previously, and it was clear that Giacomo—wherever he had spent the night—was not at home.

"*Signorina*," the young man said, "You have a gentleman visitor who is here at the palazzo to see you, here this morning."

I thought that a little redundant, but felt an immediate sense of apprehension—there was only one gentleman in the city who knew I was here. "And did this visitor give his name?" I asked. John was looking at me curiously, and I felt the color rise to my cheeks.

"*Signore* Charles Wilkinson," said the footman, and bowing again, presented a card, which I took from his hand. It was identical to the card that had been given to me by the gentleman himself just yesterday afternoon. What could I do but acquiesce?

"Please show him in," I said, "and ask that another place be set." I braced myself for whatever was to follow, and furiously debated as to the wisdom of confronting Mr. Wilkinson about his (to me) mysterious presence in the religious house next door, late at night, and talking (as I presumed) of me. I glanced at John, who was still watching me, and gave him a small smile. Well, at least with John here, I needn't fear being attacked, stuffed with orange peels and thrown into the Grand Canal! But now I was going to have to reveal all; I hoped that John would take the revelations with equanimity. And after all, I was certain that Mr. Wilkinson had managed John's release, and I felt my heart soften a bit at this.

The door opened, and the man himself was before me, looking as handsome and cheerful as ever he could be. His eyes lighted when he caught sight of John, and, bowing in his direction slightly, as to someone to whom he had not yet been introduced, he walked over to where I stood, I having in the meanwhile risen to greet my visitor.

"Miss Lee," he said, reaching for my hand in such a way that I didn't know how to refuse it. "I am so very glad to see you well and rested." He bent over my hand, which gave me the opportunity to see John looking at the two of us, plainly amused and wondering.

"Mr. Wilkinson," I said, with a formal air, and, taking the proverbial bull by the horns, I turned to John. "Mr. Singer Sargent, may I present to you a friend, and I believe, a benefactor, though unknown to you, Mr. Charles Wilkinson, Consular Consultant."

John rose and bowed his acknowledgement of the introduction, and looked even more confused.

"Mr. Wilkinson," I said, waving my hand at a chair next to John and across from myself, "please join our repast." I eyed him with what I hoped was equable severity. "We have much to discuss."

He looked on the point of demurring, but then took a seat. The footmen and maids were bringing in another plate and service for him, and after the bustle of setting his plate and glasses and napkin, and holding serving dishes for him to choose from, I dismissed the servants all, and began to speak most decidedly. If nothing else, I was determined to direct this conversation.

"My dear John," I said, and as I reached for my cup of coffee, I noticed that my hand was trembling slightly. Whether from excitement, or fear, or indignation, I knew not. I attempted to calm my nerves with a deep breath. "Several extraordinary events occurred yesterday, some of which you know about, and others"—here I glanced at Mr. Wilkinson, who was rather dutifully keeping quiet, though on the alert and watching me closely—"others which you do not. One of them is the appearance of this gentleman you see before you."

I took another deep breath. "The long and short of it is, I met Mr. Wilkinson yesterday while I was attempting to enter the Library of Venice—which happened to be closed—and this leading to that—I won't sport with your patience by detailing all the particulars—he and I struck up an acquaintance, partook of an excellent luncheon at Florian's, found the book I needed—Gozzi's *Memoirs*, Volume I—at Bettinelli's, and then parted for the day. However," and here I paused, nearly breathless, to sip some water. Eating anything more was beyond my ability at this point.

"However, as Mr. Wilkinson had indicated to me, his occupation tends toward the detecting sciences, as well as advising the British Consulate on Venetian matters, and so, when I arrived home only to find the palazzo in an uproar, and you, poor you, being dragged off by the *Carabinieri*, accused of murder, I availed myself of his assurances to me that he would be of assistance should I ever be in need of it." At this, I smiled at Mr. Wilkinson, and I couldn't help adding, "How prescient of you, sir, to anticipate that need on the very day!" He smiled solemnly at me, his hazel eyes careful and opaque.

"Perhaps you will be able to explain," I continued brightly, "better than I, how your efforts brought about my friend's release from the *Carabinieri*?" I was eager to hear his account, and I could see that John, somewhat assuaged by my calm recitation of the facts of the acquaintance, turned to our visitor in expectation.

"It was not the slightest effort," he said, shaking his head, and clearly making light of what he had accomplished. "I spoke with a consular official, who wrote a note, and the *Carabinieri* were advised it would be in their best interests to liberate Mr. Sargent at the first possible moment." He turned to John with an apologetic air. "I am very sorry indeed, Mr. Sargent, both for your incarceration—thankfully it was brief enough—as well as for the fact that I was not able to personally be there to explain the circumstances of your release. I hope you were not unduly concerned."

John smiled, and held out his hand to shake Mr. Wilkinson's, who clasped it firmly. "No apologies necessary, Mr. Wilkinson! To be set free, regardless of the reason or cause, was good enough for me, I can assure you. I am most completely in your debt, and do not know how I shall repay such service." Mr. Wilkinson bowed his head slightly at this expression of gratitude, but said nothing.

John was, however, now looking doubtingly at me, and then he spoke with some hesitation.

"Violet, did you...I mean, how much did you...?"

I knew exactly what he was asking, and I felt both humbled and fearful about how I would reply. John didn't know my suspicions about Charles Wilkinson, and therefore, how vexed I was with myself for pouring out every bit of the saga of murderous events at Ca' Favretto. I avoided his eyes as I started to respond, but was interrupted by Mr. Wilkinson.

"Miss Lee's particulars of the events surrounding your arrest," he said, with a quick look at me, "were very little more than I had gleaned already from the newspapers, as well as, I admit, certain sources I have of a more private nature. And of course, you may rely on my utmost discretion."

He was very reassuring, and I saw that John seemed easier for it.

But I was far from easy myself and, as discretion is not one of *my* strong points, I decided to lunge with my foil and see how nearly I could touch this inscrutable man. Was he a friend or a foe? How he would answer my next question would help determine that.

"You admit to knowing a good deal," I said, my hands pressed together tightly in my lap. "And there are two questions I have for you in regard to the sources of, and especially for, the reasons for this close acquaintance with the events at *Ca' Favretto.*"

Mr. Wilkinson turned his steady gaze to me, a message clear in his eyes: *I do not fear your questions, Madame.* There was even a hint of amusement in the slight lift of a corner of his mouth.

"How did you know that I was staying at *Ca' Favretto*, when you ordered the gondoliere to take me here yesterday?" I saw his eyes darken a little at this, and went on to my next question. "And why were you at the religious house next door last night, very late, meeting secretly with someone and talking about what I would be likely to find for you?" I brought out this last with a flourish and a high sense of the risk I was taking—I was guessing he had meant me, and if not, I would look an utter fool.

John was, by this time, looking completely befuddled. Mr. Wilkinson, however, reacted in a manner I did not anticipate.

He burst out laughing.

I was taken aback at his outburst, and he immediately sobered, and spoke quickly.

"I mean no offense, I assure you," he said, but his eyes were twinkling with mirth. "It's just that, well, there's no getting anything past you, Miss Lee! After our long conversation yesterday—I am constantly recalling the brilliant things you said—I knew I was dealing with a formidable mind, but I had no idea that you have the kind of detective sense that I pride myself on. You seem to have many hidden resources of your own."

He sighed, and drank a bit of coffee, then sat back in his chair.

"I see I'm going to have to come clean, and tell you who I am and why exactly I'm in this situation here with you."

† Summer 1776 †

Living in the Upheaval of Reform, I Write in Secret.

—Secret Memoirs of Count Carlo Gozzi

OVER THE NEXT SEVERAL YEARS, my family fortunes were on the wane, more so than when I had first returned to Venice as a young soldier. I alone seemed to be the only responsible one, my poor brother Gasparo and his nagging wife being at such odds about everything that no decision was ever forthcoming from their incessant squabbles. My sisters and younger brothers only contacted me when they needed money, and were loud in their imprecations when I told them I had little to none. Illness, too, succeeded in reducing me to a wan and trembling state year after year, which only the early years of my success could help cure from time to time, enough for me to work and write, frequent the theatres and enjoy the company of actors and friends who turned to me for play after play to boost their own fame and fortune. And, while I never charged my actors for a play, I was forced, eventually, to negotiate a percentage of the house takings, otherwise I would have been penurious indeed, practically reduced to being a beggar on the street, or forced to retire to the family estate in Friulia, which would have been an unbearable exile for me, citizen of Venice that I was!

Wearying at length of my long imprisonment in my monk-like rooms at San Cassiano, I ventured abroad against my doctor's advice, and found myself much the better for a moderate amount of exercise. This encouraged me to seek my previously frequent intellectual recreation among the company of my fellow members of our literary society, the *Granelleschi* who, among other occupations, had revived (though in deepest secret) the ideals, philosophy, science and cosmopolitanism of the Society of Freemasons, which had been interdicted and banished as an enemy of the Church some decades earlier.

And here, dear Reader, is the point at which I have begun a *Secret Memoir*, not ever to be published, or certainly not in my lifetime or that of my friends, as the risk of discovery followed by incarceration or banishment is too great. What follows herein are thoughts and events shared only with my Masonic brethren, and sometimes not even with them.

The middle and later decades of the 18th century were, indeed, a period of Enlightenment throughout Europe in science, art, medicine, philosophy and agriculture. Reform was in the air, even in poor backward Italy!

But the Republic of Venice, alas, had been on the decline for many, many decades—our centuries-old enemy, the Ottoman Turk, had despoiled our island territories a century and more past, and the rising Dutch and English merchants commandeered the spice and maritime trades. The population of our island city, proud and hard-working, diminished yearly, and the governing bodies grew ever more decadent, greedy and elitist.

It was a time ripe for revolution. In the country, peasants starved and bitterly complained against unfair levies on their crops and animals; great landlords—cash poor, like my family—ran fiefdoms of indentured servants like serfs of the Middle Ages. In the towns, there was no heart for modernisation of urban life, and greed kept the coffers empty which might otherwise have installed new sanitary and water systems, and thereby improve public health conditions.

We men of the Masonic Lodge in Venice, meeting in secret at each other's houses, or in rented rooms above shops closed for the night, spoke incessantly of how to maintain an enlightened point of view, and live a civilized life, in the midst of decadence and decay, and how to face the increasing threat from the Austrians and the French.

It was at one such meeting that I began to see how dangerous the times had become—we were talking of the American Revolution.

"Have you read the famous pamphlet by Mr. Thomas Paine?" One of my colleagues, who shall go unnamed here, held in his hand a translation of the prominent American's writing. "There is so much of heart, and justice, and enlightened thinking here! He titles it, 'Common Sense'! Is it not a good title?"

We all agreed, and bade him read part of it aloud, so he began to declaim: "The cause of America is, in a great measure, the cause of all mankind. Many circumstances have, and will arise, which are not local, but universal, and through which the principles of all lovers of mankind are affected, and in the event of which, their affections are interested. The laying a country desolate with fire and sword, declaring war against the natural rights of all mankind, and extirpating the defenders thereof from the face of the earth, is the concern of every man to whom nature hath given the power of feeling."

Now, be it admitted that, despite the British King, we Venetians looked upon the English quite as brothers—our very Freemasonry had come to us via the English chapters, founded in the early part of the century and even before, and also, we were fellow-islanders of a sort. But this did not stop us from knowing a tyrant when we saw one.

"There has been blood shed on both sides, earlier this year, has there not?" I queried, which our host affirmed. "Does anyone know what the Colonies will do next?"

Another colleague spoke up; he was connected to the British Embassy, and received all manner of confidential information which he imparted to us, his brethren, in strictest secrecy. "They will be presenting to King George a proposal asking for the recognition of American rights, along with the ending of the Intolerable Acts, in exchange for a cease fire."

"Well, one can easily imagine what the King of England will have to say to that!" The members nodded and muttered their opinions about this, and I presently spoke again to the group.

"And how shall we, as enlightened men of our time, strive to bring forward this understanding of virtue, progress and equality among all mankind, to our poor, fading Republic?" I paused for effect. "What are we willing to do, other than discuss ideas in endless sessions of presentation and argument?"

I really do not know what possessed me to be so provocative! My colleagues looked at me askance, some in astonishment, some in disdain.

"What, Count," one of them addressed me, civilly. "Are you advocating that we take to the streets? Shall we go further, and plant bombs in the Doge's Palace or in the churches?"

There were gasps around the room at this, and protests that even saying such things went too far.

"No, no," I relented, wondering at myself. "It's simply that I find myself, in middle age, realizing that there is a time for talking, and a time for action—and I fear the latter will be upon us before we are ready, and Fate will find us gathered here, chatting and arguing, while the City burns."

My comments effectually broke up the meeting for that evening, and we left the upstairs room in twos and threes, at intervals, so as not to bring attention to our gathering. I walked part of the way back to San Cassiano with a good friend, an old friend, who took it upon himself to reproach me somewhat, though gently.

"Carlo," he said, as we walked with linked arms through the quiet summer night, "our little society is founded on

Reason, on Science—on the life of the mind and the spirit—and while we can sympathize with reformers and revolutionaries who want to take action to bring about a more just and enlightened world; to topple tyranny and oppression; to raise the peasant and the poor man to a higher plane of living—we are not the ones who will play a physical part in this change—we will help bring it about with persuasion, and patience, and understanding."

I nodded my agreement, but still, in my heart I felt outrage at the stubborn greed for power that holds the hearts of most men—and most rulers—in its all-consuming thrall, and I desired to see these men humbled to the dust in the fight for universal freedom.

☙ Monday, 22 December 1879 ❧

Mr. Wilkinson has some explaining to do.

MR. WILKINSON POURED HIMSELF MORE COFFEE as he prepared to relate his history. John shot a wondering but sympathetic glance my way, and I lifted my shoulders slightly in response. But then all our attention was for our visitor.

"First," he said, "let me assure you that I truly am who I say I am, and that I am a *bona fide attaché* of the British Consulate." I nodded briefly at this; I actually hadn't doubted he was who he said he was as far as *that* was concerned, so this was not difficult to accept as true.

"Second," he said, "I must ask for your complete discretion and silence about what I am going to tell you, until this matter is resolved."

"Surely, *Signore* Favretto should be told this information," John interposed.

Mr. Wilkinson raised a hand, and shook his head. "Especially not *Signore* Favretto, nor any member of his household or family." He looked at each of us in turn. "I have your word?"

John and I exchanged glances, then we both nodded. How else were we to hear the wretched tale?

"I am sorry to have to extract that promise," he said, looking rueful, "and for that matter, to have both of you involved to such a degree—" He broke off, and ran his hand through his otherwise well-coiffed hair, and puffed out a sigh of mild exasperation. "In addition to my duties at the

Consulate, I am also one of the first of a new kind of, well, cross-border police corps, if you will, one that operates without boundaries—here, in Europe, and in Great Britain." He paused, looking at us for our reaction.

"*Quis custodiet ipsos custodes?*" I murmured, but audibly enough for him to hear. He looked at me appraisingly.

"I wouldn't have taken you for a radical, Miss Lee," he said, and I don't think he was entirely amused. "We operate under strict rules agreed upon by our various governments, and we do, I assure you, hold each other accountable." He smiled rather stiffly. "The custodians of the public safety are well monitored."

I nodded amiably; I didn't mind ruffling his feathers, but I didn't wish to antagonize him either. He continued.

"The course of our investigations primarily seeks out agitators and anarchists, those bad actors who are intent upon disrupting civil society and governments, and displacing the rule of law with anarchy and chaos," he said.

Although intrigued by this explanation, and with a dozen questions bubbling up, I held my tongue, and simply looked at Mr. Wilkinson with attentive expectation. To my surprise, John spoke up.

"And you think somehow that this murder, these strange events here at Ca' Favretto, are linked to some international anarchist conspiracy or plot?" He said this, not in a challenging way, but thoughtfully, taking it seriously.

Mr. Wilkinson nodded his head slightly. "We're not sure, at this point, but we've been—I've been, that is—keeping an eye on one particular inhabitant of this palazzo for some months now, someone known to the policing corps as an agitator, responsible for the bomb that exploded in the public square in Trieste last year."

I could no longer be silent. "Why have you not spoken of this to *Signore* Favretto, and enlisted his help in taking this person into custody—this man, I presume? Aren't most anarchists men?" I scanned over the various household staff members I had met, and lighted upon the most likely one who would be the culprit.

"It's Samuel, isn't it? The *major d'omo*?" I said. I turned to John. "Didn't Giacomo say he was hired rather recently, some months ago?" I looked again at Mr. Wilkinson, who had not answered me. "Well, is it he or not?"

"Yes, he's the one we're watching," said Mr. Wilkinson, reluctantly. He looked at me, apology in his voice. "I have had access to the Cavini monastery next door, to be near when needed, hence—"

"So it was a colleague with whom you met there last night?" I asked. I thought he looked a little strange when I said this, but he agreed to it with a nod of his handsome head. He continued.

"Samuel's true name is Luigi Galleani, formerly a student at the University of Turin, where he became radicalized and turned to criminal anarchy as a solution for humanity's ills." Mr. Wilkinson spoke this last phrase with a weary cynicism, which made me think that his occupation might be taking a toll on the otherwise cheerful spirit I had come to appreciate.

"Why is he here, in Giaco's home?" John said. "Is he simply hiding out?"

Mr. Wilkinson shrugged. "It's possible he has a connection here, or nearby, a relative or friend, who is helping him find shelter. The Turin police had been on the point of arresting him there when he disappeared, about eight months ago." He shrugged again. "Once he was gone from their jurisdiction, they weren't interested in pursuing him."

"But could he be involved with the murder of Anna?" John pressed him. "And the other unfortunate maid, the one who survived? And the mysterious notes?"

Mr. Wilkinson shook his head. "At this point, anything is possible. He's certainly not beyond murder, we know this—but there is no clear motive. Perhaps Anna was part of his network? Or she somehow found out who he was and he was forced to do away with her?"

I was watching our international agent very closely, and although I believe he thought he hid it well, he seemed caught by a deep emotion when he spoke about Anna, more than just a gentleman's sympathy for an untimely death. I tucked that away for further thought.

"You saw him yourself, yesterday, when you came to visit me," I said, thinking back over my various encounters with the *major d'omo*. "Weren't you concerned that he might recognize you, and flee? He hasn't shown his face here, by the way, since yesterday, when he brought you into the little sitting room."

Mr. Wilkinson looked rather anxious at this news. "He's gone? Are you sure?"

I shook my head. "It's simply that I did not see him for the dinner service last night, nor this morning for breakfast." I looked over at John. "Have you seen him about?" He shook his head.

"He wouldn't have recognized me," Mr. Wilkinson said. "He has no idea who I am, and I hope, he has no idea that he's the subject of such attention, internationally." He tapped his finger to his chin. "But this absence is disturbing. We must—"

He broke off as the door opened and Samuel himself walked into the room, followed by servants with empty trays, to gather up the breakfast things. I thought fast, and began to speak as if in the middle of a quite different conversation, addressing Mr. Wilkinson.

"So you actually were able to procure tickets for tomorrow evening's performance at Teatro Goldoni! How absolutely delightful!"

Mr. Wilkinson immediately took up my direction. "I thought that you, Miss Lee, would be particularly interested in seeing that theatre," he said, his most charming smile on his charming face, "so recently renovated and fitted up with gorgeous décor, after the celebrations four years ago of Carlo Goldoni's birth, although I know you are more partial to his main rival, Carlo Gozzi."

I smiled brilliantly, and looked up as Samuel came nearer to the table. But it seemed, in the absence of his master and mistress, he had decided that John was the person to address.

"*Signore,*" he said, "may we clear the table of the breakfast repast?"

John looked at me and Mr. Wilkinson; we shrugged our acquiescence, and the servants began clearing the table. I noticed Mr. Wilkinson paid no overt attention to the *major d'omo*, who was quietly directing the other servants at their tasks.

"If you please," John spoke up a moment later, "Samuel, it would be good to have some fresh coffee."

"Certainly, *Signore*, at once," the young man replied. I eyed him, surreptitiously, thinking of him now in an entirely new light, and especially as the most likely person to have engineered the attempt on my life with the marble vase. What is an anarchist supposed to look like, anyway? It's true I already was prejudiced against him, given his curt manners and dismissiveness toward me personally; but I felt as if I could discern in him the smoldering contempt and disdain which anarchists would naturally feel for the "ruling classes" or perhaps, rich people in general. How ironic that he might think of me in that class of people—for I was neither rich nor powerful, and in fact, probably had more ideas in common with him, in regard to sympathizing with the lot of the workingman (and woman), than I did, perhaps, with Charles Wilkinson!

THE LOVE FOR THREE ORANGES

The servants made short work of it, and the three of us were left by ourselves in the room once again.

"John," I said, breaking the growing silence, "do you happen to know how Samuel came to be employed at Ca' Favretto?"

He thought about it for a moment. "I believe Giaco said something about the man having been taken on as extra help for the occasion of Giaco and Caterina's wedding, and how everyone was so impressed by his abilities and organization, they kept him on." He paused. "I think he said his mother-in-law recommended him first." He looked at Mr. Wilkinson. "Could that be of any help to you?"

Our international police agent nodded, thoughtfully.

"So what are we going to do now?" I asked. "Why don't you simply arrest him?" I waved my hand toward the closed door. "There he is! What are we waiting for?"

Mr. Wilkinson looked grave. "In the first place, 'we' are not going to do anything, Miss Lee. This is a matter that goes far beyond a lay person's competence—and besides, it's entirely too dangerous. Galleani has killed people!" He shook his head. "We are hoping he will lead us to the local Venetian anarchist group, and then we can nab the whole lot of them at once."

John gave me a very worried look, and opened his mouth to speak. I just knew he was going to relate the marble vase incident, and I couldn't let that happen; Mr. Wilkinson would definitely forbid me to be part of any plan for Samuel's capture if he knew I had already been at risk.

"But surely," I interposed quickly, sending a fierce glance at John to silence him, "as *we* are right here, in this house, you can use that to your advantage! If, as you say, this Galleani has killed before, he may very well have killed Anna, and will kill again, if it suits his purposes. We must do something." I admit I was pressing rather hard—but I didn't want to be left out of the action.

"Mr. Wilkinson is quite right, Violet," John said, and I knew, by his using my full name, he was attempting his big brother act, as he occasionally had done when we were children. But I, long practiced in sibling warfare, could always hold my own against him.

"Nonsense," I said, and turned to Mr. Wilkinson. "You are not able to, what's the appropriate word, 'infiltrate' this household, you are a stranger, and there is no plausibility for it. I, on the other hand," I pursued with eagerness, "I can chat up the maids, and John can do the same with the footmen, just to see if we can suss out any anarchist sympathies or, or, anything, in short, that might bring this to a conclusion." I could see Mr. Wilkinson wavering, so I waited a moment, then played my trump card.

"That is, after all, why you 'accidentally' came to my aid yesterday in St. Mark's Square, isn't it, Mr. Wilkinson? And why you were so eager to discuss my literary accomplishments over coffee and pastries at Florian's? Come, come," I said, almost laughing at the chagrined look on his face. "I admit your flattery was well done, as I was completely taken in by your conversation and understanding of my essays—as if you had really read them!"

He smiled at me then, more like the Charles Wilkinson of yesterday than the grim hunter of anarchists today. "I did read them," he said. "And enjoyed them very much." He paused a moment, a delicate, laughing light in his warm eyes. "But please, if we are to join as comrades-in-arms, you must call me Charles." He paused again, his eyes searching. "And may I call you Violet?"

I couldn't help but blush! "You may," I said softly. I saw John looking on with some amusement, tempered by his concern for my rashness. I shook myself mentally.

"Now let's get on with the plan," I said.

† Autumn 1776 †

I harbor two fugitives at San Cassiano.

—Secret Memoirs of Count Carlo Gozzi

AS THE WARM AUTUMN DAYS FLOODED THE CITY with golden sunlight, followed by cooling nights, I could not help but feel a growing tension in Venice, and indeed, throughout Italy and the wider world. The continuing war in the American colonies, of which we received news haltingly and with great gaps of time, found echoes in the unrest in France, and Germany, and the ongoing reforms in Italy itself. Governing bodies argued endlessly over agricultural bills, and how to encourage reform, how to reduce taxes and bring about a government more transparent to the populace.

Some of the people were growing restless, and reckless as well. There were murmurs of riots and insurrections, first in the country villages, and then in the towns and cities. There was an influx of émigrés from Tuscany and even Sicily into our island city, people whose tempers flared in the cafés and bars at night, and who skulked in the alleys, forlorn and, it seemed, homeless. I felt for the wretches, mostly young men, but I had no spare money to give them, and tried, in the name of charity, to stop and discourse with them, and give them such advice as I thought helpful to their plight.

One evening, not very late, as the sun had just set, I was nearing my home, walking from the street side, and was about to open the gate to the courtyard when suddenly there burst into the narrow *calle* two people, running and breathing hard—a young man and woman, dressed poorly, with nothing but a couple of sacks for possessions, and what looked like a case for a musical instrument. In the distance I could hear the shriek of a Civic Guardian's whistle, and shouting.

The two young people, exhausted and frightened, pulled up short, stopping before they barreled into me, and realizing at the same time that this alley led only to the Canal. Wild-eyed, the young man, who though dishevelled and dirty, was quite handsome, with brilliant black eyes (which I could see shining by the light of the lantern I held), spoke to me quickly in a voice which told of good manners and a reasonably good education.

"My dear sir, I beg you by all that you hold most dear, please shelter me and my Angela, or we shall perish most unjustly!"

The girl, Angela, could only look at me mutely, her terror and exhaustion bright in her eyes. I heard the sounds of what seemed a sizeable crowd, growing nearer. I made up my mind.

"Quickly, inside, hide yourselves behind the palms in the corner, and make no noise until I speak to you."

I opened the gate and let them in, then closed the gate and locked it, quickly walking back some steps down the *calle*, then turned back, as if I were just approaching my home. I took my time, regulating my breathing so I did not appear agitated, and just as the Civic Guardian and some citizens rounded the corner, I was lifting my key to the lock in the gate.

"*Signor! Signor!*" called the officer, coming to a halt a few feet away. I looked up in amazement. "Have you seen anyone—two people, a man and a woman—pass this way?" He was out of breath, and he bent over, his hands on his knees, to catch it again.

"No, Guardian," I said, trying to sound concerned and dismayed. "There has been no one who has come past me here." Which was literally true, as the couple did not go past me, but turned into the courtyard in front of me. "What have they done? Why are you pursuing them?"

Several people who accompanied him complained loudly about having lost their quarry, and began to move back down the *calle* to follow another turn. The Civic Guardian merely waved his hand at me and followed the pursuers into the darkness.

I took a deep breath, waited until all sounds of the hunters receded into the night, and unlocked the door, curious and eager to find out more about this Angela and her handsome young man.

I found them trembling behind the palm trees in the far corner of the courtyard.

"It is all right now," I said, soothing them. "Your pursuers have been re-directed. You are safe." I watched as the young man, his arm wrapped protectively around the girl, slowly rose, supporting her firmly. They both seemed close to dropping from fear, and I guessed, hunger.

The young man, verifying my idea of his upbringing and education, gave a quick half-bow to me, and spoke.

"*Signore*, we owe you the greatest debt of gratitude for saving us from the mob," he said. "I am Artusio da Monte, at your service, and this is my wife, Angela da Padova da Monte." The young woman curtsied to me, and brushed away her tears with the back of her hand.

I returned the courtesy with a nod of my head, and introduced myself, leaving off the "count" title, so as not to intimidate them.

"You are welcome to my home," I said, deciding to take a further risk and invite them in. Their manners and courtesies convinced me they were not common thieves or cutthroats. "Please, allow me to offer my hospitality to you."

"Sir," said Angela, her voice soft and gentle, "you are most generous, but you do not even know…"

I interrupted her firmly. "There will be time to discuss the whole situation over a hot dinner and some wine."

I ushered them into the house, calling out to the housekeeper as I opened the heavy house door. It was not so late but that I would expect my two servants to be up and able to wait upon me and my sudden guests. The housekeeper came briskly forward, staring a little at the two young people.

"Giulia," I said, "here are some young friends of mine whom I've invited to stay for a few days. Could you please make up one of the guest rooms for them? And see to it that Marco lays a good fire there?"

"*Si, il Conte*, as you wish," she said. I winced a little at her use of my title, and saw at a glance that the young couple had taken it in.

Giulia threw me a questioning glance. "Will you be wishing some late refreshment, sir?"

I nodded, and gave her instructions to lay out a good dinner in the dining room with all possible speed, but to have wine and water, cheese and bread brought to us first, and quickly. She held out her hands to take the couple's belongings and cloaks, and after a moment's hesitation, they gave them over to her, including the instrument case. The poor girl was beginning to shiver in her thin dress and Giulia, good woman that she is, despite her stern exterior, stepped aside to a nearby closet, took a thick woven shawl from it and herself wrapped up the poor young thing to help her warm herself.

I led the way to the dining room, where, logs already having been laid in the fireplace, I knelt down and kindled the wood scraps with a taper until the wood caught fire. My manservant Marco appeared in good time with additional lamps and candles, and even more welcome, a plate of bread and cheese and a bottle of wine.

"Please, come sit here by the fire," I enjoined my young guests, and poured a glass of wine for each of them, and one for myself. The platter of food was placed on a low table between our chairs, and although I could tell they were nearly starving, they both maintained their good manners, and ate with restraint. After several moments of silence as we watched the fire, I could see the food and drink was beginning to revive them, and I judged it was a suitable time to begin a conversation.

Artusio anticipated me—he was a keen, intelligent young man!—and he spoke in a low, musical voice, at first tentative then more firmly as he was assured of my interest and attention.

"I am from a good family, sir," he began, "from the hills of Tuscany, and my wife," he nodded at her, "is from Modena, also from a long established family of good repute." He paused to give his wife a loving look, which she returned with a shy smile.

"The countryside holds nothing anymore for young people such as we," he said, a note of bitterness creeping into his voice. "The farms are mere slave-holdings, the villages neglected and run-down. Trade has been so disrupted by the corruption of greedy merchants that there is little of good to buy or sell." He sighed deeply, and reached for his wife's hand. "So Angela and I decided to come to Venice to try our luck here—I as a scribe, a writer and a scholar, and she as a musician." He cast her another loving look. "She is an excellent violinist, and could play anything you set before her!"

"Ah," I said, smiling at her, "I noticed a case for a musical instrument. Perhaps you might oblige me by playing for me some time, while you are here." She nodded eagerly, but said nothing. Artusio continued his story.

"Back home, our parents are on the edge of poverty, and have other, younger mouths to feed; we both felt it would be best to take ourselves out of dependence on them and try to find work in Venice, thereby enabling us to live here and also, perhaps, to send some money to them."

My heart was touched by this account of their journey. "But have you no relatives or friends here, in Venice, to receive you and help you to find positions?"

Artusio sighed again. "We thought we did, and had sent letters ahead to announce our arrival, but when we went to the address of a great-uncle of mine, we found the house shut up, the family all gone away, and no one in the neighborhood knew anything about it—or at least," he added grimly, "nothing they wanted to tell us." He put his hands over his face and was silent for several moments, then pushed on.

"That was a week ago," he said. "Luckily, the weather has been warm, so even though we had to sleep under awnings or in dark corners, at least we didn't freeze to death." That note of bitterness crept into his voice again. "What you witnessed this evening, sir, was a mob intent on capturing us for having taken some bread and some fruit from the market—we were near starving!" He looked at me pleadingly. "What little money we'd had was gone! I had applied to every church, every shop, every city department I could find, but no one is hiring any workers—for any kind of work!"

He fell silent again, and Angela reached over to stroke his arm, and murmur something to him I could not hear.

"Well," I said, as the door opened and Giulia and Marco came in with dinner, "this is hardship that no one should have to go through, and I will do my best to redeem my fair city's reputation for hospitality to strangers." I stood, and invited them with a gesture to be seated at the table.

"Come, be of good cheer, and we will see what we will see." They thanked me with tears of gratitude, and we sat down to eat with great gusto and hope—that best of all dishes that mankind craves.

Monday, 22 December 1879

Some Important Discoveries are Made.

IT DIDN'T TAKE LONG FOR THE THREE OF US to determine what needed to be done, and quickly. Mr. Wilkinson would leave the palazzo to marshall other forces if needed, and to learn what information his colleagues may have discovered about the Venetian cell of anarchists. He would return in the evening to consult with me and John about any hints or knowledge we may have gleaned from the servants in the interim. Accordingly, Mr. Wilkinson—Charles, now, in my mind and on my lips—departed with all good wishes, and urgent injunctions for us to remain safe at all costs, even to losing our prey altogether.

"I could never forgive myself, Violet," he said to me, most solemnly, and holding on to my hand, "if any harm came to you."

"Oh," I said, trying to turn away the intensity of his gaze and emotion, "I have no intention of leaving this mortal scene, at least until my book is published and universally acclaimed!"

With another serious look, he bowed over my hand, turned to John and nodded his head, then left the room. I sank to my chair again, as I had risen to bid him farewell, and looked over at John on the other side of the table.

"What?" I said, discerning in his laughing eye a most objectionable amusement at my expense.

"Nothing, nothing!" he said, hastily. I believe he knew all too well when, and when not, to pursue a subject with a lady or a friend, one of his many gifts. He slapped his hands on his thighs and stood up. "Well," he said, "we had better be about our detective work, eh? I'll see what I can twinkle out of the housekeeper and the footmen."

I nodded slowly. "I'll start with Maria, as it really seems to me that she knows more than she's been saying. Hopefully I can find her above stairs and by herself so we can have a quiet chat."

I started to rise again from my chair when we were interrupted by the door opening yet again, and were greeted most joyfully by the master of the house, with his mother-in-law in full sail behind him. We exchanged greetings all around, and seated ourselves again at the table. Servants brought in more coffee and more platters of food—at which I sighed and inwardly fretted over the delay in setting our plan in motion. But perhaps there would be an opportunity to glean a few facts from *Signora* and Giaco, without giving the game away. Moments later, *Signora* Caterina appeared in the doorway, alerted no doubt by a servant that her husband and mother had arrived. She bent to kiss Giacomo on the cheek, and murmured something in his ear that made him kiss her back, and look at her with great love. All was forgiven, perhaps.

"John, it does me good to see you looking rested, and free above all," said Giacomo, turning to his friend and clasping his shoulder affectionately; they were sitting next to each other. *Signora* mother-in-law, as before, sat at the head of the table; John was on her left, with Giaco next to him. I was on her right, and to my right *Signora* Caterina was seated; she looked a little pale but composed.

"Have you discovered anything about how or why the *Carabinieri* let you go?" Giaco was questioning John. I felt a moment's alarm, not that I thought John would give Mr.

Wilkinson away, but wondering how he would answer. But I shouldn't have worried.

"Ah, well you see," he said, "I am so fortunate as to have some attentive friends in the expatriate community here in Venice"—(which was true)—"friends who have a good deal of influence with the Embassy"—(good cover, John, not saying *which* embassy)—"so, what with one contact and another, you know how gossip flies in Venice, a word said in the right ear, and *voilà, je suis ici!*"

"But they kept your passport, is it not so?" Giaco continued to look concerned. "Which means you are not entirely out of danger."

John shrugged. "I'm sure it will all end well," he said, and smiled, a bit shakily.

Samuel had stationed himself at the sideboard, ostensibly—like a good servant—not hearing anything of the conversation of his betters (I couldn't help thinking in those terms, which amused and terrified me, knowing who he really was) and a look of complete indifference on his face. I wished heartily that he would leave, as I dared not ask any pertinent questions with him in the room.

I had carefully watched for any sign of intimacy or special connection between him and the *Signora*, as I had fancied I noted once before, and was rewarded to see her look up at him, as he poured out coffee into her cup, with a look positively smitten! Of course, she was enamored of this handsome, attentive young man! And perhaps, in the way of older Italian women and young, poor men, a flirtation had led to something more? Was he playing the *gigolo*, and hoping to finance his anarchic mission with gold from the *Signora's* coffers?

I was jolted from my thoughts by an unexpected address from Caterina, who had asked me a question in her gentle voice.

"*Mi dispiace, Signora,*" I said, turning to her. "You find me wool-gathering! What was it you asked me?"

"I am hoping that you are finding your chamber comfortable, Miss Paget," she said carefully, in English, as if practicing her pronunciation and diction. "I am mortified that I have been unable to fulfill my duties as hostess to you and Mr. John. And please, do call me Caterina." She looked so sweetly sorry as she said this that I couldn't resist taking her hand and pressing it, to reassure her.

"*Per favore,* Caterina," I said. "I am most comfortable indeed, and please do not trouble yourself with such thoughts! We—John and I—are here only to help you and your husband solve these terrible difficulties, and I believe all will soon be well." I spoke very low, cognizant of Samuel's presence in the room.

As luck would have it, a footman came to the door and beckoned to Samuel, who bowed to the company and left the room after a nod from the *Signora;* Giaco was deep in conversation with John and hadn't noticed. Here was my opportunity.

"Samuel seems an excellent *major d'omo, Signora,*" I said to the formidable woman at the head of the table. She was dressed as flamboyantly as I had seen her on previous occasions, albeit with no feather adorning her majestic head. Her dress of rustling silk was a deep royal blue, with red piping in various places for accent, and her jewels, though not abundant, sparkled ostentatiously at her throat, ears and on her fingers. Such a contrast to her daughter, I thought, whose modest ivory lace and muslin gown was adorned only by a long pearl necklace, and her lovely young face was accented by her upswept blonde hair, which revealed pearl and gold earrings. And further, I mused to myself, even more of a contrast to poor me, with my dark grey dress and white collar, and no adornment beyond my trusty little watch pinned above my heart.

THE LOVE FOR THREE ORANGES

The *Signora* was responding to my remark, with scarcely guarded enthusiasm. "Oh, yes," she said, "he is most capable! A very able young man, with many qualities," and I noted she emphasized, slightly, the words *able* and *many*. I noticed Caterina stiffen slightly but I did not dare glance at her face; but her disapproval of her mother was certain.

"I understand his many qualities were on display on the occasion of your daughter's wedding, earlier this year?" I tried my best to look and sound innocent of innuendo, and judging from the *Signora's* volubility, I succeeded.

"The reception would have been a disaster without him!" *Signora* said decisively. "He took matters in hand very competently just at the moment I began to notice things were failing." She leaned toward me confidentially. "I am so very glad that I recommended him to Giaco to take on as extra help—and that he proved himself so very capable." She sniffed. "That housekeeper of his, that Jocasta, she could no more manage a reception than I could steer a gondola." But she paused, and added, "However, she is an excellent home manager, I'll say that for her."

I tried for the most casual, indifferent tone I could muster, concealing my interest. "How on earth did such a gem as Samuel fall to your notice? What a lucky day that was for your daughter, as it sounds as if he saved her wedding reception from total chaos."

At this, Caterina coughed, and brought her napkin to her lips to muffle the sound. I did glance at her for an instant, and saw she was either quelling laughter or anger.

"Well," the *Signora* said, a trifle grudgingly, "As it happens, he is Jocasta's nephew, or so she says—I can see no possible relation there, either in looks or in intellect—but she had been tasked with finding additional staff for the event, and brought him to me for approval, along with some others." She shrugged, but there was a sensuous gleam in her eye. "I saw his possibilities immediately, and was justified in choosing him, as the event showed."

A sudden narrowing of her eyes warned me of her jealous nature, as if she were wondering if I—poor I!—had some kind of personal interest in the man! But I could see, clear as day, that her subsequent perusal of my person assured her that I could have no success in that quarter, were I to be so ridiculous as to try. I almost burst out laughing, she was so transparent.

But, Jocasta, his aunt! I must give this intelligence to John before he spoke with her; we had decided that, because he was an acknowledged favourite of the housekeeper's, he would have the best chance of wheedling some information out of her, while I was to try my luck with Maria. Then he would go on with the footmen and I would try the other maids, if need be. I began to feel impatient with sitting around the table, and eager, nay anxious, to get to the task at hand. We must not let Samuel—or anyone who aided him—elude capture!

At last the eating and drinking were over, and John and I escaped to our rooms, ascending the stairs together. I whispered to him what I had learned about Jocasta and Samuel, and he said he would try to talk with her as soon as possible. As we stood on the landing where our chambers were, I thought of the wooden panel I had discovered in Gozzi's writing room above us, but knew I could not return to it now. The maid Maria had just passed us, carrying linens and cleaning cloths, preparing to freshen up my chamber. I couldn't miss this opportunity, so I pressed John's hand in farewell, saying nothing more. It was nearing three o'clock at this point, and the daylight was fading.

Maria immediately began apologizing for being in my room when I entered, and she started to leave, saying she would come back later, as she didn't wish to be in my way.

"Please, my dear," I said, "I would much rather you stay and perform your duties now, it will be much more convenient for me, truly." I smiled at her to put her at ease. "I shall just sit over here with my book, by the fire."

She nodded, a little uncertainly, and began to make up the bed. I thought about how I would begin the conversation, when to my surprise I noticed that the girl was weeping, silent tears that coursed down her pretty cheeks, which she tried to unobtrusively wipe away with one hand.

"Maria, dear girl, whatever is the matter?" I set my book aside and waited for an answer.

"Oh, *Signorina*," was all she could say, then burst into tears. I rose and took her in my arms, making soothing noises. I led her over to the little sofa by the window, and made her sit down. After a few minutes, she composed herself and began to apologize, but I stopped her.

"Maria," I said, deciding perhaps the direct approach would be best with someone so clearly upset and anxious, "I feel that you are holding something inside that is bothering you very much, something, perhaps, to do with…with what happened to Anna?"

At this her tears began to flow afresh, but she managed to maintain her composure.

"Si, *Signorina*, it has to do with poor Anna," she said. I waited for her to continue.

"The night she died," the girl said, twisting her handkerchief in her hands, and not looking at me. "I heard her and, and someone else, in her room." She glanced at me, then away. For a moment my heart stopped, and I thought, *John*. But immediately dismissed the thought! I focused my brain on listening to Maria, and prompted her to continue.

"Do you know who the other person was?" I said.

She looked terrified, but nodded her head. "I don't like to say…I am afraid! Oh, *Signorina*, I am so afraid!"

"Maria, you are safe with me, and believe me, there are people all around you now who will protect you. Do you trust me?" I lifted her chin with my hand, gently, and made her look in my eyes. She nodded, and seemed to breathe a little easier. "You must tell me what you know, especially as this may save someone else from being hurt, or killed." I knew it was harsh, but as her eyes widened, I could see she was going to be brave.

"It was Samuel," she said in a whisper, and then it all came tumbling out. "I think he and Anna were…lovers, but they had some terrible argument, and I think he hit her, but then the door opened—they didn't see me, I was in my own room, but the door was open a crack, and I had no light—and she shoved him out of the room and slammed the door." She took a deep breath. "He pounded his fist on the door a few times, but she had locked it. He was yelling something about *you cannot betray me, you don't know what you are doing, you will be the death of me!*" She shook her head. "I don't know what he was talking about. But Anna had been acting strange for some time, ever since Samuel came to this palazzo; I just put it down to her being in love."

She fetched a deep sigh, and continued. "He finally went down the stairs, and I could hear Anna crying in her room. I didn't want her to know I had heard their argument, so I quietly closed my door and said nothing to her." She paused, and began to weep again. "And then, the next morning, they found her, in the *rio*." She looked up at me, her face haggard. "Do you think Samuel killed her? Will he kill me, too?" She started to panic, and I could see that, now that she had told her story, she wasn't going to be able to keep anyone else in the household from knowing her state of mind.

I hugged the girl and told her how brave she had been, and that she shouldn't worry, she would be safe from now on. I thought rapidly.

"Maria, do you have family in Venice?" I said.

"*Si, Signorina,* my whole family lives in San Polo, not far," she said, wiping at her tears.

"Do you think you can tell Jocasta that you are ill?" I thought she looked ill enough to pass! "And that you want to go home to your mother so she can nurse you?" I thought again. "Besides, it's almost Christmas, wouldn't you be going home for the holiday with them?"

"*Si, Signorina,* but only for the two days," said the girl. She looked thoughtful. "But I think Jocasta will let me go if I tell her I am ill; she has done so before."

"Then do it right away," I said briskly. "Gather your things and get out of this palazzo as quickly as you can. Speak to no one, and as little as possible to Jocasta."

"But *Signorina,*" she protested, "I have to finish making up your room!" She looked in dismay at the half-made bed.

I laughed, a trifle grimly. "That is of no account," I assured her. "I have made up my bed before, and besides, it may be a long while before I get to lie in it tonight."

† Winter 1776 †

Revolutionary ideals exact a high price,
and hearts are broken.

—Secret Memoirs of Count Carlo Gozzi

AUTUMN TURNED TO WINTER AND MY YOUNG GUESTS had become so much a part of my household and my life that it felt as if I had known them from childhood. Angela was sweet and attentive, and played the violin like the angel her name depicted. And what can I say about Artusio? The two of them were the son and daughter I never had, and so much better in that there were not the usual father/son or father/daughter annoyances and resentments to get in the way. But Artusio was even more—his mind and heart were alike deep and thoughtful, his wit keen and amusing, his spirit strong—if only he had been able to throw off the corroding bitterness that the modern, corrupted world had engendered in him.

Unbeknown to me, Artusio had begun to attend meetings of a radical group in Venice, bent upon revolution and the reform, if not overthrow, of the current government. These young men—they were all very young men, in age as well as temperament—were the estranged sons of *petit bourgeois*, of ruined country farmers, of younger branches of destitute noble families. I had heard of their existence, through the discussions in my Freemasons lodge; we applauded their felt need to change the current regime but deplored their apparent tactics: ranging from unruly disruption at public events to small-scale arson and vandalism. Their demands were all for the "Rights of Man," styled on the Americans—freedom, justice, equality, and better working conditions and better lives for all people.

It was hard to argue with their goals. Artusio and I discussed, again and again, late into the night, the wretched conditions of the poor and the working class; the recalcitrance of the government; the greed of the merchant class—and what could be done. I counseled education and patience—reform was a matter of persuasion, not coercion. He countered that stubborn men who do not listen need to be forced to accept change.

In the waning days of that year, once again, near the days of the Solstice, when anarchy is invited to parade in the streets and overturn virtue and tradition, this radical cohort of young men planned a most dire deed, and almost succeeded.

They had constructed a bomb, a poor thing (as it turned out) of gunpowder and nails, fuses and metal and thin wood, with which they intended to blow up the Doge's Palace, that crumbling symbol of ancient glory and modern failure. My poor Artusio was part of this plot, and it was he, among two or three others, who were chosen—or perhaps, who volunteered—to be the ones to plant and then set off this shameful product of their unhappy spirits.

Angela and I were sitting companionably at home, it was late in the evening of the Solstice, and she had just put down her violin after playing a lovely piece by Vivaldi, the "Winter" of his *Quattro Staggione*, my favourite, when we heard the house door open quickly, and someone running down the hall. It was Artusio. He burst into the small sitting room, and we saw immediately that he was in great distress—his clothes were torn and looked even burnt, with patches of black here and there; his face was scuffed and dirty, and his eyes were wild.

"Artusio! What have you done?" Angela stood and ran to him; her question made me think, on the instant, that she had suspected him of being about some nefarious task this evening—her playing had been uneven and at times, agitated.

"What has happened?" I said, also rising and confronting my young man. Before he could answer, a loud commotion was heard in the courtyard, and someone began pounding on the door. I strode into the hallway, where Marco was looking at me fearfully, as if he didn't know whether to open the door or not. I signed to him to stay back, and went to the door myself.

I can be a grand and intimidating figure when events call for it, and I assumed my most noble air as I opened the door to the fractious crowd outside, headed by two large officers of the Civic Guard.

"*Signore* Conte," one of the officers, who was known to me, spoke first, nodding his head deferentially. "We beg your pardon, but we are pursuing an anarchist who just set off a bomb at the Doge's Palace, and we followed him here, to your door." He looked most apologetic, but spoke firmly.

I was nearly struck dumb by this charge against my protégé, as I thought of him. From Artusio's condition, it seemed clear to me that he had indeed been involved in such a terroristic act. My sense of justice and my love for him and his wife were set at odds, and robbed me of speech for a few moments. It was enough to give the mob time to look in through the doorway.

"There he is! Get him!" A man just behind the officers pointed into the palazzo, and I turned to see Artusio standing in the middle of the hall, defiant and clearly willing to be a martyr for his cause.

All hell broke loose, and chaos reigned for the next several minutes. The Guardians rushed into the hall and then the most terrible and heart-rending event of my whole life occurred—I witnessed it as if it took place in a slowed-down sense of time.

Angela ran out from the sitting room and grabbed hold of her husband's arm, pulling him down the hall, toward the Grand Canal water-door. They were some fifty feet ahead of the Guardians and the mob who shoved past me, pursuing them. I saw the two open the doors at the end of the hall, and slam them shut. The crowd pressed against the doors, which opened inward, and perhaps had been locked by Angela after they exited, so it took several minutes to get the doors open again. As master of the house, I pushed and shoved my way through the crowd, yelling to the Guardians to give way and let me through. I gained the balcony and landing outside the doors—the night was inky black, as if no stars shone, and there was only a half moon to light the dark waters of the Canal.

I could see the beloved son and daughter of my heart, struggling in the choppy waters, about midway out into the Canal. As I watched, and called to them to be brave and hold out, there would be boats coming to retrieve them, their heads sank beneath the surface, their arms wrapped about one another, and though they appeared briefly once again, they were submerged long before any gondola reached them. The watery depths of the Grand Canal took them to its bosom, and their sad, young lives were ended.

Their bodies were never found.

❧ Late Monday, December 22, 1879 ☙

John and I edge ever closer to discoveries.

THE WINTRY DARKNESS OF THE SOLSTICE HAD CLOSED IN upon the watery city of Venice sometime in mid-afternoon, and by five o'clock it was cold and dim and dreary inside and out. After assuring myself that Maria had indeed made her escape to her family, and engaging one or two other of the maids in seemingly idle conversation, with no further enlightenment other than moony-eyed praise of the handsome Samuel, I went in search of John. There was no answer to my knock on his door, and when I inquired of a passing footman, he said he believed *Signore* Sargent had gone out.

Gone out! At this juncture in our investigation? I could only assume that something pertinent to our inquiries had taken him from the house, but I was worried for his welfare. He had not taken a gondola, the footman had told me, but rather had gone on foot by the street door. I stationed myself at the street entrance to the house, just inside the massive door, by a tall window behind a potted fern, from where I could look out into the cheerless courtyard, barely visible in the reflected lamplights. I was alone in my vigil, it being so late in the afternoon; I assumed that Giaco, his wife and his mother-in-law were no doubt cozied up in their chambers, resting until the typically late Italian dinner would be served. I shivered as a cold rain rattled the glass I tried desperately to look through, hoping that John would soon show.

A figure appeared in the courtyard as the great gate opened inward. I leaned forward eagerly, then discerned it was Jocasta, returned from some errand in the town. I shrank back from the window, to keep out of her view, fearful she would see me when she came through the door. But she walked past the main door, and I heard another door open and close, farther down the courtyard, a servants' and tradesmens' entrance, perhaps. I breathed again, gratefully.

Not five minutes later, John came into the courtyard, shaking the rain from his shoulders and head, and made for the front door. I eagerly stepped forward to open the door for him, preventing his ringing the bell and rousing up a footman.

"Vi!" he said, surprised, of course, to see me opening the door, as if in wait for him. I put a finger to my lips, and drew him inside.

"You have been following Jocasta," I said, and was gratified to see the increased surprise on his face, then a grim smile and nod of acknowledgement.

"We must talk," he said.

"And you must get out of these wet things," I said. "Let us go upstairs, to my chamber, where there is a good fire lighted, and you can dry out and we can tell each other what we have learned."

We headed for the marble stairway, quietly.

Soon enough we were safely situated in my chamber with a warm fire keeping the cold chill at bay. I swiftly relayed to John all that I had learned from the maid Maria, and how I had advised her to go to her family's house at once. He approved of this measure most heartily, and I was soon to feel very glad that I had done so. He had indeed followed Jocasta, after he'd had a few moments' conversation with her in the kitchen.

"I'm afraid," he said, looking rueful, "that my inept questions may have put her on her guard."

"Why, what did you say to her?" I asked.

"I said I had heard from the *Signora* that Samuel was her nephew, and congratulated her on having such an efficient and competent relation, such as had found favour with her employers."

I mused on this. "It was an innocuous statement in itself, but I suspect—especially if it is not true that he is her nephew—that she would have been immediately suspicious at any mention of him." I placed my hand on his arm. "It's no fault of yours, John, I'm sure. If she is one of the anarchist cell—Samuel's Venetian contact here—she must be exceedingly wary of anyone who mentions that man. So what happened then?"

"I left her in the kitchen," he said, leaning back in his chair. "But I was looking out into the courtyard from above—you know my window overlooks it—and I saw her when she left the palazzo, so I immediately threw on my coat and followed her."

He sighed and gave a sort of low chuckle. "I can tell you, it wasn't easy! She darted this way and that, and besides, it's become so dark and wet, I thought I lost her several times." He shook his head. "I've read and heard about the superstitions about Venice during the days of the Solstice, but this was the first time I'd ever experienced being out in that suffocating, damp miasma, in the near darkness, listening for retreating footsteps that echo off the walls of the houses."

I felt chilled by his description, but was impatient for him to go on. "As an artist, you must have profoundly felt your situation as an experience to be rendered in future paintings, I think," I said. "But you didn't lose her."

"No, by sheer luck," he said, "and then she came to a halt in the little *Campo de San Cassiano*, and went to stand behind a pillar on the side portico of the church. I managed to sneak into a corner nearby with an overhanging windowbox or something, which fortunately served to magnify some parts of the conversation she would have with another person, just a few minutes later."

He paused, took a drink of water that I had placed on a little table near us, and continued.

"She met a man, who seemed, by his posture and responses to her, to be subordinate to her; she asked several questions, most so low and rapid I had trouble making them out, and appeared to be giving him orders. I heard the name 'Samuel' repeated several times, and twice when the man said 'Galleani' she shushed him and told him not to use that name."

"So Jocasta is truly part of the anarchists' cell!" I said triumphantly. "We have found them out! Good work, John!"

He looked gratified, but worried at the same time. "When they were almost finished, I heard her say, quite clearly, 'I will have it out with him tonight. Tell the others to prepare.'"

I thought about this. "She must be referring to Samuel, or Galleani, but what does it mean? She's going to confront him about…what? And what should the others prepare for?"

John grimaced. "Perhaps we need to get word to your Mr. Wilkinson right away, so he can act upon this new information. We don't want them all to slip away in the night."

I looked at my little watch, it was nearly six o'clock, and our international agent had said he would come to us at seven. "He will be here in an hour," I said to John, thinking rapidly. "I'm sure there will be no harm in waiting until then, besides, we don't even know how or where to get hold of him, do we? Jocasta will be busy with dinner preparation, and Samuel with his own duties and supervising the servants, so it's reasonable to assume she will plan to meet him late in the evening, after everyone is settled in for the night."

John reluctantly acquiesced to my point of view, and stood up and stretched. His yawn brought one of my one to the fore, which I tried to stifle. "Well, then," he said, "I'm completely done for, and will retire to my room for the next hour to get some sleep. We'll just have to wait for Mr. Wilkinson. I'll tell the footman to come for me when he arrives." He looked at me fondly. "You should rest, too, Vi, you look like you could use it."

I nodded absently, and saw him out the door to go to his own room.

But I had much different plans for the next hour.

† March 18, 1798 †

We cannot go on always laughing.

—Memoirs of Count Carlo Gozzi

DESPITE THE TRAGEDIES AND SORROWS THAT colored my life darkly for many a long year, I had to earn some money, and so wrote comedies and plays that continued to delight my fellow Venetians. As years advanced, however, it came to me, as it comes to all, to be reminded that we cannot go on always laughing. One Sunday, at Mass, a friend announced to me in a terrible whisper, a fatal accident to one of my oldest and closest friends. Not many days afterwards I received the sad news that my brother Francesco was seriously ill; he breathed his last two days later. In a short period of time I lost successively several other relatives and friends, my brother Gasparo, who expired at Padua; my dearest and earliest friend, Innocenzio Massimo; my sister Laura, gone in the prime of womanhood. I could add other names to this funereal catalogue, if I were not unwilling to detain my readers longer in the graveyard.

But now it is time to close these *Memoirs*. I lay my pen aside just at the moment when I should have had to describe that vast undulation called the French Revolution, which has been sweeping over Europe, upsetting kingdoms and drowning the landmarks of immemorial history. This awful typhoon has caught Venice in its gyration, affording a splendidly hideous field for philosophical reflection. "Splendidly hideous" is a contradiction in terms, but at the period in which we are living, paradoxes have become the norm.

I have lived to see the destruction of *La Serenissima*. Two years ago, the Republic of Venice could no longer defend itself since its war fleet numbered only four galleys and seven galliots. In Spring 1796, Piedmont fell and the Austrians were beaten from Montenotte to Lodi. Bonaparte's unstoppable army crossed the frontiers of neutral Venice in pursuit of his enemy and by the end of the year, the French troops were occupying the Venetian state. Vicenza, Cadore and my own dear Friuli were held by the Austrians. With the campaigns of 1797, Napoleon aimed for the Austrian possessions across the Alps.

Napoleon issued an ultimatum to Venice, and our *Doge* Ludovico Manin surrendered unconditionally on 12 May, and abdicated himself, while the Major Council declared the end of the Republic. Many of us still suffer deeply at this betrayal—even if it saved our lives! By virtue of a dastardly treaty between the French and the Austrians, we are now, accordingly, the "Venetian Province," a territory of Austria. I don't know if it would have been better, or worse, to be a French territory. We'll see how our Italian compatriots to the South fare under their flag.

The sweet delusive dream of a democracy, organized and based on irremovable foundations—the expectation of a moral impossibility—made men howl and laugh and dance and weep together. The ululations of the dreamers, yelling out *Liberty, Equality, Fraternity*, deafened our ears; and those of us who still remained awake were forced to feign themselves dreamers, in order to protect their honour, their property, their lives. People who are not accustomed to trace the inevitable effects of doctrines propagated through the centuries see only mysteries and prodigies in convulsions of this kind. The whole tenor of my writings, on the other hand, and particularly my poem *Marfisa bizzarra*, which conceals philosophy beneath the mantle of burlesque humour, prove that I was keenly alive to the disastrous results which had to be expected from the revolutionary science sown broadcast during the past age. I always dreaded and predicted a Cataclysm as the natural consequence of those pernicious doctrines. Yet my Cassandra warnings were doomed to remain as useless as these *Memoirs* will certainly be—as ineffectual as a doctor's prescriptions for a man whose lungs are rotten. The sweet delusive dream of our physically impossible democracy will end in the evolution of...

But my publisher has enjoined me to staunch this flow of ink upon the paper. Let us leave to serious and candid historians the task of relating what we are sure, if we live, to see unfold.

Today is the 18th of March in the Year 1798; and here I lay my pen down, lest I injure my good publisher. Farewell, patient and benign readers of my useless *Memoirs*!

Count Carlo Gozzi

☙ Later on Monday, December 22, 1879 ☙

The Crisis, and the Denouement

I WAS SEATED IN THE LITTLE SITTING ROOM on the ground floor, nearly an hour later, when I heard noises in the great hall that announced a visitor had arrived, and a few moments' time verified my observations, as Mr. Wilkinson was ushered in by one of the footmen. I stood to greet him, and nodded to the footman. "You will please go to *Signore* Sargent's room and let him know our visitor is here." The young man bowed and left the room. The clock on the mantle chimed seven.

"Charles," I said immediately, waving to a chair for him to be seated. "We have discovered so much, there is no time to lose." He gave me a serious look, seated himself and gave me his complete attention. I relayed to him my discussions with Maria, and my advice to her to leave the house, at which he nodded his approval. Before I had finished, John entered the room; the gentlemen exchanged greetings, and John drew up a chair. He had a small piece of parchment paper with him, on which I caught a glimpse of a charcoal drawing. I invited him to tell Mr. Wilkinson what he had learned from following Jocasta. The agent gave a low cry of excitement, and nearly jumped to his feet.

"That's it!" he cried, though in a low voice. "The housekeeper, then, this Jocasta, she is the link?"

"It would appear so," John said.

"Can you describe the man she met with?" Mr. Wilkinson asked.

"I can do better than that," John said, and produced the drawing I had seen in his hand—a quite complete sketch of the man, which Mr. Wilkinson took with delight.

"Yes, yes, I recognize him!" he said. "He is one we have also had our eye on—and now you have brought them all together!" He seized John's hand and shook it heartily. "I cannot tell you how much I am in your debt, both of you," he added at once, turning also to me and taking my hand in his. "You both have shown extraordinary courage and ability in this matter."

I blushed and said nothing, though highly pleased at the compliment.

"So what do we do now?" I said, as the two gentleman again seated themselves.

"This meeting that Jocasta mentioned, this confrontation with, presumably, Galleani," Mr. Wilkinson thought aloud. "I imagine it will likely take place here, somewhere in the palazzo?"

I told him our thoughts about this, and he agreed that later that night would be most likely.

"Shall you stay, then, Charles, until late, in order to see this to the end?"

He shook his head. "I'm thinking it will be better if I leave the house soon—if my presence, or your questions, have aroused any suspicion, my absence may put them at ease. However," he continued, looking at John rather than at me, "If you, John, can be at the street door at, let's say, ten o'clock, to let me in? Do you think that would be an appropriate time?"

We both nodded agreement, and I spoke. "Dinner will be over by then, and all the servants below stairs. It is my intuition that this meeting will take place on the top floor, near Anna's room, especially now that Maria is gone, as there will be no one that floor."

"Intuition?" Mr. Wilkinson repeated, a slight smile on his face. Then he nodded. "Of all persons I feel I should trust as to their ideas—intuitive, scientific, or imagined—you are the one I would listen to first and foremost."

I bowed my head at this magnificent compliment, and caught John smiling at me.

We talked over for a while what precisely would happen when Mr. Wilkinson returned, where he could secret himself, what forces would be with them to follow his lead and take the anarchists into custody, and what role—if any—John and I might play in this adventure. According to Mr. Wilkinson, it would a preciously small role, especially for me, but I must say that I felt decidedly otherwise. Stay in my room and be quiet! We'd see about that.

I escorted Mr. Wilkinson to the door of the room, and stood watching for a moment as he walked down the hall. I don't believe he perceived me; he stopped a footman as he neared the street door, and handed him an envelope, saying something to the footman that I did not hear. The boy nodded and bowed, and Mr. Wilkinson went on his way.

I stepped back into the room, my head swirling. Who on earth could he be sending a secret message to, in this house?

Nine-forty-five arrived, and I had already been half an hour hidden in the storage closet on the top floor, in company with the ghost of Carlo Gozzi and his fair neighbor Lady Caterina, as I felt, with the door ever so slightly cracked open, so I could hear, if not see, if this infamous meeting of anarchists was to take place. My intuition and my enterprising action in thus hiding myself were amply rewarded when, just after the three-quarter hour sounded, I heard footsteps coming up the marble staircase. Someone reached the landing and stood waiting, and silent. I dared not move to peek through the crack in the door, but held my breath. A hand seized the doorknob of the very storage room in which I was hidden, and I held my breath, expecting exposure in the next moment—when Caterina opened the door and stepped inside. She stopped short, a hand to her mouth to keep herself from crying out, and then she quickly stepped further into the room. The door was opened wider, giving us light to see each other.

"Violet! What are you doing here?" Her voice was strong and unafraid, but pitched low. I admit, my mouth had dropped open upon seeing it was she, and I had to shake myself to respond. But before I could speak, she put a finger to her lips, and gesturing toward the staircase, pulled the door almost closed. We stood together, holding our breath in tense silence. My mind was in a turmoil of questions and speculations, and I longed to speak with her, but held my tongue.

In mere moments, more footsteps sounded, those of two persons, and stopped at the top of the landing. Urgent low whispering reached my ears, but I couldn't make out any words distinctly. Then, it seemed the pair must have moved closer to the storage room, perhaps to step away from the staircase, where their voices might carry, and both I and Caterina were able to hear their conversation.

"You cannot just throw me out of the company," said the man's voice; it was Samuel/Galleani. "It is because of me that the Trieste bombing was so successful, while everyone else hid and trembled." His voice held an undercurrent of disdain, and threat.

"You are a loose cannon," Jocasta shot back. "First you entangle yourself with that poor girl, and then you think, Oh Lord in heaven!"—she spoke sarcastically—"she loves me and I can trust her with the truth!" She made a spitting noise.

"So then she has to be gotten out of the way!" I felt Caterina stiffen beside me—how horrible to hear about Anna's death so bluntly!

Jocasta went on. "You are a child playing at games, for all your bombs and your guns!"

There was a moment's silence, and Galleani said something too low to hear, perhaps he had turned away. But Jocasta answered him clearly.

"Yes, you are sorry for it," she sneered. "But who has had to clean up your messes? Me, that's who! Those stupid notes to the master, as if that could throw him off the track—and you and your *Signora*, yes! I know about that, too, looking for lost treasure like a puling child!"

Galleani laughed scornfully. "I make use of whatever and whoever comes my way, and my *Signora* has contributed greatly to our treasury, though she is so stupid she hasn't an idea in her head of what that money is funding."

Jocasta dismissed this with a sniff. "That's a game that has no winners, you are just too young to know it! Nonetheless," she continued, "now, with these two idiots in the palazzo, asking questions and sticking their upper-class noses into everything, many of us think it's time for you to go! You'll ruin everything with your bravado and recklessness!"

I realized with a jolt that the "two idiots" were myself and John! But any mirth I felt at this was buried under the realization that Jocasta had been the one behind Anna's murder, probably the theft of the letters and other documents, maybe shoving that other poor maid into the canal as well as toppling that vase down the stairs at me.

"You can't do this to me," Galleani said, his voice deep and angry. "You think you are in charge, you simple old woman! We who are young are paving a new way, and I will be their leader."

At that, we heard Jocasta gasp, and sounds of struggling, as if she had fallen to the floor. Perhaps he was strangling her! I could no longer sit still, and shoving past Caterina, burst through the door to see the very sight I had imagined—Jocasta writhing on the floor, her hands clutching the young, strong hands that were closed around her neck.

Without thinking, I threw myself upon Galleani, and together we rolled off his victim. From a quick side glance, I saw that Caterina applied herself to restraining Jocasta, who was struggling to rise. At that same moment, I heard the sound of voices far below, at the entrance to the marble staircase, and I screamed as loud as I could.

Galleani looked at me, hatred filling his eyes and distorting his face. Jocasta had rolled away, choking and gasping, but Caterina held her fast in a tight grip. I heard the clamor of people racing up the stairs—hoping it was, of course, John and Charles—and I smiled triumphantly at Galleani.

"Your game is up," I said.

But I spoke too soon.

Galleani pulled a knife from his pocket and clicked open the blade with a single movement, then before I could resist, he grabbed me, turned me around, and held the knife point at my neck. We were poised like this when John and Charles reached the landing. They both had lanterns with them, which painted the scene in lurid light and shadows. I could feel my heart pounding, and the force of Galleani's strong arm across my neck made it hard to breathe. The knifepoint pricked at my skin.

"Stay back," he warned the two men, who were carefully entering the landing space, and sidling off to one edge of it, while Galleani moved toward the staircase, clinging hard to me. "If you attempt anything, this woman will die." And we all knew he meant it.

I saw Charles's eyes widen as he took in Caterina on the floor with Jocasta, and I could have sworn that he nodded to her, as if approving her actions.

Galleani started down the staircase, dragging me with him. Charles stepped off the landing but Galleani called up to him. "You must stay up there, or she's a dead woman!" He retreated a step.

We gained the main hallway of the palazzo at last. In my terror, I couldn't tell whether Charles and John had actually stayed on the top floor or were silently making their way down to my rescue, as I most fervently hoped they were.

Galleani made for the door that led to the water landing on the Grand Canal. He flung open the doors, and a gust of salty, fishy air and wind blew in our faces. It was then I heard more voices and the sound of running behind me. Galleani looked back in desperation, and I thought it was the end for me. But he continued his harsh hold, and dragged me outside. Banging the door shut behind him, to further delay our pursuers, he paused, leaning against the railing, and took several deep breaths. Closing the knife and putting it back in his pocket, he made me a strange, formal little bow, laughed maniacally, and proceeded to toss me over the railing like a sack of grain into the hideous black waters of the Grand Canal! He leapt in after me, and as I rose to the surface from my initial plunge, I could just discern him swimming strongly away into the darkness, making no sound that could be heard over the wind and the lapping of the water.

I don't know how to swim, but I don't fear being in water. I paddled my arms in front of me as I had seen dogs do when swimming to retrieve fowl shot down over lakes, and that at least kept my head above water for a few minutes. But I could feel the weight of my sodden clothing start to drag me down. I tried to keep my head and make for the stairs where the gondolas would pull up to let passengers in or out.

Light burst out of the suddenly opened door above me, and men clambered down the stairs toward me. I closed my lips tight as the filthy canal water splashed in my face, and made one mad lunge for a railing that seemed within reach, but which was not.

The next thing I knew was the feeling of a strong arm around my waist, and a hand under my chin, holding my head out of the water, then I was being inelegantly but sturdily pulled out of the water onto the stairs, where John embraced me as if he would never let me go, followed by Charles clambering out of the water—it had been he who had jumped in to rescue me!—and holding on to me as well. I managed to remain conscious, and not swoon, even as a tremendous shivering overtook my whole body, but before long we were all inside the palazzo.

Galleani had escaped. Whether the black and oily waters of the Grand Canal ultimately took him, or he managed to swim to safety, time would tell.

☊ Tuesday, December 23, 1879 ☋

Nearly all mysteries are revealed.

AFTER A LONG AND REFRESHING SLEEP, I rose feeling quite healthy and invigourated, despite my exposure to the treacherous canal waters. Mr. Wilkinson had been invited to luncheon at Ca' Favretto, in order to help explain to us all, as much as he was allowed to, the nature of the events that had taken place. The various police and agents who had stormed the house during my ordeal (as I termed it) and who had stayed for some time, questioning the subdued but defiant Jocasta and other members of the household, had finally left sometime long after midnight, leaving the master of the house in no little distress at all the uproar.

I was eagerly looking forward to this luncheon, when all the disparate threads of this exciting tapestry could be gathered together and resolved; plus, I had one stupendous announcement of my own that I was quite dying to make to the assembled company.

Luncheon was served early, and Mr. Wilkinson joined us as the family, and I and John, entered the breakfast room, and we all sat down in eager anticipation of hearing what he could tell us. He looked infinitely tired; I expect he hadn't slept much if at all, but he looked satisfied that inroads had been made upon the Venetian anarchists. I made sure that all of the servants left the room before he began to talk.

"We have rounded them all up," he said. "Little thanks to Jocasta, who wouldn't tell us much of anything." He nodded at John. "But your sketch, John, was of inestimable use in identifying the man, and he proved to be more of a talker than Jocasta, and so we were able to find all of them—except of course," he added wearily, "for Luigi Galleani, who, it has been reported, managed to swim away down the Canal, and was seen climbing aboard a boat that carried him away to the mainland." He drank gratefully from his coffee cup. "But we will find him again, and put a stop to his murderous programme."

I was immensely curious as to one issue in particular. "Mr. Wilkinson," I said, "we now know that poor Anna, sad girl, was murdered by Jocasta, to keep her from revealing Galleani's true identity." He nodded acquiescence. "But did she tell you anything about why she put those orange peels in the girl's mouth?"

"Ah," he said, leaning back. "Yes, actually, that was one thing she was willing to talk about. She laughed quite crazily when we asked her, and she said something about it being 'vengeance on Carlo Gozzi, the beastly cur and villain who had destroyed the reputation of her ancestor, Goldoni the playwright.' She also said she knew about *Signore* Favretto"—here a polite nod at Giacomo—"being a distant descendant of Gozzi's, and therefore had no scruples about entangling him and his family in murder and mayhem." He looked at me quizzically. "I daresay you would know a good deal more about that ancient quarrel than any of us might, Miss Lee."

I laughed, and shook my head. These Italians and their centuries-old grudges! I have never met a race like theirs, who do not forget an insult even through centuries. "But what about the ghost, and the scent of oranges?" I was ready to laugh these off as due to my over-eager imagination, so said it lightly.

At this, *Signora* di Contadini, the formidable mother-in-law of our host, spoke in a low and somewhat humble tone. She appeared to be in a state of shock. "I have a confession to make," she said, looking quite wretched. "I have to admit that I enlisted Samuel to help look through this palazzo for my ancestress's jewels, and he, being a clever one, manufactured the ghost in order to keep the other servants, or any guests"—here she looked meaningfully at me—"from pursuing anything their curiosity might lead them to."

Caterina, who sat beside me, pursed her lips and shook her head at her errant mother. Which made me, mischievously and suspiciously, ask another question of Mr. Wilkinson. I had been thinking this through in the long reaches of the night before, as I tried to calm myself enough to fall asleep.

"Mr. Wilkinson," I said, commanding the attention of all the room. "If you are at liberty to tell us, although I think you owe all of us a thorough explanation, what exactly was the role that both Anna and Caterina have played in this escapade of yours?"

Shocked silence filled the room. Giacomo looked at me in astonishment, then turned the same gaze upon his wife, who was blushing three ways from Sunday, and looking rather disconcerted.

Mr. Wilkinson put his hand to his forehead, and sighed.

"Miss Lee," he said, shaking his head. "Does nothing get by you, ever?" Sighing again, he spoke to the company.

"I cannot tell you very much, and I must, once again, extract a promise of complete secrecy from all of you in this room." He looked each one of us in the eye, especially the *Signora* di Contadini, and waited for a nod of acquiescence, before he went on.

"When we knew that Samuel—Galleani—had taken up residence here at Ca' Favretto, one of our agents approached young Anna about being an informant."

Giacomo and his mother-in-law both gasped at this, but did not speak. I noticed that Caterina only looked sad and resigned.

"She was in need of ready cash, and was happy to report to us any overheard conversations or odd behaviour that she noted, Galleani's as well as any one else."

I interrupted. "Did she know why you were watching him, what kind of person he was?"

I thought Mr. Wilkinson looked abashed at this question, and he shook his head. "We merely told her he was a person of interest to the government." He sighed. "She had no idea that she might be in any danger and…" he paused, then went on. "As strange as it may seem, the two of them apparently did fall in love!" He glanced then at Caterina, who nodded slightly. "As you overheard from his argument last night with Jocasta, he had indeed entrusted her with the truth of his identity, which shocked her exceedingly, and she foolishly told him she would turn him over to the police."

"Do you think he knew she was acting as your agent?"

Caterina spoke up then. "I believe not," she said. She looked around the curious faces at the table. "Anna and I spoke often about the situation, you see, because I too am an agent of Mr. Wilkinson's—and have been for a few years now. She truly was in love with him, but she"—Caterina faltered, tears in her eyes—"she wouldn't listen to me when she learned who he really was, she thought she could save him." She shook her head sadly. "It all went so wrong."

I looked to Giacomo to see his reaction, and was surprised to see shock and disbelief soon replaced by a wondering kind of admiration, but mostly of love. He took his wife's hand and kissed it, but she spoke again, mostly, it seemed to him alone.

"This was to be my last assignment, dearest," she said to him. "Now that we are married, I am no longer in need of that means of support for Mama and me." He kissed her tenderly. Artists, I thought, open to just about anything.

A sudden thought struck me. "Then it was you, Caterina," I said, looking at her closely, "who met with Mr.

Wilkinson in the Cavini monastery next door, yes?" I recalled the response Mr. Wilkinson had given, mentioning guilt and responsibility, and I presumed that she had been expressing her feelings about Anna's death.

She nodded but did not speak.

Her mother, however, didn't take it so quietly. "What! My own daughter! A spy? A police agent? What on earth has the world come to!" She poured herself a very large glass of wine, and passed the bottle down the table, where several of us availed ourselves of the potent comfort.

"And the first young woman who fell into the canal?" John queried. "Was she too part of all this?"

Mr. Wilkinson shook his head, a smile at last breaking through the gloom. "I received a report just this morning," he said, "from an officer I had sent to Mestre to interview the girl, where she had returned to live with her parents. Apparently she was at last ready to admit that her own clumsiness was the cause of her tumble into the water, and she was too embarrassed to admit it, so she made up the story about being pushed." He looked apologetically at Giacomo and Caterina. "It seems she wasn't satisfied with service here in Venice anyway, and used it as an excuse to return to her home."

After a long time exploring details, though many were not affirmed by either Mr. Wilkinson or Caterina, the *Signora* made a final statement.

"And so, we are to gather, that nothing of any of this had to do with my poor ancestress's ruination by Carlo Gozzi, and the jewels he stole from her? This is all about criminals and anarchists?"

"I'm afraid so, *Signora*," said I.

She sighed deeply. "I had hoped that someday we would be able to discover the truth of the matter," she said. "And finally avenge my poor ancestress, Lady Caterina."

I rose from my chair, and turned to her, then looked around the table at the gathered company. "Not all hope is lost, *Signora*," I said. "But I'm afraid that if you hear the real truth, it will not make you very happy."

"What are you talking about, Vi?" John asked, looking askance at me. "Let's hear it! Have you found something?"

I laughed, giddy with delight, and drew forth from my pocket a few pieces of parchment, and a small velvet bag.

"Let us listen to Carlo Gozzi tell you himself what the truth was."

When I had taken that one hour to myself the day before, I had returned to Gozzi's writing room, the little storage closet, and managed, with some difficulty, to break through the wooden panel by the window, behind which was an unlocked door to a little safe! Inside it were a few pages of closely written script, and the little, worn velvet bag.

I won't sport with my readers' patience at this point—the script was an alternative version of what Gozzi had published in his *Memoirs*, differing from the public account in that it detailed the true nature of his encounter with the scheming Caterina, and his decision to return all her jewels to her, with the exception of the bejeweled miniature, as a sign and warning to her that he knew what kind of woman she was, and what she had done.

Of course, the *Signora* was indignant at hearing this, and proclaimed that Gozzi lied in this version as he had done in the published one, but when I placed the velvet bag in her hand, and she drew forth the jewel-bedecked miniature of Caterina del Rosso, she was silenced. Everyone exclaimed over the beauty of the piece of jewellery, and after a moment, the *Signora* put it gently into the hands of her daughter, who looked at her wonderingly, and accepted the gift.

The Favrettos entreated us—John and me—to stay with them through the Christmas holidays, but we both felt we were required to be on our separate ways—I back to

Florence to accompany my mother and brother to the *Contessa's* Christmas Day dinner, and John down to sunny Morocco, where he longed to return to his painting. I couldn't blame him—the dreary, wet chill of Venice was enough to drive anyone away, but especially to warmer climes with enchanting spices wafting on the breeze! I told him I expected great paintings from this Moroccan adventure, and he promised it would be so.

We both took leave of Mr. Wilkinson in the great entrance hall, after luncheon. He was most earnest in his *adieus*, especially to me, and when I joked him about running across him perhaps in another European city, in pursuit of traitors and anarchists, he only looked arch and said, "I don't think I shall ever lose sight of you, dear Violet, and may very well turn up at an unexpected moment."

And so ended our Solstice adventure in the dark City of Venice, on the Grand Canal—a city called *La Serenissima*, but whose questing, rebellious soul has never been truly at peace.

৯ EPILOGUE ৶

I CANNOT RESIST ONE FINAL WORD OR TWO. My detecting adventures with my dear friend, John Sargent, encompassed some twenty years of our lifetime, after which we went our increasingly separate ways, parted by duties, and avocations, work and loves and life, and sadly, some differences of opinion too great to be overlaid by the fabric of a friendship that was fading but was still true at heart. But during those twenty years, from 1877 to near the turn to the great next century, John and I met up in city after city, at seaside resorts, in the capitals of great countries, and once even in America, that new, raw land of promise and ambition beyond description.

The next adventure I will write about happened in Paris, where John was gaining quite a name for himself, and had already had several paintings accepted at the Salon. Patrons were clamoring for him to immortalize them in oils, and he was never without an invitation to dinner or the theatre. I, too, was becoming better known as Vernon Lee, although many people knew my actual name, and I divided my time between London, Paris and Florence. It was during this period that I had also met the person whom I have always considered to be the love of my life, and I believe John encountered someone similar. I invite you, if you will, to meet us in Paris to hear the tale of *The Unicorn in the Mirror*.

Violet Paget

ᛦ Author's Notes ᛉ

In any work of historical fiction, there are two parts: The Historical Part and The Fiction Part, and readers always want to know which is which. John Singer Sargent and Violet Paget (aka Vernon Lee) are real people whom I've set to solving fictional mysteries. In this book set in Venice, Giacomo Favretto is a real person, an artist and friend of Sargent, who actually did live in the Ca' Favretto as described. (It is now a wonderful small hotel—my husband and I stayed there some years before I knew I would be writing this story!) He did have a wife and presumably a mother-in-law, but the characters in my book are not intended to be a faithful representation of those two ladies.

In the "past" part of the story, not only is Carlo Gozzi a real person, about whom Violet wrote in her *Studies in 18th Century Italy*, but nearly eighty-five percent of the Gozzi Chapters are verbatim from his own *Memoirs*, as translated by John Addington Symonds, a late 19th century literary light and a friend to Sargent, Paget and Henry James. The playwrights of Gozzi's time, Carlo Goldoni and Pietro Chiari, were very real, as in fact are all of the people he mentions in his *Memoirs* as I have presented them here. His "secret memoir," however, is entirely fictional except for the revolutionary fervor and Gozzi's membership in the Freemasons.

The issue of anarchists and revolutionaries was a very frightening and real part of life in the 18th and 19th centuries, particularly in Europe and Great Britain. Luigi Galleani was one such real anarchist, who escaped from Italy in 1879, lived in France for twenty years, then returned to Italy where he was captured and imprisoned for five years. He managed to find passage to the United States in 1901, was deported in 1919 for criminal activities, and returned to Italy.

THE LOVE FOR THREE ORANGES

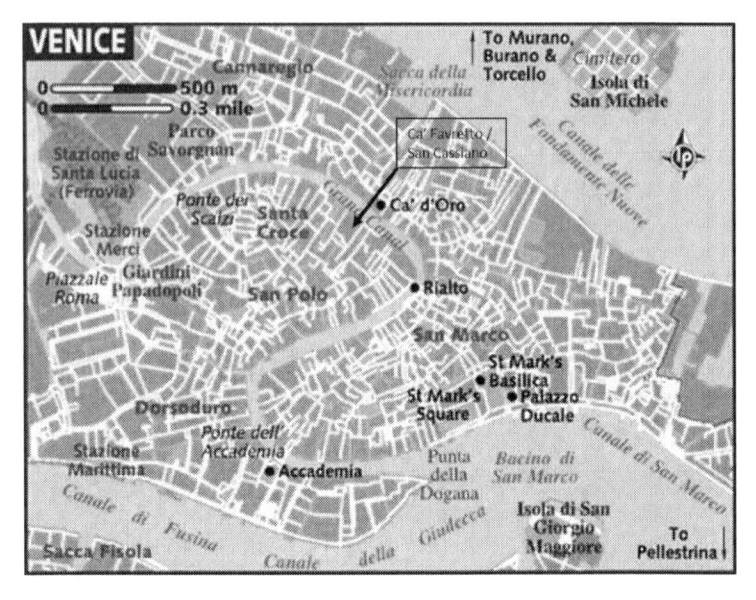

Giacomo Favretto, self-portrait

Carlo Gozzi

If you enjoyed *The Love for Three Oranges,* we hope you will review it on Amazon or Goodreads!

Other books by Mary F. Burns

Portraits of an Artist:
A Novel about John Singer Sargent

The Spoils of Avalon – Book One
of the Sargent/Paget Mysteries

Isaac and Ishmael: A Novel of Genesis

J-The Woman Who Wrote the Bible

Ember Days

To see book trailers, contact the author, and order these books, please visit the author's website at www.maryfburns.com.

Made in the USA
San Bernardino, CA
01 February 2019